"I can't find my orange puck!" thickening flurry.

"It's over there." Jason waved to the far end of the pond where a flash of orange peeked through the swirl of flakes. "Hurry up, Pumpkin." He loaded the net and sticks in the back of the truck and dug around in the cargo area for their boots.

A deep, loud cracking sound reverberated across the ravine, quickly followed by Mishayla's scream.

At first, Christina thought a gun had gone off. Instinctively, she flinched and looked wildly around for her daughter. The noise of splashing confirmed her next fear. She spun toward the noise and bolted across the pond with quick, sure strides.

Jason's urgent voice cut through the thudding panic in her head. "Get down!" he commanded. "Get on your stomach before you break through!" She threw herself on her stomach and crawled closer to the hole in the ice.

"I don't see her!" She plunged her arms into the black, icy water and without hesitation, swung her skates over the edge and slid into the hole.

Jason's voice was high and urgent as he yelled, "Chrissie, no!" She took a deep breath anyway and submerged her body. Her skate blades sank in the muddy bottom of the pond—it must have been about shoulder deep for her but too deep for Mishayla.

The water quickly penetrated her clothing and was so cold her skin felt as if it was on fire. An incredible urge to gasp took hold but she fought it. She opened her eyes as wide as she could in the gloom, waving her arms slowly in front of her. Something hard hit her fingers—Mishayla's helmet—then something soft—her jacket. Freezing fingers refused to close, so she enclosed her arms around her daughter, gathering her close to her body. She bent her protesting knees and pushed upward. Her head abruptly made contact with the underside of the ice. She winced and cried out. When she opened her eyes again, she saw the bubbles from her silent shout race to the surface and spread out against the ice. She must have misjudged her position. Running out of air, she followed the crawling bubbles with her fingers until she found the opening. A hand grasped her wrist and pulled.

She broke through the surface, gasping with the cold. Her blurry, ice-encrusted vision slowly cleared until she saw Jason's panic-stricken face looking at her.

Champagne Books Presents

Bad Ice

By

Sandra Cormier

This is a work of fiction. The characters, incidents and dialogues in this book are of the author's imagination and are not to be construed as real. Any resemblance to actual events or persons, living or dead, is completely coincidental.

No part of this book may be reproduced or transmitted in any form or by any means, electronic or mechanical, including photocopying, recording, or by any information storage and retrieval system, without permission in writing from the publisher.

Champagne Books
www.champagnebooks.com
Copyright © 2008 by Sandra Cormier
ISBN 978-1-897445-16-7
July 2008
Cover Art © Christopher Butts
Produced in Canada

Champagne Books
#35069-4604 37 ST SW
Calgary, AB T3E 7C7
Canada

Dedication

To Dad, who turned his daughter into a hockey fan.

One

Ian Pollard hesitated and stared at his reflection in the big glass doors. Taking a shaky breath, he entered the vast sports complex through the players' entrance.

A security guard glanced up from his magazine. "Working late, Mr. Pollard?"

Ian raised his hand briefly, not trusting himself to speak. He strode briskly past the guard and entered the elevator leading to the executive offices above the corporate boxes. He rocked on his heels and watched the blinking lights, counting the levels upward with agonizing slowness.

The elevator doors slid open to reveal a carpeted hallway lined with identical doors. The boom, boom, boom of rock music filtered through thick walls, competing with his galloping heart.

The deserted passageway unsettled him. His colleagues were likely at home with their families or enjoying the game from one of the private boxes surrounding the hockey arena. He wished the hallways were crowded with bustling suits; perhaps then, he'd have an excuse to change his mind. Just as well, he didn't want to deal with curious co-workers tonight.

Once inside his office, he leaned against the door and realized he hadn't taken a proper breath since he had entered the building. He inhaled deeply and moved toward the filing cabinet against the wall. As he grasped the drawer handle, his sweating fingers slipped, and he tried again. This time the drawer opened. He searched behind the hanging file folders and pulled out a small handgun. After he slipped it into his trouser pocket, he left his office and made his way to the nearest doorway providing access to the stands.

The concrete landing was at a dizzying height near the myriad of crisscrossing ceiling rafters and catwalks. The players circled on the ice below, the names on their uniforms barely recognizable. He knew he had to get closer, but he hesitated again. It had taken a week of turmoil to work up the nerve to go through with his plan. He shook his head. *It's too late to back out now.*

He felt jittery enough, and the curious glances of the fans didn't help. They stood against the back wall, staring at his obviously expensive suit. They probably wondered what a guy like him was doing way up here in the cheap seats.

I couldn't help but raise ticket prices so those losers can't afford the good seats. After all, those selfish jocks need their millions. He swiped the back of his hand across his sweating upper lip and shuffled down the steps, closer to the action.

His eyes darted across the ice, focusing on and discarding player after player, until he saw him.

There he is. Number Twelve. Jason Peterson. Ian suddenly felt light, as if he had left his body behind.

That bastard will finally pay for what he did.

He watched as Peterson streaked down the ice, charged past a defender, and snapped the puck over the goaltender's shoulder. The rubber disk found the gap and slammed against the netting, knocking the water bottle off the top of the net.

Ian stared at the winger as he glided to the bench and slapped his glove against those of his teammates. He was getting closer. *Wait. Wait until he sits down.*

He raised his eyes to the giant screen suspended from the vast ceiling. The Jumbotron showed an extreme close up of Jason's face as he laughed and focused his intense blue eyes on the action. The athlete's shoulder pads rose and fell as he breathed rapidly through clenched teeth.

I'm going to wipe that smile off your face.

He drew his gaze downward and focused on the back of Jason's head only thirty feet below. His shoulders tensed as he readied himself.

~ * ~

Christina Mackey squirmed with impatience at the refreshment kiosk. She knew the play had resumed and didn't like leaving her daughter alone in the stands.

At least Mishayla was safer in the platinum seats than in the nosebleed section. Christina reminded herself to send a thank you note to her boss for providing the tickets to the game. What a treat to watch from ice level instead of her usual perch in the greens, far above the action. Even the cheap tickets were as rare and expensive as real platinum.

Two drinks and a tray of nachos teetered precariously in her arms as she reentered the seating area. She paused to shout with delight when the horn sounded for the home team's goal, almost upsetting her load of snacks.

She resumed her trip further down the concrete steps then found herself forced to halt again as a man stopped in front of her, blocking her way with his broad back.

"Excuse me, please." She barely heard her own voice above the noise of the raucous crowd. She tried again, louder, but the man didn't move. She tried to move around him, annoyed, when he stretched his arms in front of him, pointing down the steps toward the home players' bench.

She glanced over his shoulder and realized with a gasp that he held a gun.

Instinctively, she pushed her tray of refreshments in front of her. The icy soda and hot cheese sauce splattered against the back of the man's head. Too late. He had already squeezed the trigger.

Everything happened at once. Nearby spectators jumped out of their seats at the sound of the loud crack, the man toppled down the shallow concrete steps, and the large sheet of safety glass behind the home players' bench exploded, shattering into a thousand flying pieces.

Christina stood frozen with shock, hardly aware of the dripping remains of the ruined nachos still hanging loosely in her hand. The man had lost his grip on the gun, but he scrambled on his hands and knees to grab the weapon that had skittered across the floor. Horrified fans shouted and called for security. No one seemed inclined to lay their hands on the man as he rose to his knees and looked up at her.

He had fallen only a few steps, and she clearly saw by the look in his eyes he was in a rage. *He's crazy.* She felt naked as she stood on the steps with no place to hide. Her eyes locked with the gunman's, and without further hesitation. He grimaced and swung the instrument toward her.

What the hell? She dropped the tray and raised her hands in a crazy attempt to protect herself. She didn't hear her own instinctive shout of protest, drowned by the rush of astonished noise from the surrounding crowd. A much louder voice bellowed from behind her, "Get down!"

Two more explosions sounded. She was instantly aware of a burning sensation in her hand and shoulder that quickly expanded to excruciating pain. *He shot me. That bastard shot me.*

She squeezed her eyes shut and when she opened them again, she realized she was lying on her back. Three or four concerned faces filled her line of vision. Suddenly, she felt tired, more tired than she ever had in her life. A bizarre notion entered her fuzzy thoughts. *Even after eighteen hours of labour, I've never been so damned tired.* She closed her eyes again, and the noise subsided.

~ * ~

At the sound of the first explosion, Jason instinctively ducked. Granular bits of safety glass rained like gravel on his helmet and scattered on the floor, diamonds in the bright stadium lights.

He looked behind him. In the confusion, he saw a partial view of a kneeling man at the bottom of the steps. The man pointed something at a woman standing about ten rows up. He held a gun.

He's going to shoot her. He had an urge to vault over the shattered glass to tackle the man. A hand gripped his shoulder, holding him back.

Two more sharp cracks rang out. A puff of smoke burst from the man's weapon, but he'd already been hit. He spun backwards and sprawled on the concrete.

Screams and shouts erupted all around Jason. He swept his gaze around the arena. Security personnel were suddenly everywhere, pushing past him at the bench and spilling down the aisles.

He straightened further and peeked over the shattered bits of glass. The team trainer had already scrambled over the boards and worked on the inert man. He used a team towel in a vain attempt to stem the blood flowing from the man's chest. The assistant had grabbed the jump kit and fired it up.

Jason glanced further up. The scene repeated itself as arena medics positioned a gurney next to the fallen woman. *Oh, God, she was hit.*

A small girl grasped the woman's outstretched hand, tears streaking her cheeks. He saw her lips move, mouthing, "Mommy!" but he couldn't hear her in the din.

Bertie, his line mate, nudged him and pointed at the figure on the floor. "I don't think he made it."

"I hope she does," Jason murmured, staring at the gurney twenty feet upward.

After a quick consultation with the referee, the coach moved back and forth in the narrow area behind the bench. He slapped the players' shoulders and brushed bits of glass from their uniforms. "Okay, guys, game's over. Let's get to the dressing room."

Jason followed his mates as they moved toward the exit at the end of their bench. He strained to see the activity in the stands, but there were too many bodies in the way.

For a brief moment, the din receded. The athletes walked single file along a narrow hallway, the sound of skate blades muted by the rubber floor. All he heard was the rustle of fabric, the clunk and rattle of sticks, and the hard breathing of his teammates.

As he entered the dressing room, excited voices resumed and rang against the walls. It was going to be a while before everybody calmed down. His own heart thumped furiously; the adrenaline that normally coursed through his veins while on a breakaway seemed like a nap in comparison.

Bertie Gauthier paced the room in his skates. His sharp gaze darted uneasily from player to player. "Man, that was close. What the hell was that guy thinking? How did he get the gun into the building? He could have hit any of us. Mon Dieu, my Corinne could be a widow right now."

A voice cut in from the end of the bench, "Who could possibly hit your pointy little head?" Adam Noole, the captain, prodded the man next to him and laughed raucously at his own joke.

Bertie thrust his chin at the grinning captain. "I can tell you, my friend, he wouldn't have missed your ass—it's as big as a Zamboni."

"C'mon, guys, this is serious shit." Jason yanked off his helmet and tossed it behind him on the shelf above his seat. He sat down on the bench in front of his locker and rubbed a towel over his short, auburn hair. He went over the scene that had just played in the arena. A mental recollection wasn't necessary since a small monitor, mounted near the ceiling and at one end of the room, repeatedly showed the event, providing different angles and detailed comments from the television personalities. Apparently, all cameras had swung toward the incident, ignoring the activity on the ice in the dying seconds before the play stopped.

He gazed upward at the monitor. "It didn't take long for everyone to clear out."

The television showed a brief shot of the area around the scene. Uniformed officers and men in suits, probably detectives, interviewed a few witnesses.

The gurneys were gone. Yellow tape surrounded the area, stretched tightly around the cushioned platinum seats.

He wasn't aware how long he stared at the monitor, but the perspiration rolling into his eyes reminded him he should be getting showered and changed. Nevertheless, he remained seated, occasionally blotting his eyes with the towel.

The uproar settled to a murmur as two detectives entered the dressing room. They made their way around the perimeter of the room asking questions. Jason tried to recall what had happened, but his story wasn't much more detailed than those of his teammates.

"How's the woman...the one in the stands?" He couldn't shake the image of the little girl from his head.

"We don't know, sir. Thanks for your assistance." The detective moved on, scratching a few notes on his pad.

Jason returned his attention to the monitor. He felt a rush of relief when he learned the woman, a single mother, was only slightly wounded in the fracas and was expected to make a full recovery.

After several replays, the network returned to the live scene. The announcer stood on the steps above the players' bench. Officials still worked behind him, and a few fans remained.

"The alleged gunman was not so lucky. When arena security opened fire, he was critically wounded, then pronounced dead upon arrival at St. Michael's Hospital. Names have not been released, but it's been reported he may have been an employee of this building. Police Services will be investigating the incident."

Jason raised his eyebrows and glanced up at Bertie. "That's how he got the gun in, I guess." He shook the sweat from his hair. "Man! What a close one, huh? Who would think somebody could go postal in a hockey arena?" He finally began to unlace his skates.

"Jason."

"What?" Jason looked up again at Bertie's face. His friend's eyes focused on a point just above Jason's head.

"Take a closer look at your lid, man."

Jason stood and took his helmet from the shelf. A narrow groove traced along the left side of the helmet, about a half-centimeter deep and a few centimeters long, just above the gap where his ear would have protruded.

If he had been looking to the left or downward, the bullet would have penetrated his head or the back of his neck. Even if the glass slowed it down, Jason knew any impact in the temple area or the base of the skull could be fatal—or worse, career ending—whether by elbow, stick, puck, or bullet.

Jason shivered and sank back to the bench, staring with round eyes at the helmet.

"Holy shit." He felt a ghostly tingle and rubbed the back of his head. "I could be dead right now. Shit."

He reached to trace the groove, but Bertie stopped him. "That's evidence, don't touch it."

"Who do you think the bullet was for?" Jason rubbed his damp hair and looked at his fingers, satisfied his hand came away clean.

"Not for me, that's for sure. Everybody loves me."

Jason scowled at his friend and returned his gaze to the helmet. Bertie sat beside him and nudged him. "I guess you'd better go and pay those cops out there another visit, eh?"

Jason felt as if the world had receded for a moment, and Bertie's voice slowly surfaced as he repeated, "You'd better go talk to the cops."

"Yeah…yeah, okay," he murmured as he turned the helmet over and over in his hands.

~ * ~

Jason finally emerged from the elevator in the underground parking garage. He had changed into jeans and a loose sweater, worn under a cracked, brown leather bomber jacket. He shifted the garment bag containing his pre-game suit over his shoulder.

The police had taken his statement and had accepted his helmet as evidence. The authorities informed him that the dead man was Ian Pollard, a man he had seen around the complex during his twelve-year career with this hockey club.

Ian was a member of the team's finance outfit with an office in the upper region of the arena. It must have been how he got the gun inside. Security would never have let something like that slip if he'd been some fan trying to get the thing through the doors at game time.

Despite the late hour, Jason couldn't decide whether he was tired or pumped from the excitement. His initial shock had gradually worn off, and he looked forward to a couple of days off after the next morning's practice. He made a mental plan to find out what hospital the injured woman was at so he could send her flowers after practice.

He pointed his keychain remote at his BMW and debated whether he should go home right away or find a bar that was still open.

The car's alarm blipped, and the blinking lights briefly illuminated a figure that stepped from behind a concrete support. With a sharp intake of breath, Jason dropped the garment bag.

"Jesus, Sheila, you scared the crap out of me! What are you doing here? I thought you were in Barrie." His thudding heart slowly quieted.

His girlfriend stood with her arms crossed tightly against her chest, and her fur-clad shoulders hunched against a cold draft that curled around the concrete pillars. With a cry, she rushed forward. Jason left the garment bag on the floor and wrapped his arms around her.

He peered down at her. "What's wrong?" She couldn't have heard the news about his own close call with the gunman. The media had already left by the time he had gone to the police with his scored helmet.

She pulled away and ran her manicured fingers through her long blonde hair. He tried to meet her gaze, but she wouldn't look at him. She began to pace, the stiletto heels of her boots clicking on the pavement. The sound echoed through the nearly empty parking garage.

"I didn't think he'd do it, he's crazy! I never thought it would go this far."

"What the hell are you talking about?"

"Ian." She stopped pacing and appeared to study the peeling paint on the side of a concrete support with intense interest.

"What about Ian?" He squinted at her. Still facing the pillar, she shuffled and scraped her boots against the salt-encrusted concrete floor. "Did you hear something about Ian Pollard?"

"I heard about it on the radio on the way down here. Is he okay?"

"Why do you care?" Suspicion took hold. Sheila was a serial flirt, drawn to suits like a cat to a nut-counting squirrel.

"Um, we were sort of seeing each other, and…uh, I guess he was jealous of you."

It figured. He had been dating Sheila for only a few months and didn't expect an exclusive relationship, but he also didn't expect competition with a nut bar holding a gun.

The discovery he was an actual target made him feel sick. "Hang on, it wasn't an accident? He was aiming for me and you knew about it? And you didn't warn me?" *Christ, whatever happened to a simple Dear John letter?*

Sheila continued to evade his gaze and looked everywhere except his face. She hesitated and blurted, "I didn't know he was going to do anything like this. He kept joking he wished you were out of the way and I guess I just kind of laughed it off."

She studied the oil stains near the toes of her pointed leather boots and shrugged, whispering with a pout, "I'm sorry, sweetie, I was such an idiot. I'll give him the boot first thing tomorrow. Now, how about a late drink?"

She stepped close to him. He retreated, his back pressed against a concrete pillar. She slid her hands around his waist, under his jacket, and underneath his sweater. He felt her long fingernails graze the skin along his ribs.

He held his breath and closed his eyes. He felt her warm breath graze his jaw before her teeth nipped, and he shuddered, fighting for control. It was like this every time. She pissed him off and then wrapped herself around him. He clenched his fists at his sides and let his breath out in a *whoosh.*

Unbelievable. For the last six months, this woman had taken him for quite a ride, and he desperately wanted to get off the crazy train. She was far more than he could handle, and he was sick of her mind games.

With a massive effort, he grasped her wrists and pulled her hands from under his sweater. His grip tightened as he held her away from him. She glanced at his whitening knuckles with a perplexed frown.

"I guess you don't know he's dead," he said quietly.

Sheila backed a step, her gaze connecting with his for the first time. Her eyes widened as she drew a ragged breath. "What?"

"The cops shot him. It's all over the news already so I might as well tell you now." His words felt like shards of splintered wood. They scraped his throat but he ignored the pain. He feigned indifference and pushed her away, releasing her wrists.

Her expression hardened as she raised her chin and declared, "Well, isn't that convenient. Now he's out of your way, so you can have me all to yourself."

He backed away, appalled by her callousness. "Jesus, Sheila. Can't you at least be sorry a man is dead? I guess the word regret isn't in your vocabulary."

She's using again. He wondered if she'd ever stopped, although she repeatedly promised to go straight. He felt the last shred of his feelings for her drift away in the drafty underground parking lot.

She must have known she'd gone too far. She reached for him again.

"You don't understand, Jason, sweetie...I love you. He was just... just a friend who did things for me that you wouldn't."

"I suppose he did your drug shopping for you."

"Baby, those days are over. I'll never touch the stuff again. I promise. I just—I don't want to lose you." She raised her hands to her mouth and began to sob.

Jason watched her face. She wasn't the same person he'd met six months ago—a girl with a creamy complexion and bright, shimmering eyes. He didn't realize at the time she was high.

As the months passed, her skin paled and stretched over prominent cheekbones. Her gaze lost its focus. In this harsh overhead light, a thick application of makeup failed to hide the blue shadows under her eyes.

He crossed his arms and waited. She wailed and cursed, her beautiful features marred by rage. She was probably faking again, and his suspicion was confirmed when she peeked at him through her fingers, likely appraising his reaction. There was no trace of tears in her eyes.

At that moment, he felt the bottom drop out. For twelve years, he'd been spinning his wheels, surrounded by beautiful women, getting nowhere. What the hell did he expect? Did he really think he was going to find another Brenda?

"Sheila, it's over." He picked up the crumpled garment bag and stepped around her.

Her heels rapped against the concrete as she followed him. "Every week, it's over. By this time tomorrow, you'll be back. You're always back. You don't have the balls to be alone."

"I'm sure as hell gonna give it a try." He slid into his car and slammed the door. Her hand slapped against the side window as he gunned the engine and plunged his foot on the gas pedal.

His last glimpse of her revealed a face contorted with rage. He could imagine the torrent of curses pouring from those red lips.

The garage door rumbled open, barely clearing the sleek windshield of his BMW as he accelerated up the ramp and into the snowy night.

Jason blew through two red lights in the deserted streets before he took a deep breath and pulled to the curb. His fingers felt glued to the steering wheel. Stiffly, he peeled them away and flexed them before cutting the engine.

He leaned on the headrest and stared through the windshield. Snowflakes drifted aimlessly downward, disappearing when they hit the warm glass. He felt like a thermometer about to burst. He waited. After a few minutes, the heat drained from his forehead and cheeks, and he no longer heard his pulse pounding in his ears.

He restarted the car, headed for the nearest highway on-ramp, and drove sedately northward.

The brightly lit highway eventually became a darkened strip, slicing through rolling, snow-covered fields. He exited, drove eastward and eased the vehicle along a curving driveway, until his century farmhouse emerged like a friendly ghost from the blackness. He climbed out of his vehicle and stood in the driveway for a moment. The silence surrounded him.

He trudged through the snow to the dark barn. The heavy wooden door slid easily, well-oiled wheels rolling on their track with a small squeak. He pushed his face into the opening and peeked inside to ensure all was well.

Warm air blew outward and caressed his face, accompanied by the familiar fragrance of hay, ammonia, disinfectant, and dung. A welcome feeling of peace washed over him. Comforting sounds drifted from the dim, yellow light within—a soft snort through sleepy nostrils, a hoof scraping through wood shavings on the wooden floor. Satisfied, he pulled the wooden panel shut and headed for the house.

The kitchen phone rang as he kicked off his shoes in the mudroom.

"Finally, you're home. Corinne made me call to make sure you were all right." Bertie's North Shore accent was thicker than usual.

"Yes, Big Brother, I'm just fine. The police had plenty of questions about that Pollard guy, but I didn't have much to say other than the fact he was an accountant. You been drinking? I can hardly understand you."

"You know damn well I ain't been drinking. Corinne's been hounding me all evening, and I'm dead tired. Do you think that guy was aiming for you?"

"As a matter of fact, I know he was aiming for me. Sheila showed up as I was leaving and our conversation was very enlightening."

"What do you mean?"

"She was boinking the accountant."

"What?" His friend's voice squeaked with astonishment. "Moron, you gotta lose that woman. She's bad news. Did you tell the cops?"

"What would be the point? It'd be her word against a dead man's. Oh, and just so you know I broke up with her tonight."

"Yeah, how long will it last? This time next week you'll be back together. You're always pulling that crazy woman out of whatever hole she digs herself into. You're not a goddamn babysitter."

Jason rubbed his forehead and sighed. "Sorry, Bertie—it just seems like she needs one. But this time she's on her own. I just hope she finds someone with more patience. Mine is all dried up."

Bertie chuckled. "You've always been too soft. I'm surprised you don't have a houseful of lost puppies. You can't rescue every girl who's on the wrong path, my friend."

"It seems I'll never catch up with you, Bert. I'm destined to be single and childless forever."

"You don't look in the right places, moron. Bars and clubs don't produce family material. Okay, gotta go. Corinne will be relieved you're home."

"You can't fool me, Bertie. I know it was you checking up on me. Hug the kids for me. I'll see you at practice tomorrow."

As Jason hung up, he smiled. Bertie acted like a mother hen sometimes, but he wouldn't trade his friendship with the quick, dark Acadian for anything. They'd been best friends since their rookie year.

Bertie played and lived passionately, and he had a strong romantic streak. The day the NHL drafted him, he proposed to Corinne. They had had four young children and were still blissfully married.

Jason's life had taken a different direction as they'd matured. While his best friend settled down, Jason felt like he was still stuck in a college dorm, drifting from one woman to the next. He didn't seem to have the same magic formula to find his match.

He'd screwed up royally with Brenda, and since then he'd been searching in vain for a substitute. He hadn't any trouble attracting the opposite sex, but in the last few years it had turned into a parade of the wrong kind of woman. Women like Sheila; all hair, nails, and lipstick but no substance.

He remembered his first date with Brenda—horseback riding. The bright, cold and sunny day had quickly developed into a blizzard halfway through the ride. She hadn't complained; she only laughed when the wind whipped around them. She expertly corrected her mount when it slipped and stumbled on the ice. They'd cut the ride short, but the relationship had blossomed. Any other woman would have let him have it for taking her on such a loser first date, but not Brenda.

He imagined what it would have been like to have her by his side. Maybe his life would have been more like Bertie's.

Sighing, he rubbed his tired eyes and went to the fridge to pour a glass of milk. There was no point in speculating a life that would never be. It was better to be alone. He'd been alone anyway, even with a parade of beautiful women on his arm.

He sat on a stool beside the kitchen island and watched bubbles pop in the glass. *Maybe this is bugging me more than I thought.*

He jerked upright, startled as his cat jumped on the counter to inspect the contents of the glass.

Picking up the tumbler, he held it toward the feline in a silent toast and remarked aloud, "Well, Max, this certainly wasn't a typical day at the office."

Two

The coach's whistle blasted and Jason sprinted toward the blue line on the ice, scraped to a halt, and plunged forward once again.

The close-call had stayed on his mind far into the night, but he pushed dark thoughts away and juked between his teammates with the puck balanced delicately on his stick. His skates skimmed over the scarred ice with barely a scrape, and the ads on the boards blurred as he sped past them. He dodged behind the net and wrapped the puck around the post.

The netminder raised his stick and shouted, "How am I gonna practice, Peterson, if you don't give me a fuckin' chance?"

Jason grinned and slapped the blade of his stick against the goaltender's pads. "How're you gonna get better if you don't practice, Mego?" He swiveled and skated backwards, facing the goalie. He pointed his gloved fingers at his own eyes. "Watch me and learn."

He picked up another puck and this time barreled straight down the centre of the ice. He lifted one leg as if he was aiming left and fired the puck to the right, roofing it.

Mego dropped his stick, tilted his mask on top of his head, and headed for the bench for a drink of water. Just like a cat. Trying to act like it doesn't bother him but it does.

He skated after the goalie and gave his pads another friendly tap. Leaning on the boards, he said, "Don't let it get to you, Mego. You're going to see move after move, and soon you'll have them all memorized. You won't be a backup for long, trust me. You're good."

The netminder grunted and slid his mask over his face. "Okay, Peterson, show me some more." He skated back to the net, picked up his stick, and got into position. This time, the puck stayed out. Mego's victorious grin peeked through his cage.

As Jason skated back to the bench, Bertie slid alongside. "That was a gift. You must be feeling pretty generous today."

The big winger plucked a plastic bottle from the half boards and squeezed water on his face. He shook his head, refreshed, and blinked the liquid from his eyes. "I'm feeling very much alive today."

Bertie laughed and skated toward the blue line to join his mates. "Yeah, nothing like a brush with death to make you feel alive."

As he placed the water bottle back on the boards, Jason's gaze drifted to the steps behind the bench. The cleaning staff must have scrubbed away the evidence of last night's fiasco, but yellow tape still clung to the seats. The pebbles of safety glass had been swept away, but the big sheet hadn't been replaced yet.

Why try to kill me? Was it just jealousy or something more? That guy must have been unhinged to bring a gun into a crowded arena. Again, he shivered and scanned the seats, looking for any movement.

After practice, he barely heard the buzz of conversation as the team prepared for a free afternoon. As he settled on his bench to wipe the perspiration from his new helmet, he felt Bertie's eyes on him. Jason ignored him and gave every rivet on the helmet his undivided attention. He knew his friend had something to say when he stood like that, legs apart and hands on hips.

Bertie cleared his throat.

Here it comes.

"I think some of us should visit that lady in the hospital. Maybe get a little present for her kid or something," Bertie lifted one black eyebrow and stuck out his tongue, pretending to drool. "Hey, the mom might be cute."

Jason grimaced as he stood up to place the helmet carefully on its shelf. "I already planned to visit her before heading home. You're welcome to come along but don't start fixing me up with the poor girl. I'm off women. Besides, she's probably got enough on her mind right now."

In spite of his reservations, he thought of the brief moment last night when he had glimpsed a slender hand stretched toward a crying child.

Bertie reached forward and punched him lightly on the chest. "Come on, you wimp, get back in the saddle. No rest for the wicked, you know?"

The winger flung a towel at his friend's head and laughed good-naturedly. "All right, all right, but just for a few minutes, I have to get back to the farm. I've been neglecting my boys enough these days." He thought of his three horses, retired thoroughbreds he had adopted and rode as often as he could. The team had recently returned from a long road trip, and the horses needed some exercise.

"Get Mel to ride them for once."

"Mel's a great barn manager and groom, but he can't ride worth shit," Jason said with a smile as he shrugged into his jacket.

Later in the afternoon, the two men arrived at the hospital, armed with a bag stuffed with autographed team memorabilia. The attending administrator's eyes widened with recognition, and she cheerfully checked her computer and directed them to a room on the third floor.

Jason dug out his wallet and extracted a credit card. "If there's anything I can do to make this girl more comfortable, let me know."

She raised a hand in protest. "Don't worry; your bosses took care of everything."

A riot of color met his eyes when he pushed the door open. Flowers and stuffed animals filled the large room, and it took a moment for him to locate the patient. She sat propped up in bed, her head bent to whisper to a little girl beside her.

A few relatives stood near the window and their low murmurs ceased for a moment when the athletes entered.

The little girl regarded him with wide eyes and shrank closer to the woman. He hesitated, suddenly feeling like an intruder. The purpose for his visit seemed false. He could see the headlines now: *Famous hockey player visits hospitalized victim.*

What great PR. He felt a twinge in his chest. He was doing this because he wanted to, not because the media expected it of him. Somehow, he figured most critics would agree with the media, simply assuming he'd visited the hospital only for publicity purposes.

A thick mane of dark brown hair obscured the woman's face and fell about her shoulders, covering most of her pale blue hospital gown. The small point of her nose and dark lashes were barely visible beyond her cheekbone. A sling secured her heavily bandaged left hand against her body, and a thick square of gauze peeked from the edge of the gown at her shoulder.

She followed her daughter's gaze and looked up at him. When her gray eyes connected with his, Jason felt a buzz travel down his spine and a small jolt in his chest.

Apparently, she didn't feel the invisible connection. Her expression was cool as she appraised him. In fact, it bordered on mistrust. *What did I do?* Usually, hockey fans treated him with unbridled enthusiasm, but today he felt like he was on a job interview.

I'm not here to impress her, he angrily reminded himself. Still, he had an irresistible urge to set her at ease.

He sidled around the bed to shake her good hand.

"Hello, I'm Jason Peterson."

"Of course you are. I'm Christina Mackey." She indicated the little girl leaning against the bed, "And this is Mishayla." Her gentle voice held a formal tone.

He hunkered down and offered his hand to the girl. Wide, hazel eyes peeked at him from beneath honey colored curls. "Hello there, young lady. Do you like hockey?"

His initial unease doubled when she stiffened and crossed her arms.

Children usually took to him immediately.

"I don't think I like hockey anymore. Too many guns."

"Mishayla!" Christina protested. She glanced at Jason, blushing. "I'm sorry, she's usually so friendly. In fact, she plays hockey and watches you on television every chance she gets."

"It's okay; it's only natural she'd be upset after last night." He tried to make eye contact with Mishayla, her gaze darting about the room. "That kind of stuff almost never happens at a hockey game. The team would never want anything bad to happen to your mom. We're very sorry she got hurt."

She eyed him with a small frown. Her glance flickered briefly and finally rested on the bag in Bertie's hand.

"We've got presents." He felt like a traitor using toys to win an ally, but what the heck.

"Really? Hockey stuff?"

Bertie stepped forward and tipped the bag so Mishayla could see inside. He raised a questioning eyebrow at Christina, and she smiled and nodded, a dimple creasing her cheek.

He pulled out a jersey with the team insignia. "My daughter is your age, and she has a hockey sweater just like this one."

Mishayla detached herself from her mother and sank to the floor to help Bertie dig through the bag. It wasn't long before she visibly relaxed and exclaimed over every piece of treasure.

A trickle of relief washed over Jason as he saw her smile. He hated to see unhappy children. He had no trouble taking a stick to the face without so much as a wince, but every time one of Bertie's children skinned a knee, Jason often felt like joining in their tears.

He returned his attention to Christina. She was watching Bertie and Mishayla with a half-smile on her face. Her dark hair and lashes were a direct contrast to her creamy skin and gray eyes. Although she must have been tired from her ordeal, he thought she had an aura of freshness about her. He wondered why she was single. Somebody must have really messed up.

He could have used a number of smooth lines to help the conversation along, many successful conquests being the proof, but he knew this wasn't the place for such nonsense. It was time for him to grow up, anyway. All he could come up with was, "How do you feel? Does it hurt much?"

Christina shrugged with her good shoulder. "No big deal. It just grazed me and should heal in no time. I think I was more mad than hurt. Look at the bright side; it earned me a paid vacation."

Jason grinned. *Tough girl.* "I'm sorry you had to go through all this for my sake."

"To tell you the truth, I had no idea you were the target. I heard on the news you were hit."

"Just my helmet, not my noggin." He glanced at Mishayla. She held a Bobblehead doll, giggling at the replica of Bertie's face. Jason always thought the dolls looked ridiculous, but Bertie always bought one when he had the chance. "Your daughter plays hockey?"

"She had a natural aptitude for hitting things with sticks, so I thought she should have an outlet. It's fun watching her play; she's already tearing up the ice like a natural."

She sounded like she knew her sport. "Do you play hockey?"

"Goodness, no." She laughed and waved her hand at her family. An older man stood near the window. He waved and threw a wink in their direction. "That's my dad." Two women were involved in a lively discussion at the foot of the bed. "My sisters. After having two girls, I think my dad desperately wanted me to be a boy. He enrolled me in hockey when I was a kid, but I couldn't skate to save my life. Anyway, he gave up and we just watched games together." She grinned. "I used to play a bit of pond shinny in my boots with some of my high school buddies, but when I gave Carl Hickey a fat lip with a puck, I decided the world was safer without me on the ice."

Jason visualized a pretty brunette in boots and jeans unloading a slap shot at an unsuspecting youth and laughed. At the same time, his cell phone chimed. "Excuse me," he said, chuckling as he flipped the phone open. When he heard the voice on the line, his good humor quickly faded. He rose from the chair and took a few steps away from the bed.

~ * ~

Christina glanced across the room, catching her mother looking at her with a speculative gleam in her eye. The older woman raised a brow and gestured toward the broad back of the hockey player.

With a small frown, Christina raised a finger to her lips and shook her head; she'd have none of that nonsense. She had nothing against a visit from her idol, but she wasn't about to start flirting with some high and mighty sports god, no matter how rich and insanely good-looking he was.

Trying to ignore the way his jeans fit snugly across his hips, she turned her attention to her daughter. Mishayla peered at the pages of a children's book about a hockey sweater and giggled while Bertie read aloud in his lilting French accent.

She looked at Jason again. She found it difficult to ignore him—his presence filled the room. He had turned to the wall and covered his free ear so he could hear the person at the other end, but she clearly heard his end of the heated conversation.

"I told you, Sheila, I don't want to talk about it. It's your problem, not mine." After a few seconds of silence, he said, "You can be as sorry as you want to be, it won't make any difference to me. What the hell do you expect me to say? You blew it. We both did. Yeah. Bye."

He made a groaning noise and flipped the phone shut. When he turned around, he looked tired and a little sad.

He settled back into the bedside chair and smiled. "Sorry about that."

Christina wondered if she should say something, then pressed her lips together and studied the bedcovers, giving a little shrug. *None of my business.* She glanced at his face. The sprinkle of doubt she felt must have appeared in her eyes because he flushed and raised his hands.

"Oh! I am so sorry. I hope you don't think I got some girl into trouble or something." He laughed nervously. "I have to be honest with you…I'm getting over a pretty bad break up. Sheila's a great girl, but she got a little mixed up, and I couldn't deal with it."

She offered what she hoped was a reassuring smile. *Yeah, he's a typical athlete, all right. I wonder how many girlfriends he's broken up with this week? What a life.*

The door opened one more time. Phil, the male nurse, filled the doorway, his broad shoulders almost touching the doorjambs. He breezed into the room and clapped his hands. "Okay, everybody! Visiting hours are over! Come on, hit the road, our little heroine needs some rest." He waved his big arms, a wide, white grin on his dark face.

Christina laughed. "Do what the man says." Nurse Phil had proven his talent for clearing a room several times. She suspected her family was afraid of him.

A general noise of dismay drifted around the room. Christina's parents, sisters, and their spouses gathered their things and took turns bidding their invalid goodnight. Mishayla wrapped her thin arms around Bertie's neck and planted a kiss on his stubbly cheek. She hugged her mom and skipped toward one of her aunts.

"Mishayla. Stop." The girl skidded to a halt and looked inquiringly at her mother. Christina raised a brow and tilted her head toward Jason, who still sat beside the bed.

Her daughter received the message loud and clear. She trotted to Jason and threw her arms around him. "Thank you for all the great presents, Jason." She glanced at her mother and added pointedly, "I already thanked Bertie."

Jason's strong cheekbones reddened slightly, and his eyes crinkled. "You're welcome, young lady." He waved as she left, gripping her aunt's coat sleeve.

Christina watched his face as the last guest slipped through the door. His eyes had lit up when Mishayla thanked him, but the light faded as if he remembered something sad. She waited. He sighed, stood and offered his hand again. "It was nice meeting you. Get better soon. If there's anything I can do—"

"Everything's fine. It's all taken care of, thanks to your head office."

He still appeared concerned. "Does your family have a place to stay?"

"It's all right. They live just a half hour north of the city."

She watched him slip through the door.

Phil returned, fluffed her pillows and leaned toward her with a jerk of his head. "Them hockey players are still out there. Probably fighting over you." His cheeks expanded in a blooming grin.

She gave him a playful slap on the arm. "Phil, you're a sweetheart." Curious, she strained to see through the window beside the door, catching a glimpse of Bertie's face as he gestured furiously at the door.

Jason reentered, his head dipped sheepishly.

Phil kept himself busy at the other end of the room, shifting vases and stuffed animals on the windowsill while humming tunelessly.

Jason glanced at the nurse and shifted from one foot to the other. He mumbled something she couldn't quite catch.

She raised her eyebrows. "Excuse me?"

He tried again. "Could I take you out for coffee or lunch or something after you get out of here?" His stage whisper was clearly intended to escape Phil's attention, but the nurse only chuckled and hummed louder.

Christina thought about the phone call. She silently argued with herself, but eventually, curiosity overcame caution. She leaned back on her pillow and said, "Hmmm." *What the hell, I'm all grown up. I can take whatever comes my way. It's only coffee...or lunch...or something.* "Of course, I'd be delighted."

Jason's blue eyes lit up. "Great! I'll give you my number. Or you give me yours. No, you won't be home yet. I'll give..." He patted his pockets, searching for something to write on.

"Don't worry, I'm not going anywhere for a while." His flustered behavior amused and surprised her. *Not your typical super jock.* "Just drop by again in a few days. We'll probably have something written down by then."

He sketched a brief salute and pushed at the door. It didn't move.

"I think you're supposed to pull it," she said, hiding her smile behind her hand. He glanced at her with a shy, embarrassed grin and violently yanked the door open to rejoin his friend.

She glanced across the room at Phil. He raised his eyes innocently to the ceiling and sauntered from the room. Off-key strains of "Love is In the Air" drifted from the hallway before the door closed with a soft clunk.

Resting her head on the pillow, she closed her eyes for a moment and savored the silence. She loved her family, but they were a loud bunch. She hadn't a moment's peace all day and looked forward to a nice, long nap. She shifted a bit, trying to make herself more comfortable as her hand and shoulder throbbed lightly.

She gazed around the room at the flowers and gifts. She would never have been able to afford a private room with her insurance and under the circumstances, was grateful for the team's offer to upgrade her coverage. It was unnecessary; anyone would have done the same thing in her situation, but she was glad she had accepted the offer.

That poor man. What could possibly drive an accountant to wave a gun around in a crowded arena? He must have been a real nut case.

Death was hardly a punishment for a couple of scratches, though. She was lucky to be alive. The thought of her little girl without a mother made her shudder, and she forced herself to think of happier things.

Her mouth curved upward as she thought about Jason. This place wasn't exactly a nightclub or a setting for a posh party, but when he'd stepped into the crowded room with his buddy, she'd expected him to flash those incredibly blue eyes and come up with a cheesy pick up line.

Perhaps it was just a preconceived notion she had built up in her mind after living and breathing hockey since she was a little fan. Being dumped in college by a promising player had reinforced her prejudice, but getting pregnant by the bastard made things worse.

For years, nobody could sway her from her opinion that hockey players were rich, spoiled bags of testosterone, leaping with grace from one bed to the next. *But they sure are fun to watch when they leap over the boards and on the ice. I'm such a sucker for punishment.*

She recalled Jason's crinkly smile when Mishayla hugged him. Stop the presses! He was a rich, outrageously popular sports hero, and he seemed normal.

Three

"Why did you say yes? Are you nuts?" Heather folded a nightgown with quick precision, slapping a hand across the fabric to smooth it. "You said you'd never, never date a hockey player again."

Christina responded mildly, "I've had time to heal, and I'm not dating him." She shrugged the sling off her shoulder and reached for her slippers under the bed.

"Put that thing back on! The only reason they're letting you out early is because you promised to keep the sling on for two weeks." Her sister's expression softened. "Listen, Baby Sis, I'm not trying to give you a hard time; I just wish you'd exercise a little caution here. Especially after the fiasco with Mishayla's father."

"He wasn't a pro. At least, not yet—they'd just signed him. From what I hear, he still hasn't made it into the NHL. He's on some farm team out west. I think he drank away his big contract. It's a shame, he was really talented." She eased her stiff shoulder back into the sling and sat on the bed with a plop.

"Besides, Reggie gave me the best three years of my life. I don't regret any of it for a moment." She picked up a stuffed bunny from the pile of gifts on the bed and thoughtfully caressed its purple ears.

Good old Reggie, he hadn't hesitated for a moment when she'd cried on his solid shoulder.

Big, soft Reggie with his brown eyes and booming laugh. Wonderful Reggie, with his pathetic slap-shot and bumbling skating stride. Gentle, loving Reggie, who made tea and gave her crackers when she moaned with morning sickness. For two wonderful years, he'd been a great father to Mishayla.

She still felt responsible for not being there to keep him awake on that fateful night. He'd fallen asleep behind the wheel on the way home from a late night amateur game. His car had plunged over an embankment and crashed through the ice of a deep, frozen pond.

Heather sat beside her and gently placed an arm around her.

"Sweetie, I know the last four years have been hell, but are you sure that trying to bag Jason Peterson is the right solution?"

"Don't you listen to me? I'm sick of Mom trying to fix me up with every man who crosses my path, and then you telling me nobody's good enough for me. I'm grown up. I can handle whatever comes my way. Besides, I haven't been trolling for husbands since Reggie died, and I'm not about to start now. It's only lunch."

"You're just setting him up for disappointment."

"Why in the hell would a hockey player be disappointed if I reject him? Stop making this more than it is."

Heather took the stuffed bunny from her sister and stuffed it into a paper bag. "Why the sudden change of heart, anyway? Why are you willing to go out with him if you're so sure he's going to dump you?"

"I don't know…curiosity, boredom, hope. Why do people jump out of planes? This is my version. I'm tired of playing it safe."

Her sister smiled and laid a reassuring hand on her cheek. "Whatever you do, just be careful." She stood. "Speaking of future, if Mr. Wonderful doesn't show up soon, I'm driving you home now." She headed for the door. "Otherwise, I'll do a bit of shopping at the Eaton Centre and you can call me on my cell to drive you home. I'm going downstairs to sign you out. Back in a few minutes." She gathered a few remaining toys and swept from the room in her usual, businesslike manner.

Christina struggled to jam the last of her clothing into her bag with her good hand, effectively ruining her sister's effort to maintain neatness. At the sound of a soft knock on the door, she called out, "Come in," while attempting to zip the bag shut.

Jason pushed through the door. "What are you doing? You should let someone else handle that." He dropped a bouquet of flowers on a side table and stepped forward to help her.

His big hands flew as he expertly rearranged the top articles of clothing, and he zipped the bag with swift efficiency. He was obviously used to packing—all those road trips would make anyone an expert.

As she watched him, a ridiculous notion entered her head. He's touching my under-things. A hockey player is manhandling my bra. She stifled a giggle and told herself to grow up.

In an attempt to appear stern, she glanced pointedly at her watch. "Ten more minutes and you would have missed me. My sister's downstairs right now. She threatened to drive me home, but I kept stalling. Somehow I knew you'd be here today."

"Sorry, we were on a road trip." He picked up the flowers and thrust them toward her. "Somehow I knew you knew that."

"Yup, and evidence was up there." She pointed at the small

television mounted near the ceiling and grinned. "Five goals in two games! Congratulations."

She took the flowers, held them to her face and inhaled deeply. The velvety rose petals caressed her cheeks. Handing the bouquet back to Jason, she said, "You might as well take those down to the car and put them with the others."

His face fell. "You don't like them?"

"They're beautiful. Of course, I love them. Don't worry, they'll have a place of honor in my humble home. Are we still on for lunch? My sister left my car downstairs, and I've got some free time before Mishayla's out of school."

"Are you sure you're up to it?"

"Piece of cake." She slipped one arm into her wool overcoat and tried to pick up her purse and overnight bag with one hand. Jason quickly stepped forward, helped her with her coat, grabbed the bag, and tucked a bear and a huge horse under each of his arms.

Heather arrived at the same moment, with Nurse Phil in tow. He pushed an empty wheelchair into the room.

Christina eyed the wheelchair with dismay. "C'mon, I'm not getting in that thing. It's embarrassing. Besides, there's nothing wrong with my legs."

The big black man shrugged apologetically. "Sorry, Ms. Mackey, it's policy. Pleased to see you again, Mr. Peterson." He nodded to Jason and helped Christina into the chair.

Heather handed Christina her purse and swept her gaze over the hockey player, barely visible behind the giant stuffed animals. "It looks like your date decided to show up and he's got everything under control, so I'll take my leave. Call me on my cell when you're ready to go home."

"Yes, Mommy." Christina reached up to kiss her sister's cheek.

The elevator was packed. Heather hung back and waved the others ahead. "I'll take the next one. Bye, Jason," she said coyly, waving as the doors closed.

"Sorry about the plushie invasion," Christina said with a smile, as two doctors and an orderly were forced against the back wall of the elevator.

She leaned toward Jason and peered up between the horse and the bear. "Coffee or lunch?"

"Lunch, if you're up to it. There's a great place a couple of blocks away with a high definition TV."

She grinned. "Afternoon game?"

His deep, warm chuckle tickled her insides. "Bruins and Senators, I think you already know me." He wrestled the bear to one side and peered at her. "You don't mind?"

She laughed. "Me? Do I mind watching a hockey game? You don't know me very well, do you?"

His head disappeared behind the bear. "I plan to." His words sent her heart sideways. *Don't do it, girl. You need a plumber or a roofer, not this guy.*

Phil liberated Christina at the sliding exit doors. He leaned down, enveloped her in a gentle hug, and slapped Jason on the shoulder. "Take care of her."

After they stuffed Christina's belongings in the trunk of her car, they strolled through the gray afternoon and stopped in front of a replica of an old Irish pub. The hum of the lunchtime business crowd filled the room. A bright fire glowed in an oversized fireplace at the far end of the room.

After they settled in a dark polished booth near the flames, she perused the menu. "What's good here?"

"Everything."

She wiggled her sling. "I think I'll stick with something that doesn't involve a knife. Damn, I wish I could lose this thing."

"Wear it for a little longer and eat Shepherd's Pie. It only involves a fork." He gave her a knowing grin. "I've had plenty of experience with shoulders in slings. I can think of lots of things to eat with one hand."

"I remember. Two years ago you had that separated shoulder during the playoffs."

"Hmm, I think I gained ten pounds in pasta."

As they chatted and ate, Christina felt the occasional streetcar rumble by, causing the floor to shake and the cutlery to rattle gently. She loved the city and its noises, smells and sights, but its charms paled in comparison to the little village where she lived.

She loved the little bungalow on the quiet, tree-lined street in Schomberg. Keeping up with repairs, raising Mishayla and working full time in a dentist's office was draining but worth every nicked finger and banged knuckle.

Jason Peterson probably had a jazzy condo in the center of all the action.

She caught him staring at her. It felt odd looking directly into the intense blue eyes she had admired, even ogled, on the television screen. Seeing those eyes returning her gaze with the same, if not more, intensity was a strange feeling. Disconcerted, she tried to focus elsewhere.

"Normally, I'm the culprit staring at television screens in restaurants," Jason commented dryly after she glanced for the fourth time at the game on the wide screen above his head.

"Just checking to see what your enemies are up to." She sipped her pint and forced herself to look at him without blushing. Surprisingly, his face seemed relatively undamaged from the rigors of the sport. All that interrupted the smoothness of his skin was one small scar, just above his upper lip. The imperfection was somehow appealing.

He possessed rough-edged good looks, strong in brow and jaw line. His eyes, although deep set, seemed prominent in their intense blueness. Unlike Bertie's conspicuous and crooked nose, Jason's was straight and fine.

"You don't seem to have too many scars. It's a good thing you keep out of trouble on the ice," she remarked.

"Well, I'm a lover, not a fighter."

She raised an eyebrow at his cocky response. *That's not going to work, buddy.*

He must have sensed her skepticism. He dropped his gaze and shrugged. "Sorry, force of habit." He picked up his pint and started again. "I don't fight, but I've seen a few pucks close up. I guess I'm just a good healer."

"Thank goodness you never got hit on the nose."

"Yeah, then I'd look like Bertie."

She laughed, remembering the bobble head doll. "Nobody can possibly look like Bertie."

Nibbling on her shepherd's pie, Christina asked offhand, "So, who's this Sheila?"

"A mistake."

He had a look on his face that didn't invite any further inquiries. *Oops, bad subject. Jilted female, maybe?* It was too late to switch gears, so she pressed on. "None of my business," she said lightly, "it just seemed like you were pretty upset the other day." She could only guess what it must be like for someone in the public eye to maintain a private life. He probably had a whole string of girlfriends, anyway.

He simply offered, "She was seeing someone else."

She cast her doubts aside for the moment. *Maybe I'm not being fair.* "Well, thank God that only happened to me once and it was a long time ago." She forced another reassuring smile and took another sip of her ale.

He seemed to hesitate and then ventured, "Um, your husband…?"

"No. Not my husband. Just an unfortunate incident during college." She regretted mentioning the man who'd abandoned her before Reggie offered to marry her. Her good mood deflated.

His next question increased her discomfort. "What happened to your husband?"

"I lost Reggie four years ago. Car accident." Christina still found it difficult to say the words aloud. She switched her gaze to the large screen and stared blankly at a beer commercial.

He murmured something consoling.

A minute of silence followed as they both concentrated on their meals. She glanced at him and caught him peering at her face with apparent interest.

She blushed. "What?"

"You've got a little something..." He reached for her. She straightened in her chair and backed a little. "No, just a bit of mashed potato." He brushed her lower lip, gently.

She felt her stomach flip. *Oh, God, I think I'm in trouble.*

Jason cleared his throat. "When do you have to get home?"

"Huh?" Slowly, the buzz in her ears receded, and she heard the hum of conversation around her.

"Home? When?" He waved his fingers as if he was using sign language.

"Oh! Yeah...um, my sister's doing some shopping, then taking me back to Schomberg in a couple of hours. Mishayla will be home from school by then."

"Do you want to see the rink? I mean, really see the rink?"

This day is looking up. "Would I!" She proceeded to shovel the rest of her mashed potatoes and peas into her mouth with gusto. Jason smiled and followed suit, quickly finishing his fish and chips.

"We'll go in my car, it has a parking pass," he offered as they left the restaurant. "Yours is too crowded."

Christina settled in the BMW, sighing with pleasure when she felt the heated seat warming her back. "Nice car," she murmured. She glanced further down the block where her Escort was parked. It was older than her daughter.

"It gets me there. Personally, I like the SUV better." He wove easily through the afternoon traffic and turned into the arena's underground parking facilities.

They walked from the parked car to the elevator, their steps echoing through the deserted garage. At surface level, he led her through a warren of hallways that eventually opened behind the players' bench.

Christina gazed upward, struck by the size of the place, especially when devoid of fans. Muted, yellowish light shone on the ice surface, giving it a haunted feel. She brushed her fingers against the gleaming, new safety glass and turned to look up at the steps where the shooting had taken place. It seemed so long ago, yet it had been little more than a week.

She hesitantly glanced at the foot of the steps near her feet, relieved that the blood had been scrubbed from the concrete floor where the gunman had died.

She noticed Jason staring at the same spot.

"Did you know that accountant?" she asked.

He seemed to pull himself out of some kind of trance and turned to focus on her face. His lips twisted in a poor imitation of a smile. "Yup. Sort of."

"I heard he was aiming for you. Why do you think he'd do such a thing?"

"Jealousy, I guess."

"Jealous of whom?" A tiny seed of doubt took root once again. *Did Jason have an affair with the accountant's wife?* She gave her head a mental shake. *Give him a chance. He's nice.*

He leaned against the half boards and gazed down at the ice. "Remember when I told you Sheila was seeing someone else?

Oh, now I get it. "He was the other guy?"

Jason straightened and briskly headed for the entrance to the tunnel. "Yup."

A trickle of relief washed over her as she followed him. She couldn't imagine why; she'd probably never see him again, anyway. He'll do his duty and move on.

He pushed open a door, revealing the dressing room. She slowly walked around the perimeter, taking note of the small plaques above each open locker. Everything seemed shiny and bright compared to the old blue and white chipped paint she remembered on a tour of the old Gardens.

They rode upstairs, snuck into a corporate box, and raided the refrigerator, settling into a couple of stuffed armchairs near the observation window.

She leaned forward and peeked downward. "Now this is a more familiar viewpoint for me. I can't believe people pay thousands of dollars to watch a game when they can barely make out the numbers on the backs of your jerseys."

Jason laughed and gestured with his beer bottle at a flat screen television mounted on the wall. "They can watch that."

She snorted. "What would be the point?"

"I guess that's the way businesspeople do business. Better than entertaining your clients in your rumpus room or a sports bar."

They checked out the media booth before he took her back to the parking level. She watched his profile as he hummed along with the elevator music, and he looked down at her with a grin. Again, a long forgotten but delicious feeling slithered down her hips. She quickly slid her gaze to the blinking lights.

A repeated beeping sound increased in volume as they approached the garage level. The doors slid open, and Jason held an arm out to keep Christina from stepping toward the car.

Straining to see around his back, her eyes widened with dismay when she saw the condition of the BMW. A gaping, jagged hole had replaced the sweeping windshield, and the headlights and taillights dangled by their wires, shattered. Glittering bits of glass surrounded the lonely vehicle.

She held her hand to her mouth. "Oh, my God, Jason..."

His expression was grim as he turned Christina by her good shoulder and steered her back into the elevator. They rode to street level, and he jabbed at his cell phone. In a cool voice, he gave the police the details and arranged for someone to come take a report. Now at street level, he strode briskly to the exit, and Christina trotted to keep up. He slowed down and took her elbow.

"Sorry to cut this short." Jason guided her to the sidewalk's edge and waved down a cab.

She reluctantly slid into the taxi. "Are you going to be okay?"

He ignored her question. "Would you rather have the cab take you home or back to your car?"

"I'm meeting my sister at the Eaton Centre, and she's driving." She braced the door with her hand before he could close it. "Are you sure you don't want me to stay with you? It could have been a gang or something."

For a fleeting moment, his expression softened and a little crinkle formed at the corner of one eye. "I think I'll be safe. Thanks for the offer. Anyway, your sister's waiting." He spoke to the driver, giving instructions to take her to The Eaton Centre.

"Everything will be fine. This stuff happens all the time." He handed the driver the fare in advance with a generous tip. "Thanks for lunch, it was great." He seemed to provide the farewell as an afterthought and firmly closed the door.

Christina gazed through the salt-encrusted glass of her side window. He stood alone on the sidewalk with hands stuffed in his pockets, then plucked his cell out. His expression swiftly changed to one of irritation. She sighed and turned to face the back of the cabbie's head. Well, it started out to be a great afternoon.

~ * ~

Disappointment coursed through him as the cab pulled away. What a crappy ending to a great afternoon.

His cell phone buzzed and he flipped it open, expecting the police.

"Jason? Sweetie? It's me." *Shit. Sheila.* He made a move to flip the phone shut but hesitated.

She spoke quickly, as if sensing he would hang up on her. "Are you free tonight? Maybe we can get together at that nice restaurant in Yorkville. They say it's simply stuffed with movie stars. Honey pie, you know I'm so sorry about the other night. Really, I had nothing to do with it. Can't we just let bygones be bygones and start fresh? Jason?"

"Sheila, I've got a lot more on my mind than your social life. Leave me the hell alone!" Passing pedestrians glanced at him nervously. He flipped the phone shut, spun on his heel, and headed back into the arena to await the police and the tow truck.

Later in the evening, when he returned from the barn, she called again. She immediately launched into another campaign to set up a date. "What happened that got you so upset?" she asked with what seemed like genuine concern.

Jason let his guard down for a moment. "My car got smashed this afternoon."

"Oh, you poor baby," she cooed over the line. "Are you sure you don't want me to come over and comfort you?"

"Sheila, for Crissakes, I broke up with you. When's it going to sink in?"

"I don't see why you're being so hostile. I didn't ask Ian to go after you. He must have had his own reasons. It's not my fault."

He sighed and rubbed his forehead. *Why am I so hostile? She's weak. She doesn't know what she's doing half the time.* Other than being an insensitive, self-centered bitch, Sheila wasn't exactly evil.

He steeled himself. "Listen, Sheila, I'm not backing down. You and your lifestyle don't agree with me. I'm tired, just plain tired. I can't keep up with you."

Her voice had an edge as she retorted, "You can't keep up with me? The big strong hockey player hasn't got the energy? You sure seem to have enough energy for the chick who rescued you. That's it, isn't it? Just because I didn't stop Ian, you dump me and go for some simpleminded hick. Who is she, anyway?"

"It's none of your business who she is." He wasn't ready for this. *I hardly know Christina, and I've already managed to get Sheila's sights on her.* He could only imagine what Sheila would do to a nice, small town girl.

She pressed on, her voice now high and shrill. "Did you slam her right there in the hospital? Did you have enough energy for that?"

"Shut up."

"I hear she's got a kid. Is that the attraction? You like kids. Too bad it's always someone else's kid and not your own. Not your own, because you fucked up all those years ago with Brenda."

"Shut up!" He slammed the phone down with vehemence. Startled, the cat sprang off the kitchen stool and darted into the living room.

~ * ~

Sheila heard the rattle and click, and slowly rested the receiver into the cradle. She waited for her heart to settle down, but it didn't. It still pounded like the drums at the Seven nightclub. She restlessly drifted to the console in the dining room, poured a gin and tonic, and lit a cigarette. A rush of heat swam up her neck and bathed her face with perspiration. Suddenly, she felt greasy. Gulping, she pushed open her balcony door and stood on the tiny platform. At first, the blast of cold air was welcoming, but the moisture on her skin stiffened. She took a deep drag on her cigarette. Headlights blurred through the intersection below—cars full of happy worker bees going home to fuckin' happy mates. *Fuckin' saps.*

I wish I was one of them.

She couldn't wait to talk to him again, just to hear his voice, but decided to wait a while before bothering him. He was obviously in a bad mood, and she knew why.

She'd felt an incredible rush when she'd smashed in the windshield and lights on his fancy car. There's nothing like a good old-fashioned baseball bat to do the job, much better than a stupid hockey stick. It served the bastard right for trying to break up with her.

She hadn't expected him to be so uptight about the car. After all, he's rich. He can afford to get it fixed. Besides, he has another one on reserve. She'd give him a chance to cool off and call him again tomorrow.

Chilled, she returned to her living room and draped herself on the sofa. As she took another gulp of her drink, she squirmed with boredom. *It's too bad Ian went and got himself shot. He would've been a nice diversion tonight.*

She wondered what had made Ian go after Jason with a gun. After all, Ian knew she was already dating the hockey player. He slept with her anyway. Jealousy wasn't his forte. She thought back to their last conversation but couldn't pick out anything significant.

Maybe it was the thing about Brenda, one of Jason's old girlfriends. She recalled Ian's face going red when she had mentioned, laughing, that the big boy was prone to nightmares, and she had cheerfully given Ian the details. *Maybe Ian knew the girl.*

She shrugged and got to her feet. Draining her drink, she moved to the bathroom to prepare for a bit of bar hopping.

She reached for a ceramic talcum powder jar resting on the top shelf of her medicine cabinet. Under the powder puff was a tiny plastic bag of white powder, but it wasn't talcum. She frowned, noticing the amount had diminished over the last few weeks. As she prepared a couple of lines, she wondered how she was going to get some more. When Ian was alive, he had been obliging and kept her in good supply. He wasn't cheap, but he sure delivered. Now he was gone.

Sheila had no shortage of drinking buddies and acquaintances, but she didn't have any real friends. Ian had been her best source for cocaine, but he'd remained aloof, only doing favors for her when he was sure he could get something in return.

Jason, however, had no patience for her choice of recreation. *He just doesn't realize how much I need this.* She sniffed and wiped her nose. *He's such a goody-goody, no fun at all.* She touched up her makeup.

She wondered if Jason would be willing to help her out, but the notion died as soon as it entered her head. She knew Jason didn't go in for that kind of stuff, and he had never failed to remind her she was on a bad road.

Still, she vaguely recalled moments he took her home when she overindulged, held her hair when she was sick, and stayed with her while she sobered up. They were hazy, blurred recollections. The clearer memories were of his lectures, his glares of anger, and his declarations that he washed his hands of her.

She remembered the silence when he hung up on her. She also remembered his rock hard body, his lips, and his smile. She felt a brief surge of guilt, wondering if he would have stuck around if she'd stopped the drinking and drugs, but the feeling slid away just as quickly, like a wave that licked the shore of a beach. The obsession was too powerful to toss away.

I'm not giving up my lifestyle for him. Maybe I can talk him into helping me get more cocaine. Some of those losers on his team must be users, all that energy can't possibly be natural.

If he couldn't supply her with drugs, maybe she could hit him up for some money. Her dress shop was high end but also high overhead. Her assistant was already giving her strange looks when the till was short. It was too risky.

Maybe he'd help her if offered the right reward. The problem was finding an incentive. Her charm had held him for a while, but obviously the attraction had worn off. *I can't be what he wants me to be. He wants an angel.* She brushed her blonde hair behind her ears and checked her teeth for traces of lipstick. *And I'm no angel.*

She smiled as she slipped her fur coat over her shoulders and grabbed her purse. *To Hell with him, I'm having fun tonight. To Hell with him.*

The cab dropped her off at The Seven Up, a dance club on Yonge Street. It resembled a solid black monolith, its gleaming surface broken only by a recessed, rectangular hole at street level.

Inside, the music pounded her eardrums and slammed against her chest. Bodies moved in rhythmic unison; intermittent flashes of orange, blue, and green light illuminated identical faces. She moved to the primal beat before she reached the bar.

She spent the evening sampling each of the seven dance floors. At each level, she scanned the crowd carefully, searching for a likely partner. The drumbeat didn't change; only an occasional guitar lick or keyboard riff separated one so-called song from another.

The patrons didn't change, either. They all looked the same—scantily clad females thrusting their perky breasts at sweating gentlemen in various stages of wool-suit abandonment.

At Level Three, she leaned against the bar and casually glanced around. A man stood apart from the layers and layers of gyrating bodies. Pulsating flashes of red and blue light revealed a thin face punctuated by large eyes and a dark moustache. His suit was obviously expensive but it hung from his shoulders as if a stouter frame had once supported it.

He seemed to be looking in her direction, so she lifted one leg and carefully crossed it over the other, making sure the slit in her skirt was clearly noticeable.

She turned her face away and watched him from the corner of her eye. Yes, he was staring at her. He picked up his drink and approached the bar. She watched the man run his finger across his mustache, lean across the counter, and give instructions to the bartender. The big man behind the bar nodded and poured a gin and tonic. He placed it in front of Sheila and jerked his head toward Mr. Moustache. She smiled. She had a winner.

She sidled up close and placed her lips against his ear. In a raised voice she asked, "Want to dance?"

He squinted at her, and in the dim red light she saw all the signs—a thin sheen of sweat on his forehead may have been from the pulsing heat, but the way he repeatedly ran his finger along his upper lip told her he might have something she needed.

After a hip grinding session on the dance floor, she led him to the ladies' room and asked him directly, "Got any?"

He grinned and drew a small package out of his pocket. Sheila noticed the bulge in his pants and remarked, "You're well-equipped, and I don't mean the mirror and straw."

He laughed and they took a couple of hits each. He picked up the small mirror, ran his finger across the surface, and allowed her to lick it. Sheila pressed close to him and tugged on his tie. He kissed like a lamprey, his lips surrounding hers until she was sure he'd sucked off all her lipstick. Too much saliva flowed into her mouth.

"Time to pay for your candy," the man mumbled. He slid his hands up under her blouse and fumbled for her breasts. Sheila winced as he tweaked a nipple as if he was trying to dial in Seattle.

She relied on the rising euphoria to mask her revulsion. Before the feeling passed, she led him by his tie into the nearest stall.

Afterward, she managed to lose him in the crowd and hit the next level. She found a new partner, shared another hit and a few more drinks before hitting the stairwell again.

It was a good thing there was no windows. A sudden urge gripped her, to sail from the uppermost level and fly to the street below. She imagined the colorful lights sweeping past her in a blur before she hit the bottom.

She giggled. Hit bottom. Jason said that a lot.

Jason's voice in her head suddenly sobered her. The lights became garish; the constant boom, boom, boom of the drums jarred her nerves.

She pushed through the crowd of dancers and staggered down the multiple staircases. At the bottom, she broke a heel. Swearing, she snatched her shoes from her feet, bypassed the coat check, and stepped out onto the icy pavement to hail a cab. She ignored the dampness seeping through her pantyhose as she clutched her shoes in her hand.

A taxi pulled over and the driver yelled out the window, "Where's your coat, lady?"

Sheila stared at him, nonplussed. At the same moment, a server burst through the front door of the club with Sheila's fur coat. She snatched it without a word and climbed into the cab.

It was afternoon before she awoke. She didn't know how she got home, but there she was, in her own bed. She ran her hand along the sheets beside her. Alone. Thank God.

What day is it? Shit. What day? Am I supposed to be at the store? Gotta wake up. Gotta get back in gear.

She rolled over and groped for the phone. She haphazardly jabbed at the fuzzy keypad. "Oakville Farms," a voice replied.

"Damn," she muttered, and disconnected. She tried again and finally heard his low, sexy voice.

"Baby," she drawled, "I need you to do something for me or I'm just going to go crazy. Would you be a doll and take a little trip down to Jarvis Street for me? I have a friend there who has a package for me, and I'm afraid to go there by myself."

She heard him groan. "I thought you told me you weren't using any more. Why would you ask me to do something like that for you, anyway? You know damn well I'd never buy drugs for you or anyone else."

"Come on, baby, you don't want me to get attacked, do you? It's a nasty neighborhood. You're so big and strong; they won't give you any trouble. Besides, I didn't say the package was drugs. Did I say that?"

"Sheila, you've got to get yourself cleaned up. You're dealing with thieves and creeps. Some of them would think nothing of killing you for your watch."

"Why should you care what happens to me? You don't give a shit."

There was silence. She wondered if he was still there. Finally, his voice drifted across the line. "We're not together anymore, but I still give a shit."

"Not enough." Her throat tightened and she felt the prick of tears behind her eyes. This time, the tears were real. Not that it mattered. She was losing him.

He sighed. "I can give you the number of our team counselor, but that's as far as I'm going to help you. If you refuse to follow my advice, you're on your own. Your choice."

He disconnected.

Sheila dropped the phone on the carpet and sat up, running her fingers through her tangled hair. She wished she knew the identity of his mysterious rescuer. No pictures in the paper, just a name. *Christine. Christina...something. She's taking him away from me. That bitch has it coming...when I find her.*

First, she had to find a way to teach Lover Boy a lesson.

Four

Jason seriously considered changing his phone number and flushing his cell down the toilet.

Sheila's calls increased in number and vehemence. She threw everything at him—more tears, threats to end his career—she even threatened the cat. The problem was, she didn't really make any demands, other than the occasional, half-hearted attempt to get him to accompany her to a show or charity dinner. He wondered where the hell she was getting the money for all that stuff, considering what she was probably already spending it on.

After a particularly exhausting exchange involving a trip to Casino Rama, the calls abruptly stopped.

He thought his troubles were over until two weeks after his lunch with Christina. As he suited up for morning practice, Adam Noole burst through the door and stopped in front of Jason, his fists clenched.

"You son of a bitch!" he shouted. "You couldn't keep your hands off her while my back was turned, could you?"

Jason stopped tightening his skates and looked up at Adam, confused. Raising his eyebrows, he asked, "What the hell are you talking about?"

"My wife, you asshole! Stay away from her or you're dead meat!"

Jason stood. He felt a flush of anger, and he fought to keep his voice steady. "Jenny and I are friends. We've been friends since before you met her. What makes you think it's any different?"

"I hear you've been more than just friends…behind my back!" Adam's voice rose, and the veins stood out from his neck. He stepped closer until their chests almost met. Jason heard the men muttering, and he glanced at Bertie, who jumped to his feet with a flash of anger in his eyes. Jason held up his hand, and Bertie settled back on the bench.

He turned back to the captain. "Adam, I don't know where you got your information, but I've never been anywhere near Jenny, except at team functions," he said quietly. "This isn't the time or the place to get into this; let's talk about it later, over a beer." He deliberately turned his back on the furious captain and proceeded to slide his jersey over his shoulder pads.

"Look at me when I'm talking to you!"

Jason fixed his gaze on the wall, waiting. He felt Adam's eyes burning into his back. Fighting the urge to turn around, he plucked his helmet from the shelf and inspected every bolt and joint with intense interest until he heard Adam grumble and move away.

During practice, the only sounds were the echoes of stick against puck, with the occasional resounding boom against the boards. No ribald jokes, and no loud challenges. They passed the puck and performed their drills in a desultory manner, barely looking at each other. After forty minutes, the coach gave up and sent the men to the dressing room.

Jason stayed behind and skated in slow circles around center ice. He picked up a stray puck with his stick and wound up. The puck slammed against the boards with a satisfying bang. He gathered it up and slapped it against the scarred wood again and again.

The rest of the team had left by the time he entered the dressing room to shower and change. On his way out, the coach called him into his office.

"We have to take this seriously," the coach said, rubbing his chin nervously. "Adam is pretty upset, and I can't have the captain off his game."

What does he think I am? The towel boy? "Have you ever considered the consequences if the top goal scorer was off his game? Where the hell did he get this crazy story, anyway?"

"There was an anonymous call to their house yesterday."

Jason was incredulous. "How could something like that possibly have any solidity? What does Jennifer say about it?" He hoped Adam wasn't giving poor Jennifer a hard time.

"Of course, she denies everything, but it doesn't mean it isn't true."

Jason had never heard anything so ludicrous in his life. The coach had only been on the job since the beginning of the current season, and they had never been on close terms. In spite of his lack of experience with this team, Coach should have known Jason would never allow himself to be involved with a married woman, even though he had certainly entertained a succession of single women in the years since the beginning of his career.

"You are one piece of work." He turned to leave the office, muttering, "Christ, what an asshole."

The coach called out, "Watch your mouth or you might find yourself in the minors!"

Jason waved a hand in disgust and kept walking.

That night, as the players prepared for the game, it was the first time he wished he were somewhere else. He pushed through the gate, onto the ice, and the spotlights assaulted his eyes. Blaring rock music jarred his ears. As the game progressed, he felt rather than saw his captain's glaring animosity and the furtive glances from the rest of the team.

The situation should have been handled in private. He was furious Adam had voiced his concerns in front of the guys. With the exception of Bertie, it seemed the other men sided with their captain. *I've been with this team for over ten years and never gave them any reason not to trust me. Funny how loyalty can change in an instant.*

He felt like he was alone on the ice. Gaining possession of the puck was no small feat—he received more passes from his opponents than his own team, with the exception of Bertie. When he finally cradled the puck in the curve of his stick, he suddenly forgot what to do with it.

In the dressing room, during the first intermission, he heard Bertie berate a defenseman. "Peterson was wide open on the last shift, and you didn't give him the puck. Now we're two goals down, moron, because of your stupidity."

The defenseman didn't respond. He faced Adam as if for guidance, and Adam simply glared at Jason from the other end of the room.

"We're a team, damn it, and the playoffs are just around the corner." Bertie jerked his thumb at the glowering captain. "Concentrate on the game and not that fool's delusions. You should know Peterson's not the kind to break up a marriage."

Adam retorted, "You can trust him with your wife because she's so bossy nobody would dare try anything with her, you hen-pecked little frog."

Jason jumped to his feet just in time to stop Bertie from leaping on the captain.

"Settle down. His opinion doesn't matter anymore." Jason surveyed the room. All eyes were downcast. "Apparently, mine doesn't either."

The team lost by an embarrassing margin. After the game, he waited until the bench was empty before he left the ice. In the passageway, a bright spotlight blinded him momentarily.

Great. Another on-camera interview. For the first time since his rookie year, he didn't know how to respond to the host's pointed question.

"Jason, can you tell us what happened tonight?"

He hesitated only a second before falling into the tried and true. "We just weren't concentrating like we should have. I let the team down tonight, and I'm sure the next outing will be a thousand percent better."

Mercifully, the host ended the interview, and Jason wasted no time changing and leaving the arena.

~ * ~

"Heather! Mishayla! Dinner!" Christina pulled the casserole dish out of the microwave. She lost her grip and it slipped and landed on the countertop with a loud clunk.

Her sister swept into the kitchen and shooed Christina out of the way. "I told you I'd take care of it. Sit down, I'll serve this up."

Christina watched Heather scoop lasagna onto serving plates and held a chair out for her daughter. Mishayla rested her chin in her hands and eyed her plate balefully.

"Lasagna again? When can we have tortillas?"

"Tortillas require a little more dexterity than your mother has at the moment," Heather replied as she sat down.

"Dex what?" Mishayla regarded her mother with a perplexed frown and poked the crusty brown edge of her lasagna with her fork.

"Never mind. Eat." Christina picked up her fork and tasted. It was a little dry, but serviceable. She felt her daughter's frustration. "What I wouldn't give to ram some stuffing into a chicken right now. Everyone's been wonderful with these microwave meals, but a roast chicken would be a real change. I miss cooking."

Heather assured her, "Be patient. The bandages only came off a few days ago. You're still a little weak. After more physio, you'll be as good as new. Then you can cook for me for a while."

Christina raised her hand and flapped her arm. It still felt stiff but she felt barely any pain. "Look, Mishayla, I'm a chicken."

Her daughter giggled. "You couldn't do that last week. Maybe by next week you can tie my skates so Uncle Eric doesn't have to."

"I sure hope so. I miss tying your skates. The blisters have almost healed, and I need some new ones."

"Do you miss work, Mommy?"

"Not in the least. I'm having too much fun with you."

In truth, she felt guilty missing her duties at the office, but the dental practice where she worked had a policy about not returning until the patient was fully recovered. She needed both hands to handle the delicate work of cleaning the teeth of a long parade of anonymous mouths, anyway.

Endless rounds of lunches with the girls and physiotherapy were broken only by the occasional hockey game. She attended Mishayla's games and practices, allowing a sister or brother-in-law to handle the skate tightening duties.

After tucking Mishayla in bed, Christina settled on the sofa with Heather to view the pros on the television. Her favorite pastime took on a whole new meaning as she heard the noise of the crowd swell every time Jason leaped over the boards and took possession of the puck.

Tonight, she couldn't help noticing, although he made his usual gargantuan effort, things weren't going his way. He wandered around the perimeter of the action and never seemed to have the puck. Once, he ventured into the corner to compete for possession but none of his team-mates followed him. Inevitably, he lost the puck, skating slowly with his head low as he headed for the bench.

On the rare occasion when he managed to get his stick on the disk, he missed the net when he should have made an easy goal. His play seemed lackadaisical.

The game ended in a lopsided win for the other guys. Christina cringed as she listened to the television commentators criticize the hockey star's apathy.

Heather put down her wine glass and squirmed with boredom.

"Great, the game's over. Change the channel."

Christina wasn't listening. Jason's handsome, perspiring face filled the screen as he listened attentively to the on-ice interviewer. The athlete's usually flashing eyes seemed to have lost some of their light as the interviewer asked probing questions about Jason's uncharacteristic lack of enthusiasm.

"I think you've got the hots for that guy," Heather said. She began to sing, "Chrissie and Jason, sittin' in a tree, K-I-S-S—"

Christina shot her an irritated look and told her, "Shhh, I want to hear what these guys are saying."

"Who cares what they're saying? They're just a bunch of empty-headed jocks."

"They're not all like that. Some of them are really nice guys, family men," Christina replied with a frown.

"I'll bet even the family guys stray once in a while. Look at them," Heather waved at the television. "All muscles and sweat. They spend half their careers on the road, away from their families. Women follow them everywhere, drooling over them. Christ, they're not gods; they're only humans. You, of all people, should know that."

Christina felt a stab of annoyance, not necessarily aimed at her sister. She had to admit Heather's comments contained a grain of truth. After all, Christina had her share of crushes on mullet-haired heroes when she was a teenager and innocently ignored the rumors about professional athletes and their conquests. That is, until she met Mishayla's father. He managed to topple all her fantasies with one indifferent farewell after he got what he wanted.

Since then, she'd read about high profile divorces, about players sleeping with other players' wives. It was common knowledge.

But one guy shouldn't ruin it for the rest of them. "Well," she muttered aloud, "I think this one's different."

"Be careful, Sis. Not every man out there is another Reggie."

Christina tore her gaze from the television. "Give it a rest. I already had an earful at the hospital. I told you before, it was just a thank you lunch. I'm not trying to bag another hockey player."

"Well, after Dave dumped you, you and Reggie had something special. Can't you pick somebody a little…safer?"

"Safer? Heather, I didn't pick Jason, we just went to lunch. I'm not marrying him. I just want to get to know him. He deserves a chance, at least." *Now I sound like I'm a prize or something. I'm nothing compared to those beautiful blondes in the wives' section.*

"Just be careful. I'll go look in on Mishayla, so you can watch your lover boy on television." Heather dodged the cushion Christina tossed at her and ventured down the hall.

She's beginning to sound like a broken record. You'd think she was the one wronged, not me. Christina returned her attention to the broadcast. The play-by-play announcer argued with the color commentator about the star player's frame of mind. One of them thought Jason was distracted, and the other said something about a disagreement with the coaching staff.

She wished she could talk to him. *Something's bothering him. I don't know him that well, but even I can tell something's wrong.* As far as she was concerned, she was just another fan. *It's his life, and it's none of my business.*

The next day, the phone rang in the middle of the afternoon. Expecting a call from one of her sisters, she was surprised to hear Jason's low voice.

"Hello, Chrissie. How's the hand?"

"It's coming along just fine, thanks. How's the car?"

"Yeah, about that…I'm sorry we had to cut our afternoon so short. I had a great time at lunch in spite of how it ended."

"I understand. It must have really thrown you off. Did the police find out who did it?"

"Well, I filled in the report, but they didn't find out who did it. The car's been fixed and it's as good as new."

"You seem pretty casual about the whole thing. If anything like that happened to my Escort, I'd be livid. Did the security tapes show anything?"

"Nope. Nothing."

She gave up and changed the subject. "You seemed a little preoccupied at the game last night. You should have heard what the commentators were saying."

"Well, I guess I just wasn't concentrating like I should have. I'll snap out of it next game." His low chuckle trickled over the line. "Maybe a certain brunette was distracting me."

"Don't blame it on me!" She felt a warm flush rise from her neck to her cheeks.

"We're in Montreal tomorrow. It should be a real treat. Will you be watching?"

"Of course. You're talking to your second biggest fan."

"Who's the first? Me?"

"Mishayla."

They both laughed. Jason said, "Speaking of Mishayla, Bertie has a nice place in the country near Unionville, and we have a couple of days off after we get back from Montreal. I think this is the only weekend all year when we don't have a game. Do you think you and Mishayla would be able to join us on Saturday for a bit of skating on Bertie's pond? He and Corinne have four kids, they'd love having Mishayla around."

Christina visualized her little girl skating on a winter pond. She would enjoy it so much. "We'd love to come. Just let me know the time and place."

"How about you, are your hand and shoulder okay?"

"The bandages and stitches came off last week, so I can wave my arms around a bit to keep from falling. I'll just take it easy and be careful to fall on my butt instead of my face."

"So, you're actually going to skate? I thought you didn't like skating."

Christina laughed. "I'm sure going to give it a try. It's been about ten years, so just be prepared to catch me if I fall." She realized too late how flirtatious she sounded. *Damn, he's making this too easy.*

"I'll stick really close," Jason promised. Christina made a mental note to aim for his arms if she lost her balance, or maybe his waist, or maybe lower. Her own thoughts shocked her, and she blushed again, alone in the kitchen.

Five

The team, if Jason could call it a team, made the train trip to Montreal Friday morning. He felt good, making plans with Bertie for the skating party and looking forward to seeing Christina again after his return. His euphoria was short lived as he became aware of the strained atmosphere in the train.

He leaned toward Bertie and asked quietly, "Did you notice nobody's talking to us?"

Bertie straightened in his seat to scan the faces of his teammates. Some glanced nervously in their direction and quickly averted their gaze, while others talked to each other in low voices. Bertie sat down again and snorted with disgust. "Looks like the poison is spreading," he murmured through the side of his mouth.

The Montreal fans kicked up their enthusiasm a notch or three when Toronto was in town. Resounding boos jarred Jason's ears when he stepped on the ice.

Cripes, now I'm getting the business from both sides of the rink. The game was a carbon copy of the last one. He was open for passes on several occasions but lumber and puck rarely connected.

In the third period, Adam brought his stick down sharply on Jason's foot during a crowded scrum in front of the opposing net.

"What the fuck was that?" Jason growled through clenched teeth, following the captain to the bench.

Adam didn't turn his head. "It was an accident." He threw his legs over the boards and sat at the other end of the bench.

The night belonged to Montreal.

~ * ~

Home never felt so good. After his return, he spent Saturday morning coddling and riding his horses in the outdoor arena next to his barn and later having lunch in the farmhouse. He tried to put last night's game out of his mind and looked forward to an afternoon of pond skating.

The small red light on the answering machine blinked. *Probably*

Sheila again. He ignored it.

Eager to get going, he gathered his skates and a spare stick and climbed into his SUV, ready to pick up Christina and Mishayla at their home in Schomberg, ten minutes away.

Turning off Highway Nine, he wove the vehicle through the small village until he drew up to Christina's house. He stepped out of the SUV and admired the surroundings. Most of the homes were red brick Victorian houses, but Christina's home was a single storey Arts and Crafts home with sleek gables and a wide front porch. Mature trees lined the street, their branches bare and curled against the pewter sky.

As he strolled up the walk, the front door swung open. Mishayla stood on the threshold.

"Hi, how are you?" Jason paused in the doorway.

"Mom's under the sink."

"I beg your pardon?"

"She's under the sink. She dropped Daddy's ring down the drain." The girl beckoned him into the small foyer and shouted, "Mom! Jason's here!" She wandered toward the living room off to the right and left Jason to kick off his boots and search for Christina on his own.

Her muffled voice emitted from just beyond a wooden stairway. To the left was a dining room and to the right was a small entranceway. He stepped through the arch and found himself in the kitchen.

He felt as if he'd stepped into the sixties. A faux brick wall encased the area around an ancient electric stove, and a small window illuminated a red Formica countertop. With no room for a table, he could easily traverse the kitchen in two steps.

Looking down, he saw a pair of slender jean-clad legs sticking out from under the kitchen sink. His gaze settled on an enticing little strip of midriff between her jeans and her cropped sweater.

He bent down and inquired, "Need any help?"

"Nope, I got it." A grunt, a rattle of metal against plastic, and Christina sighed in satisfaction. "Yup, got it." She emerged with a victorious smile.

Once again, her beauty struck him. She had gathered her dark tresses into a ponytail, and she wore a sky blue cable knit sweater with her slim-fitting jeans. There was no trace of a sling or bandages.

"Sit down and have a coffee before we hit the road," she invited, scrambling to her feet. She dug around in a cupboard and produced a couple of mismatched mugs.

They sat in the dining room while Mishayla dragged her hockey bag across the floor and dug inside to retrieve her skates and helmet. The short visit relaxed him even more, and the disturbing events of the previous week began to slip away.

"Let's see the hand," he said.

She presented her hand across the table, palm side down. He reached out and cradled it, turning it over to inspect the tiny red scar that remained. As he brushed his finger gently across the raised surface, he heard her slight intake of breath.

"Does it hurt?" he asked with concern.

She gazed at him intently, her full lips slightly parted. "No," she breathed.

He wanted to bite that full lower lip.

Something in her eyes changed. She looked down at the table and cleared her throat. "I—I guess we should get going before I lose my nerve."

He raised his eyebrows in surprise. *Lose her nerve?* "What are you afraid of?" *Not me, I hope.*

She shrugged. "The ice, I guess." She offered a reassuring smile. "Don't forget, I haven't skated in a long time. I don't want to embarrass myself."

Mishayla appeared at her elbow. "I'm ready now. Let's go, let's go!"

He offered to take her equipment to his SUV, but she gripped the bag tightly. "I can do it. I always take my stuff."

After he stowed her bag, he opened the back door for her. "Wow! Cool, it's so big in here." She crawled across the back seat, dragging her Hello Kitty backpack behind her and bouncing with delight.

Christina admonished her, "Don't get your dirty boots all over the upholstery."

"Don't worry about it." He glanced at the dark green Escort wagon. In spite of its age, it seemed to be in fair condition. Only a few flakes of rust appeared on the rear fender and hood.

During the trip, Mishayla chirped constantly from the back seat.

"Let the man drive," her mother admonished mildly.

"Let her talk. I'm used to it." He loved to listen to the chatter of children. It was a refreshing change from the trash talk in the dressing room and the raucous flattery of fans. He was used to the chatter; he spent plenty of time with Bertie's four children, often recruited to babysit when his best friend took Corinne out on 'date nights'.

"I got two goals last night," the girl informed him proudly.

"Great, that's two more than I got."

They bantered back and forth, making inane jokes and singing silly songs.

Finally running out of steam, her chatter slowed until she merely responded with the occasional monosyllabic, "Yeah."

Soon, an electronic beeping sound replaced conversation as she concentrated on a handheld video game she had extracted from her backpack. He glanced at Christina, who looked at him with an indefinable expression.

She self-consciously tucked an errant strand of hair behind her ear. "Did you have a lot of little siblings? You seem to enjoy kids a lot."

"Nah, I just spent a lot of time with Bertie's kids and got used to it," he said with a grin and a quick glance in the rear view mirror at the busy girl in the back seat. "She's a smart one for her age. I'd like to see her play hockey sometime."

"It's a date," she promised.

As they hummed eastward along Highway Nine, Jason glanced at Christina curiously when she stopped responding to his small talk. Her smile had faded and her usually plump mouth tensed in a straight line. They approached a long curve in the road that ascended as it gradually bent left. At the base of the curve, a small dirt road intersected the highway, leading southward and skirting a deep, tree-lined pond.

The locals called it Glenville Pond, named after a nearby village. He knew this curve well. A few years ago, this stretch of highway was only two lanes wide, and there had been many accidents at this location.

He peered at her again and inquired, "Are you okay?"

She turned her face toward the passenger window. Her fingers clenched in her lap, and she didn't speak until they had passed the curve. Only when the road had straightened out again did she exhale. She relaxed her fingers, and her gaze returned to the road. He glanced at her again and thought she looked a little pale.

She brushed his forearm lightly and gave him a tight smile. "It's all right." She cleared her throat. "That was the curve where Reggie had his...accident."

"I remember. You told me about an accident."

"He fell asleep at the wheel. He went through the barrier and into Glenville pond. The car broke through the ice." Christina turned to check on Mishayla. She had donned a small pair of earphones, effectively muting the high-pitched sound effects of her video game. She was deeply engrossed, her tongue sticking out as she concentrated.

"Every time we pass this curve, Mishayla looks down at the pond and asks me if we could go skating on it. It's so pretty, she says. I don't know what to tell her. We never really got into the details about her father's death. Every time she brought up the subject of skating on that pond, all I could ever say to her is 'it's bad ice' and 'I don't want to go down there.'"

"Well, Bertie's pond isn't deep, and I promise you it's good ice." He wondered if that was the real reason that she was nervous about skating again, rather than mere embarrassment from lack of practice.

She spoke hesitantly, as if trying out the words for the first time.

"Sometimes…sometimes I blame myself."

"Why?"

"He played men's league hockey at midnight on Wednesdays. When we first got married, I went with him every week to watch. After Mishayla came along, I stopped."

"And?"

Her voice gained strength. "I should have been there to keep him awake. If I'd been there, he never would have fallen asleep and gone over that embankment and through the ice."

He was silent for a moment, thinking of the many things he could have changed in his own life. "You can't blame yourself. The blame grows and gets stronger. It bangs on the door and eventually gets in. It eats into you until there's hardly anything left. Squash it, before it's too late."

She stared at him with a look of wonderment on her pretty face. He mentally squirmed under her scrutiny. "What? What are you looking at?"

"That was kind of deep, coming from a hockey player." She must have realized how she sounded, and she immediately apologized. "Sorry."

He gave a wry laugh. "You're right. The game is simple enough, but the players aren't just a bunch of plastic pieces on a board. Life can get pretty complicated. Some of us have more regrets than others, and we have to work extra hard to keep the blame at bay."

~ * ~

When they pulled into the long driveway at Bertie's home, three of his children were already playing in the front yard. As Jason stepped out of the vehicle, the youngsters simultaneously vaulted toward him. He allowed himself to topple to the snow, exclaiming in mock protest as they piled on top of him.

Mishayla climbed out of the back seat, watching the wrestling match for only a moment before joining the fray.

Christina leaned against the SUV and beamed, her melancholy left behind. It seemed Jason had no trouble communicating with children; they obviously adored him.

She climbed up the wide stone steps to meet Bertie's wife, Corinne, a petite, dark, Frenchwoman with intense brown eyes. The woman held a baby that looked about seven-months-old. Christina liked Corinne immediately. She seemed to exude an electric energy even when standing still.

Corinne zipped the baby's jacket with a practiced flick and skipped down the steps. "Bertrande, get the nets and sticks. There's room in Jason's truck. Be careful, children, you don't want to end Jason's career with your carelessness. Come here and meet Miss Mackey."

She must keep everyone on their toes, Christina thought as Corinne rescued Jason from the pile. She handed him the baby, and he raised the laughing child above his face, making airplane noises.

Corinne lined up the remaining children and introduced them. The eldest was Eric, and the two girls were Jeanette and Lorraine.

Jason held the baby up and declared, "And this is little Barbara, the light of our lives." He handled the child as if she were his own, with pride and confidence.

Bertie was already hard at work, dragging nets and sticks and stowing them in Jason's vehicle.

After a bit of organization, the brood tumbled into the two vehicles and headed down a winding, evergreen lined track. A pond rested at the bottom of a sloping ravine behind the grey stone farmhouse.

It's beautiful. A mixture of pine and birch trees surrounded the spring fed pond and rose in steep hills on three sides.

"It looks like a Christmas card," she commented as she laced her old skates. "I hope it's safe."

Jason pulled her to her feet and guided her onto the lumpy surface. "I'll keep you safe." His blue eyes sparkled. "Now for a warm up lesson before we start our game."

~ * ~

For the rest of the afternoon the pond was alive with the muffled sound of metal blades scraping on windswept, uneven ice mixed with chatter and laughter. Occasionally a cracking sound echoed off the densely treed, steep hillsides when two wooden sticks collided. The sun, a pale white disk, barely succeeded its feeble attempt to penetrate the icy haze in the platinum sky.

Jason took his turn tending goal at one end of the pond. He leaned against the chipped metal hockey net as the action heated up at the far goal. He loved watching young people playing pond hockey, it took him back to his own childhood. *No referees, no grouchy coaches, no shit-disturbers chirping from the opposing players' bench...or my own bench, for that matter.*

Watching the children in carefree play, as he often did, he felt a mixture of contentment and loss. He wondered what it would have been like if a child of his own had been among them. *Well, maybe I'll never know.*

He picked out Mishayla, her flowing, honey-colored curls bursting from under her helmet. *Then again, maybe there's hope.*

She kept up with the Gauthier children with apparent ease. *She'll make it far.* Maybe by the time she hit her teens, a professional women's league would be ready to welcome her. *Christina, on the other hand...*

He laughed when Christina awkwardly pushed the puck past Bertie at the other goal, obviously by accident. She raised her arms and squealed with delight. She almost lost her balance, and Bertie dropped his stick and reached out to prop her up.

Jason skated over to join the others as they offered congratulatory back slaps.

The daylight turned from light silver to steel blue, and a few snowflakes began to drift about. Jason squinted upward and called across to Bertie, pointing at the sky.

Bertie waved in assent and placed his whistle to his lips. He blasted a call that ricocheted off the pine trees. Corinne, who had been at the edge of the pond attending to little Barbara, beckoned to the children.

"It's getting dark, my children. I can hear the cocoa calling me all the way out here. Wrap it up, time to go."

With moans of protest, the Gauthier children gathered their sticks, dumping them on the snow at the edge of the makeshift rink. They climbed on the tailgate of the SUV, and Corinne helped them to exchange their stiff, frozen skates for chilly boots.

Jason skated toward his friend. "I'll take these two ladies in a few minutes. I think our novice here needs one more lesson."

Bertie glanced at the still struggling Christina, inching along the ice and using her hockey stick for balance. Mishayla skidded around her, laughing as her mother squealed in protest. "Yeah, she looks like she could use some help, but I don't think she'll be an expert today."

"Not that kind of lesson, idiot."

Bertie raised his eyebrows. "Oh, that kind of lesson. Don't forget, this is a family rink." He winked. "Don't be too long. Can you grab the net and sticks, please? There's no room with this brood. See you back at the house."

The 4x4 bumped along the track toward the house on the hill, red taillights eventually fading in a swirl of bluish white snowflakes. Jason signaled to Mishayla, it was time to start collecting her things.

"Aw, c'mon, Jason, just a few more minutes, please?" Mishayla grinned and started to skate backwards. "I wanna practice just a little more." She tilted her head to the side and showed her dimples to advantage.

Jason raised his eyes to the sky and patted his gloves against his chest. "Be still, my heart, I can't resist you." He turned toward Christina. "I can't say no to that kid."

"It's easy. You just shake your head and frown." Christina called out to her daughter, "You can skate for just a couple of minutes. It's starting to snow pretty hard, and hot chocolate is waiting." She gave Jason an impish grin. "Now, where's my lesson?"

"What lesson? You're a pro."

"I don't know who you've been watching but it certainly wasn't me.

I'm surprised my ass is still attached, falling on it so many times."

Mishayla scrambled along the rough ice and pushed a puck before her with her tiny stick. As the girl knelt to dig the errant disk from a snow bank, Jason skated over to Christina. She stood on unsteady legs, holding on to the top of the goal net. Jason grasped her uninjured hand and pulled her behind him. Turning sharply, he held her waist and began to spin her around.

Christina squeezed her eyes shut and laughed breathlessly. They spun faster and faster until she pressed her forehead into Jason's chest and yelled, "Stop! I'm getting dizzy. I'll fall."

Jason scraped to a halt and held Christina against him to stop the spin. She clutched his sleeves and fought for balance, squinting against the drifting flakes and peeking up.

Jason felt as if she was drawing him in. Her cheeks, flushed with the afternoon's exercise, ached for nuzzling.

"Okay, here's your lesson." He hesitated before slowly lowering his head almost to her level. The vapor from her warm mouth intermingled with his own, floating between them. Their lips almost touched.

Jason felt a tug on his jacket. "Hey, Jason, spin me, too!"

Damn. He gave Christina a rueful smile and took hold of Mishayla's mitten covered hands. "You betcha, kiddo."

~ * ~

Christina closed her eyes and drew in a deep breath, exhaling slowly. If she stood very still, she might regain control of her liquid knees. She crossed her arms and watched the two spinning around the ice, laughing as they fell in a heap to the surface.

She wanted this silver blue afternoon to last forever but glanced at the darkening sky and remembered it was getting late. The woman inside her took a back seat to the mother, and she called out to her daughter, "Okay Mishayla, get your stick and puck and come over to the truck."

Jason picked himself up from the ice and dragged the net toward his SUV. Gliding over to Christina, he smiled at her with a look of promise in his eyes and took her elbow to guide her to the vehicle. Mishayla was still poking around a snow bank at the edge of the pond.

"I can't find my orange puck!" Her plaintive call drifted through the thickening flurry.

"It's over there." Jason waved to the far end of the pond where a flash of orange peeked through the swirl of flakes. "Hurry up, Pumpkin." He loaded the net and sticks in the back of the truck and dug around in the cargo area for their boots.

A deep, loud cracking sound reverberated across the ravine, quickly followed by Mishayla's scream.

At first, Christina thought a gun had gone off. Instinctively, she flinched and looked wildly around for her daughter. The noise of splashing confirmed her next fear. She spun toward the noise and bolted across the pond with quick, sure strides.

Jason's urgent voice cut through the thudding panic in her head. "Get down!" he commanded. "Get on your stomach before you break through!" She threw herself on her stomach and crawled closer to the hole in the ice.

"I don't see her!" She plunged her arms into the black, icy water and without hesitation, swung her skates over the edge and slid into the hole.

Jason's voice was high and urgent as he yelled, "Chrissie, no!" She took a deep breath anyway and submerged her body. Her skate blades sank in the muddy bottom of the pond—it must have been about shoulder deep for her but too deep for Mishayla.

The water quickly penetrated her clothing and was so cold her skin felt as if it was on fire. An incredible urge to gasp took hold but she fought it. She opened her eyes as wide as she could in the gloom, waving her arms slowly in front of her. Something hard hit her fingers—Mishayla's helmet— then something soft—her jacket. Freezing fingers refused to close, so she enclosed her arms around her daughter, gathering her close to her body. She bent her protesting knees and pushed upward. Her head abruptly made contact with the underside of the ice. She winced and cried out. When she opened her eyes again, she saw the bubbles from her silent shout race to the surface and spread out against the ice. She must have misjudged her position. Running out of air, she followed the crawling bubbles with her fingers until she found the opening. A hand grasped her wrist and pulled.

She broke through the surface, gasping with the cold. Her blurry, ice-encrusted vision slowly cleared until she saw Jason's panic-stricken face looking at her.

~ * ~

No, no, no, Jason's mind raced when Christina's head disappeared under the frozen slush. He lowered himself to the ice, mindful his heavier weight could create another cave-in. He used the hockey stick as support and shimmied closer to the hole.

Mere seconds had passed but felt like hours. He was about to slide into the hole when he saw bubbles break to the surface, then a hand.

Thank God! He reached out, grabbing Christina's wrist and pulled. Two heads broke the gelling surface of the black water. He held the stick across the edge of the hole, and Christina used it to steady herself while heaving the little girl's limp body out of the water.

Jason reached out, grabbed a handful of sodden hood, and pulled Mishayla out of harm's way before holding out the hockey stick for Christina to grip. Kicking furiously, she hauled herself out of the water.

Christina knelt and yanked at Mishayla's wet jacket. She finally pulled it off. Jason had shed his coat and quickly wrapped the little girl in it. He peeled off his wool sweater and handed it to Christina.

"Take off that wet jacket and put this on. Is she breathing?"

"I—can't tell."

He pulled off Mishayla's helmet and put his ear to mouth. He couldn't tell if she was breathing. Laying his hand on her chest, he felt no movement.

He immediately started resuscitation. Again, time stood still until Mishayla began to cough and cry.

Christina's relieved sobs mixed with her daughter's wails. She bent and kissed Mishayla's forehead.

Jason reached out and cradled Christina's cold cheek in his hand. He had to get them to the house. He gathered Mishayla into his arms. "Come on, let's go. Can you get to the car?"

"I—I d-d-don't know…" Christina's hair had loosened from its ponytail and freezing tendrils obscured her eyes, although he easily saw her lips tremble.

Jason shifted Mishayla to one arm, enclosed Christina in the other and skated as he'd never skated before. The snow pelted his bare chest and arms, but he hardly felt the cold.

His silver SUV materialized out of the grayness, offering shelter. He let go of Christina long enough to reach up and slam the hatch shut and guided her to the passenger side. He jerked opened the door and ushered her toward the opening. Christina made a helpless sound, so he used his free arm and lifted her into the front seat.

He deposited Mishayla in her lap, adjusting his jacket to cover mother and daughter, scrambled around to the driver's side, and started the engine, cranking up the heat to full.

He realized he was still wearing skates.

"Shit!" he muttered, trying to untie the wet laces with cold fingers. Swearing again, he reached across to the glove compartment, blindly feeling around inside until he found a penknife. With an anxious look at Christina as she shivered and pressed her cheek against Mishayla's wet hair, he slashed at the laces of each boot and peeled the skates off, hurling them into the back seat.

Jason pressed his socked foot on the accelerator and drove like a madman to the house at the top of the hill, holding the steering wheel with one hand and stabbing at his car phone with the other in an effort to reach Emergency Services. All he heard was a gurgling sound from the phone—no service. He threw the phone behind him to join the skates.

Finally, Jason ploughed to a stop in the driveway of the big stone house. The front door opened, spilling warm, yellow light and Bertie's silhouette onto the front steps.

~ * ~

Bertie stepped outside and peered through a snowfall that was quickly developing into a blizzard. He flipped on the exterior light and his heart jolted when he saw a bare-chested Jason plugging through freshly fallen snow in his socked feet. In his arms, wrapped in his red jacket, was a bundle. Christina hurried close behind, hugging an oversized sweater to her body, her hair plastered and half frozen to the sides of her face. Her skates scraped against the flagstone walk.

Mon Dieu, not again. "Corinne!" he shouted over his shoulder, "Mishayla has gone through the ice! Get blankets and towels!"

He ushered the trio inside. This wasn't the first time a little one had fallen through a weak spot. He berated himself for not checking every inch more carefully that morning.

He took one look at Jason's face. His friend looked devastated. "Don't worry, moron, Corinne will know what to do." He attempted a light grin. "I leave you alone for a minute and this happens?" He pushed Jason with his precious cargo toward the warm family room.

Christina attempted to follow, but Bertie grabbed her arm. "No, no, my dear, you stay right here. We have to get those skates off. Corinne will strangle me if the floor gets scratched."

"How can you joke at a time like this?" Christina sobbed. She brushed her damp hair from her face and plunked on the bottom step of the oak staircase.

"Because it's all I can do." Bertie's insides churned, but he kept a smile on his face. Swearing softly in French, he struggled with her ice-encrusted skates until he got them off, while his wife dashed down the stairs with an armload of blankets.

She paused long enough to drape one over Christina's shoulders. "Go straight up to our room at the end of the hall. There are pajamas in the top drawer of the high dresser," she said over her shoulder, rushing to the family room with the rest of her bundle.

Bertie helped the trembling girl to her feet and tried to guide her upstairs. Christina resisted, attempting to head for the family room and her daughter. The sound of shouts and wails burst through the open doorway.

He grabbed her shoulders and turned her firmly toward the stairs. "Get changed first, you're soaking and freezing. Jason and Corinne are taking care of Mishayla. Don't worry, we've been through this before. One of our kids went through the ice two years ago. Do you need help with your head?"

She looked blankly at him for a moment. "Why?"

"You're bleeding."

She touched her forehead, shook her head and gave him a half smile through her tears. He watched her as she hurried up the stairs and he strode into the family room.

The four Gauthier children crowded around their mother as she wrestled a weeping and shivering Mishayla into a warm pair of flannel pajamas. Four-year-old Lorraine reached through legs and arms, stroking Mishayla's wet hair with concerned fingers, telling her in a tiny voice that everything was going to be okay. Jason stood to one side, shivering, his muscular arms folded tight against his chest. Shock etched his face.

"Get upstairs and find one of my track suits," Bertie ordered Jason as he reached to pluck little Lorraine from the crowd and deposited her on a chair with a little shake of his finger.

Jason didn't respond.

"Hey! Moron. Go get changed."

Jason's eyes slowly regained their focus, and he turned his gaze to Bertie. "Nothing you own will fit me," he retorted.

That's more like it, Bertie thought.

Christina returned, dressed in red fleece pajamas, wet hair encased in a thick towel. A small bandage covered the scraped forehead. Her cheeks were still flushed and her nose red from the chill, but she already looked better.

Lorraine had already slipped from the chair and was back in the fray. Muttering to himself, Bertie scooped her up again. "How can your mother do anything with you under her feet? Sit."

His daughter chirped in a fine imitation of her mother, "She needs my help. I'm the best comforty girl here."

He passed his hands over his mouth to hide his smile and said sternly, "You will be the best help if you sit here." He gave her a quick kiss on the forehead and turned to Jason.

"Moron. Get dressed. You'll get my wife all excited looking like that."

~ * ~

Christina walked up behind Jason and laid a shaking hand on his forearm. Her fingers were freezing cold, but his skin was colder.

He slowly turned to look at her, and his expression softened.

"Are you okay?" He glanced anxiously at her injured forehead.

She wanted to wipe the worry from his face. She reached up and touched his cheek. "I'm all right. We're both all right." She reassured him with a smile she didn't feel, and he turned his head to lightly brush his lips against her thumb.

She felt the electricity travel down her arm. She withdrew her hand and held her wrist against her chest with her other hand.

"Go cuddle your little girl." The corner of his mouth lifted in a little smile. He shivered again, rubbing his shoulders.

"Get something warm on," she whispered and turned to her daughter.

Mishayla had stopped crying and finally allowed Corinne to do up the last button on her pajamas. At the sight of her mother, she raised her arms and looked as if she was going to start wailing again.

Christina gently brushed the children aside and slid onto the sofa to take her little girl in her arms. Corinne draped blankets over the pair so their bodies could warm each other. "Both of you should warm up slowly, not too quick, so stay at this end of the couch."

"Why? Shouldn't we get warm as fast as we can?"

"You don't want to shock your system."

"You're the boss."

Corinne chuckled. "You bet I am."

As little Lorraine attempted to climb in with Christina and Mishayla, Corinne clucked and shooed her children from the room, shouting instructions. "To the kitchen, *mes enfants*, let's finish making that big batch of chocolate. Eric, go entertain Barbara, she's crying enough to wake the dead. Bertrand, please get some more firewood for later. Jason, go upstairs and find something that will fit you and I'll put your things in the dryer." She blew out of the room like a little tornado, calling out behind her, "Nobody is going anywhere tonight. This snowfall is going to be a blizzard. I think there's enough chicken soup for everyone."

Christina cradled her daughter in her arms and watched her face. Mishayla's sobs had finally subsided to little sniffles, and her eyes drooped sleepily. Her shivering eventually stilled and she snuggled deeper into her mother's arms.

Ghastly images played repeatedly in Christina's frozen, befuddled mind.

Ice. Bertie's pond. Glenville Pond. Damn ponds! Fucking, damned ice took Reg. Almost took my baby.

She leaned her head against the back of the sofa and closed her eyes. *Why does the damn ice keep calling me back? In this country, you can't escape it, may as well live with it.*

"It's my fault."

She opened her eyes. Jason sat cross-legged in the chair on the other side of the coffee table. He wore a grey fleece tracksuit, too tight for his large frame. A wool blanket hung over his shoulders. The sleeves of the sweatshirt crept halfway up his forearms, and his muscular calves showed between pant legs and clean white socks. His eyes intently focused on Mishayla's sleeping face. Christina frowned, puzzled. "What's your fault?"

"I shouldn't have told her to go back to get the puck. It should have been me."

She straightened in her seat. Stiffness had set in, and her joints protested. "Everyone must have skated over that spot thirty times this afternoon. It could have collapsed at any time. There was no way you could have known the danger. None of us did." She frowned. "Besides, you're the one who gave that great advice about not assigning blame. Leave it. It's over now, and everything's all right."

Bertie entered with more firewood, took one look at Jason's outfit and burst into high, cackling laughter. "You look like the Incredible Hulk in that getup!" He dodged past Jason as the big man stretched his legs out in an attempt to trip him.

Jason quipped, "It's not my fault, I had to choose from a bunch of clothes that belong to The Keebler Elf."

Christina smiled. *They sound like Heather and me when we fight.*

Corinne swept into the room, frowning and shushing the men. She bent to check on Mishayla.

"She looks fine. I'll take her temperature and then, if everything's all right, we'll let her sleep a bit before having some soup to warm up some more. Is that okay with you, my dear?" She raised her eyebrows questioningly at Christina.

Christina nodded. Corinne slid an electronic thermometer into Mishayla's ear. The tiny Acadian woman inspected the instrument and smiled in apparent satisfaction. She bent and lifted Mishayla's eyelids, inspecting the pupils carefully.

Christina was still worried. "What if she's not okay? What if there's a setback or something? What if there's brain damage?" She looked out the front window. The snow had intensified.

Corinne waved a hand in dismissal. "We went through this before. I was a nurse and I know what to look for. We'll keep an eye on her temperature and when she wakes up, we'll get some soup into her. If there's a problem, I'm sure Bertie can get her to the hospital faster than an ambulance in this snow."

Only partially reassured, Christina settled Mishayla into the sofa and followed Jason and Corinne to the kitchen.

The family already sat around a long, scarred harvest table. Jason slid a chair back for Christina and opened a cupboard door. He grabbed a couple of bowls and ladled some thick chicken soup for both of them.

The chatter and laughter reminded Christina of her own large family. Corinne and Bertie exchanged cruel banter and loving glances, and the children egged them on.

Jason was quiet. He sat with his arms folded on the table, staring at his untouched bowl of soup. When Christina caught him glancing furtively at her, his gaze quickly switched to the doorway.

Suddenly, he smiled, and Christina looked behind her.

Mishayla stood in the doorway with her blanket trailing behind her. She rubbed her eyes and announced, "What's all the noise? I'm hungry. Can we have tacos?"

A general cheer rose from the table and Mishayla happily settled on Jason's lap for a share of his hot chicken soup and soft warm bread.

~ * ~

Jason's relief was palpable. He encouraged Mishayla to eat and laughed gently at her jokes. She seemed unaffected by her spill in the icy water.

He couldn't help going over the events of the afternoon in his mind. He should have taken the girls back at the same time as the Gauthier family. He should have gone to get the puck himself.

Christina laid a hand on his forearm again, giving it a little squeeze. He looked at her and all he saw in her eyes was warmth and gratitude.

"You handled everything perfectly, mister," she said with a smile. "Everything's fine now. Don't worry."

Jason relaxed a little, rested his cheek on the top of the little girl's head, and grinned back. "You did most of the work. I was just the courier. Hey, do you realize you were skating like a pro when you went after her?"

Christina's eyes widened with surprise. "I was? Wow, maybe there's hope for me after all."

After dinner, he helped Bertie load the dishwasher while Corinne and Christina settled the children in bed. He heard the squeal of laughter and the thump of running feet.

"They want you to read them a story." Christina stood in the kitchen doorway.

Bertie pushed past Jason, but Christina stopped him. "They want Jason."

"Ha!" Jason threw his sponge at Bertie and draped his arm around Christina's slender shoulder. "Let's read Cinderella. I'll be Prince Charming, and you can be Cinderella. Corinne can be the Ugly Stepmother."

"I heard that!" Corinne's voice drifted from her son's room.

An hour later, peace finally wrapped itself around the house. Jason entered the family room to find the women already draped on the long sofa, each holding a snifter of brandy. Bertie stretched in one of the leather chairs flanking the fireplace, his eyes drooping.

He poured a glass of brandy for himself and settled in the other chair near the fireplace. With a sigh of contentment, he swirled the amber liquid and inhaled its fragrance. For a few moments, the only sound was the ticking of the hall clock and the crackle of the fire.

He noticed a folded arrangement of bedding on the end table beside the sofa.

"Who's getting the sofa?" He already knew he was elected, but couldn't resist getting a rise out of Corinne. She had a strict policy about decorum in her household, not that he'd ever had a chance to break it.

Corinne arched an eyebrow and quipped, "Your lady friend gets the guest room tonight."

"Couldn't we have flipped for it?" He winked at Christina. She lay curled at the end of the sofa, wrapped again in a soft wool blanket. She had removed the towel from her head and her dark hair spilled onto her shoulders in unruly curls. The firelight reflected warmly on her lovely face and in her eyes. The tension in her face and shoulders had finally disappeared. She raised her brandy glass and smiled.

He wished Corinne would get her skinny butt off the other end of the couch so he could take her place.

He knew his hostess too well. Until now, she had never allowed his past girlfriends to pass through the front door. Except for Brenda, so long, long ago, back when he and Bertie were rookies.

He gave Corinne a baleful look, and her only response was a wicked grin and a wink.

"I think everyone should call it an early night," she announced in a voice that didn't invite any protests. She gave Jason a particularly stern look. "After today, everybody needs to get some sleep."

Jason sighed. As usual, she was right. She was always right.

~ * ~

Christina lay in the darkness of the guest room, looking blankly at the ceiling. No artificial light crept through the high windows, but the reflection from the snowy night gave the room a ghostly glow.

In all the excitement, she'd almost forgotten the moment of closeness between her and Jason, just before Mishayla went through the ice. He had looked at her with an expression she'd seen before—the heated, passionate intensity she usually witnessed when he was in the middle of a game. When he had looked at her that way, the sight had left her frozen but not from the cold. She wished the afternoon had stopped right there and lay suspended, so she could absorb his gaze.

But this wasn't a game. It was real life and she couldn't afford to get mixed up with a man who might only have a passing interest in her.

She could tell he was attracted to her. She was attracted to him, too. But so were thousands of other women.

Mishayla liked him. Hell, she liked him. She turned over and punched her pillow, trying to get comfortable.

She thought about her first serious boyfriend, just before she had met

Reggie.

I liked David, too. He was popular, handsome, and a wicked good hockey player. He had decided he had to have her, and like an idiot, she had succumbed to his charms. As soon as he'd gotten what he'd wanted, he moved on in a flash.

I was an idiot.

Thank God for Reggie. He had swept in and provided a solid shoulder to cry on and the rest was history.

But like Heather said, Jason is not Reggie. Hopefully, he wasn't like David.

She rolled on her back and silently screamed at the ceiling. *Make up your mind, woman!* She concentrated on the image of his strong arms sweeping up her child to carry her to safety. She recalled the look of concern and tenderness on his face after delivering Mishayla to Corinne's capable hands. She still felt the burning tingle in her palm when he had brushed his lips against them.

Remember though, he just broke up with his girlfriend. His only girlfriend? Hockey players are bad news. Bad news... But maybe not this one.

~ * ~

Jason gazed through drowsy eyes at the dying embers in the big stone fireplace. When Mishayla kissed his cheek and allowed her mother to tuck her into bed, he had felt a rare peace. Now, alone, his old fears resurfaced.

My God, if anything had happened to her or Christina, she'd never forgive myself. She didn't think she could go through that again. He deliberately steered himself away from such thoughts. *Everything's okay now, nobody's lost, and everyone is fine...except me.*

He was afraid to fall asleep. The nightmare would come back again, especially after today. He turned to his back, concentrating on the dancing light on the ceiling until his racing heartbeat slowed to normal.

He thought of Christina. In spite of the frightening events that day, he was glad he had invited her to spend time with him. She was different. She didn't seem like the kind of woman who liked him just because he was a hockey player. Well, maybe it was because he was a hockey player but not because of the money.

She seemed to love the game for itself, not for its fringe benefits. It was a deep, intangible love for the game that had deep roots in their country's past. To him, the game represented everything that was Canadian—in winter, anyway. Summers were precious and somehow surreal. When winter set in, one either hid from it or embraced it—the cold, the snow, the sportsmanship and camaraderie, the speed, the toughness required in order to survive…and win winter hockey.

The women he had dated in the past didn't seem to see beyond the lights, the crowds, and the money, but he had a feeling Christina shared his passion for the game in her own way. She must have showed it by rolling out of bed at four thirty in the morning to take her daughter to an early morning game, by enduring the calluses caused by tying countless skate laces; the cold fingers and sleepy eyes revived by a paper cup of vile coffee from the nearest vending machine.

He was sure she could imagine the rush a winger felt when his partner fed him a jewel of a pass that stuck to his stick like glue, the breakneck speed at which a player sped from one end of the ice to the other, and the strength required to stop on a dime.

Just like she'd claimed, she didn't play the game. In fact, she played badly. But her eyes had shone with glee that afternoon when she'd shoved the puck past Bertie into the old net and hobbled around on her skates, dubbing herself the next Lemieux.

He smiled when he recalled her leaning on a battered goalie stick when it was her turn to tend goal, looking like a diminutive version of the old goalie legend, Ken Dryden. He was sure she only leaned on the stick for support, but the image made him smile in the dark.

He remembered with admiration her quick action when Mishayla was in danger, throwing herself in harm's way without thinking about her own safety. He saw her face again in the firelight, swirling her brandy and peeking at him from under her lashes.

From what he had witnessed today, he drew a conclusion. She was steady, she was deep, she was brave, and by God, she was beautiful.

Sleep still evaded him. He twisted around on the sofa until the bedclothes wound around his legs. Irreversibly awake, he kicked the mangled sheets from his legs, sat up, and rubbed his eyes. He moved through the darkness to look out the living room window. The storm had passed, and a navy blue landscape met his eyes.

He turned his head to gaze at the shadowy, oak staircase just visible through the hallway entrance, thinking of the woman alone upstairs. For a moment, he entertained a fleeting image of himself knocking softly at her door. He imagined the door opening with her welcoming invitation. He looked down at his ridiculous outfit, the borrowed tracksuit, so tight he felt like a tick about to pop.

No. He shook his head. *I'm thinking like a goddamn teenager. There's lots of time to get to know her…plenty of time.*

As he returned to the sofa, his cell phone chimed from the narrow table near the front door. Groping his way across the room, he cursed as he stubbed his toe against a chair leg in his rush to answer the phone before the voice mail kicked in. He was too late. As he listened to the message, he felt his heart pick up speed.

It was Mel, the barn manager. "Jas, the barn's on fire. I called the Fire Department and tried to put the damn thing out with a hose but it's spreading. I'm trying to get the horses out. Get your ass out here!"

Christ. He dropped the phone and ran to the laundry room. His freshly laundered clothes sat neatly folded on top of the dryer. He dragged his jeans and sweater over the sweat suit. After leaving a hastily scrawled note on the hall table, he was out the front door in a flash, wading through the freshly fallen snow to his SUV.

He thanked God for snowplows. The roads were clear and deserted. He must have broken a speed record because only twenty minutes passed before he detected a red glow behind a silhouette of trees. Winding up his driveway, he was horrified to see the front of the old barn almost engulfed in flames. He slid to a halt and vaulted out of the truck, sprinting up the driveway.

The intense heat at the front of the barn drove him back, and the massive sliding door was impassable. He ran around to the rear where the flames had not yet reached. Squinting into the light, he saw the barn manager's outline as he pulled and yanked at the lead of a terrified horse.

Jason struggled closer, shielding his face from the blast of heat. He shouted, "Where the hell is the fire department?"

Mel unclipped the lead from the halter of the panicked horse. It bolted toward the far side of the paddock and trotted back and forth, snorting and shaking its head.

He turned back to the barn and shouted over his shoulder, "They were on a call; they're on their way!" He ran back toward the door.

Christ, only one horse out. Jason reached down, took a handful of melting snow, and rubbed it on his head. The cool wetness lasted only a few seconds as he followed Mel, grabbing a lead from a hook just outside the door. Already, he felt the broiling heat.

The crackle and roar of the fire mixed with the terrified screams of the two remaining horses. The flames had leapt up the far wall and raced across the hayloft, sending bits of glowing hay and ash floating downward. Jason grappled with the latch of one stall as Mel opened the other.

In the box stall, the chestnut gelding pirouetted in circles, snorting and whinnying with terror. It hardly noticed Jason inching his way inside. The animal's shoulder made violent contact with Jason and he slammed against the oak panel.

He recovered his balance and shrugged off his jacket, waiting for his chance. As the gelding made another circuit of the stall, he tossed the jacket over its head. It slowed and stopped, momentarily confused.

Jason took the opportunity to snap the lead onto its halter and tucked the jacket around its head, keeping the eyes covered. "Come on, Jerry, you can do it."

He yanked on the lead and the chestnut finally burst out of the stall.

The smoke almost blinded him despite the glow from the flames. He had to squint through tear-blurred eyes to find his way out. He reached out with his fingers to feel his way and made contact with the rump of the remaining horse Mel was leading out of the burning barn.

Coughing and gasping for air, he and Mel released the horses into the adjoining paddock. Jason rubbed his eyes, leaned against the cedar rail fence, and watched his barn disappear.

Soon, but not soon enough, another red glow joined the chaotic scene. The fire truck had finally arrived.

Six

The next morning, Christina studied the note Bertie found on the hall table. It was brief and to the point: Barn on fire. I'll call you tomorrow.

"Is it always like this with him?" she asked, giving the scrap of paper back to him.

He shrugged. "Not in the slightest. This is starting to get really weird. I'll phone to see if everyone's okay."

He headed for the kitchen and returned with the news that the horses were fine, just a little frightened. "He and Mel got the horses out in time, but the barn's gone. I'm heading over there to see if I can help," Bertie grabbed his jacket from the hall closet. "Coming?"

Christina hesitated. "What about Mishayla?"

Corinne emerged from the kitchen, drying her hands on a tea towel. "Mishayla can stay with us for a couple of hours. They're having so much fun in the playroom anyway. Go with Bertrande. I think Jason will need you there."

"Okay, then…but I don't know how much help I'll be."

Bertie grinned and rolled his eyes. "You'll be a help, really. The only time he smiles these days is when you're around."

She felt the heat of a blush. *Get a grip, girl.* "Why wouldn't he have a reason to smile, except for what just happened?"

"Trust me; he hasn't exactly been on cloud nine lately. Things with the team have been going badly."

He helped her with her coat and they stepped into the blinding whiteness of morning. The storm clouds had moved on, and the sun sparkled on the pristine deposit of snow. It was colder than the previous day; their boots squeaked in the snow as if they were walking on Styrofoam as they crossed the parking area to Bertie's 4X4.

Christina watched the passing landscape for a few moments before she spoke. "So, what's been happening with the team? I noticed the last game was a train wreck."

"All I can tell you is the captain had a phone call from someone, saying Jason had slept with his wife."

She felt her stomach plunk. *Am I getting mixed up in a soap opera?*

"Would something like that really happen?"

Bertie flashed an incredulous look at her.

She cursed her big mouth and sought damage control. "I don't know much about these things, but you have to admit they sometimes happen."

She didn't want it to be true. Nevertheless, did it really matter if it was true? After all, she and Jason were not involved. For what seemed like the tenth time, she reminded herself Jason's private life was none of her business.

Bertie's voice held an uncharacteristic edge. "Jason would never, ever do something like that. It's obviously someone's attempt at a sick joke." He drove silently for a moment then continued more quietly, "I don't understand where these lies are coming from. I know Jason like my brother. He would never mess around with another guy's wife."

Christina thought for a moment. "What about his ex-girlfriend? From what I've heard, it wasn't a good break up. Do you think she might be trying to make his life hell because he wouldn't take her back?"

"He didn't say much about it, but I noticed he's been swearing at his cell phone a lot lately."

She remembered the day they went to lunch. "You're right. When I got out of the hospital, someone smashed in his car. He acted like it was nothing, but when I left him, he was practically yelling into his phone. Do you remember when his cell phone rang while you two visited me in the hospital? I'm pretty sure he was talking to her. I asked about her at lunch, but he didn't say much. What is Sheila like, anyway?"

"I've seen her a few times since last summer. She hung around the rink a lot. You know the type, all fluffy and shallow." Bertie made an exaggerated, mock shudder. "Not my type, you know, eh? Good riddance."

They turned off the country road and drove up a long, winding driveway lined with split rail cedar fences. The smell of charred wood still hung in the air as they pulled around the back of the house and climbed out of the SUV.

Jason stood at the head of a nervous horse, coaxing it into a waiting trailer. The horse jerked its head, pointing its muzzle at the sky in protest. Its coat covered with a fine layer of gray ash, damp and steaming with sweat. Jason pulled down the horse's halter and pressed its forehead against his chest, whispering soothing sounds into its ear. Finally, the chestnut allowed him to lead it into the trailer.

All that remained of the century old barn was a jumble of smoking, blackened lumber surrounded by a low foundation of mottled gray stone. The singed bricks forming the silo stood alone at the rear of the mess, a few forlorn bits of insulation flapping in the cold breeze at its severed summit. Blackened, muddy slush surrounded the structure.

As Jason turned to greet the newcomers, Christina felt his fatigue. His face, smeared with ash and smoke, caused his blue eyes to stand out in contrast.

He stepped forward and enclosed her in a warm hug, reaching out to shake Bertie's hand.

"You didn't have to come all the way out here but thanks, anyway," he said, rubbing his bare head with his gloved hand. "It looks like everything's under control. Mel is taking the horses to my neighbor's farm until I get something sorted out for them." He gazed at the ruin. "The fire chief says it may have started in the laneway between the stalls, near the front door. He found cigarette butts there. Mel and I don't smoke. It's a good thing there was a back door, or the horses would have been goners."

Bertie scraped a boot against a chunk of charcoal. "You know, too many things have been happening lately, and it just doesn't seem random to me."

"Don't be crazy. It was probably just some kid trying to keep warm. Come on inside, it's freezing out here, and I could use another coffee." Jason turned and crunched through the snow to the back porch of the wooden farmhouse.

Bertie shrugged, and he and Christina followed their friend.

Christina was pleasantly surprised at the appearance of the big, two-storey vertical plank farmhouse. She expected a single, professional sports athlete to live in an ultra modern condominium downtown, not in a century home in the country. A wide porch surrounded the house and scrolled storm doors covered the thick oak exterior doors. There seemed to be at least four entrances to the home, probably the result of decades of additions. They entered through the mudroom in the back that led directly into a large kitchen, old fashioned in style but equipped with contemporary fittings. Christina took in the deep honey wood, burnished copper accessories, and cobalt blue tiles, feeling immediately at home.

Jason measured coffee into a brushed steel coffee maker and leaned against the counter as the machine gurgled and spat. Soon, its delicious aroma filled the room.

Christina tapped a fingernail against a hanging pot. "Do these things get much use?"

"Do you think I can't cook?" Jason crossed his arms and lifted a brow.

"Someday, you have to try his Tourtiere St. Jacques. He makes it better than my maman," Bertie interjected from somewhere inside the refrigerator.

She glanced at Jason, puzzled. He grinned and said, "French-Canadian meat pie. It's a big Christmas Eve tradition at Bertie's house. It's always my job to put it together. You have to use fresh pork, sometimes rabbit, and just the right amount of cinnamon and cloves."

"Okay, okay, so you can cook." Christina smiled and accepted a mug of coffee.

They carried their coffee into the next room. "Oh, my God..." Christina closed her eyes in mock rapture after she took in the deep, overstuffed leather furniture, the huge stone fireplace, and the trophies lining the mantle. A high definition television stood in the corner like a great monolith. Stroking the side of the flat panel, she exclaimed, "I'll bet everybody on television hates these things. You can probably count every nostril hair."

Jason laughed in spite of the rotten night he must have spent with the fire department in the freezing night. "Put the camera on me, you'll see every capillary in my bloodshot eyes." He settled in a chair with a tired sigh, and the other two followed suit. Jason's cat immediately jumped onto Christina's lap.

She absently stroked the cat's long fur. "Listen, Jason, Bertie's right when he says things have taken a strange turn in the last few weeks. You can't keep insisting the shooting, the car, and the barn are all unrelated."

Jason tensed and shot an irritated look at Bertie who held up his hands in self-defense. "She already knew about the helmet. All the other stuff is her theory, not mine. I think she's right, though."

Jason flashed an assessing look at Christina, leaned forward, and ground his palms into his eyes. "Okay, okay. Sheila showed up just after I finished talking to the police about the helmet. She told me she'd been sleeping with the guy who had the gun. I didn't know him well, but he's been with the team for a few years." He moved over to the fireplace and poked at the flames. "I don't know how long she'd been with him, but I'm guessing it might have been before she met me. She was still seeing him."

He sat again, welcoming Max, who had vacated Christina's lap. "She had the nerve to treat the whole situation as if it wasn't important and tried her usual sob job to get me to stay with her, but I felt I had to break it off." Jason scowled, looking down at the cat while he scratched its ears. "That isn't stopping her from harassing me, though. She calls me at least twice a day. The poor kid just doesn't seem to understand I broke up with her."

Christina frowned. *Poor kid, my ass.* "So that's what all the angry phone calls have been about. She sounds like a real bitch, pardon my expression, and you've been awfully forgiving in spite of what you say." She stood and looked through the side window at the devastation outside. *Did Sheila smoke?* "Every time we mention she might be connected to this mess, you jump to her defense."

Jason frowned, shifting uncomfortably. "I realize now, she's a bit shallow and good riddance," he said, "but I honestly don't think she's capable of the things you accuse her of. Ian must have been the crazy one, jealous or something, and now he's dead. Besides, she's my problem. I can handle her myself."

"You're way too generous," Bertie remarked. "Present company excluded, some people can be pretty mean when they're rejected." He straightened in his chair. "Think about it, Jason, all this other stuff happened right after the shooting. I know you got plenty of phone calls from her and each one got hotter and hotter, then this thing with Adam! Who else would stir up trouble like that?"

"Anybody could have made that call, maybe a disgruntled fan or something. Maybe I forgot to sign an autograph and somebody's pissed off."

Christina insisted, "I still wonder if she's capable of smashing a windshield or starting a barn fire?"

Jason rolled his eyes. "Now, come on, give it a rest. I can see her making nasty phone calls, but smashing cars and starting fires? I find it hard to believe."

"Well, hopefully the fire department will find some more evidence in the barn. It's useless for them to look for tracks in the snow at this point—if they haven't been dumped on by more snow last night, they're all chewed up by the fire trucks and other footprints. Maybe one of us can talk to Adam's wife to find out what really transpired in this anonymous phone call. She must be really upset with Adam right now, and she'll want to clear her name." Christina was thinking aloud, and raised her eyes to see the two men looking at her in astonishment.

"What? You never watch crime dramas on television?" She grinned, taking a sip of her coffee.

"Wow, you're something," Jason said with a lift of his eyebrow. He settled on the sofa. "Don't get yourself all excited and mixed up in this, it's probably nothing, just a string of coincidences."

"Well, something has to be done before you turn into a wreck," she said. "If your ex-girlfriend isn't behind all this, it likely ends here. However, if she is involved, it can only get worse. Who knows what she could do next? Besides, I don't go back to work for another week, and I'm bored, bored, bored."

He grinned tiredly. "I thought Nancy Drew was blonde."

"You're not taking any of this seriously. Those horses could have died."

Jason softened. "I know, and I'm sorry. You two are great for trying to help me out like this, but I still think it's nothing to get excited about. It's all over now."

Bertie frowned. "You saw how the guys look at you in the dressing room. How much longer do you think that can go on before there's a punch up?" He joined Christina at the window and stared glumly at the scene outside.

The sound of a soft snore made her turn. At first she thought it was the cat. Jason lay sprawled on the sofa, his head tilted back. His fingers laced together across his chest, rising and falling gently.

"Looks like he finally hit the wall. Good thing there's no game tonight," Bertie commented dryly and went to fetch their coats.

Christina stood over Jason, watching his face. Worry lines that had furrowed his forehead were gone, and his mouth looked soft and relaxed.

She plucked a folded quilt from the back of the sofa, draped it over him and peeked surreptitiously behind her. Hesitantly, she reached out to touch his lips. His warm breath sidled around her fingers, and she shivered. She knelt and leaned closer, inhaling the odor of leather and smoke. Very lightly, she planted a kiss on a smudge on his cheek.

"Coming or staying?" She shot upward and whirled to face Bertie.

He leaned against the doorway with her coat in his hands. He wore a sly grin and his dark eyes danced with delight.

She glared at him. "Don't you dare tell him what I did," she whispered.

"Sure, sure, my lips are sealed…unlike yours, apparently."

She took her jacket from him and followed him into the bright day. "Well, since your lips are sealed, you can help me out. I'll need you to dig up a couple of phone numbers for me."

"Jason said to leave it alone. He can take care of it himself."

Maybe this is more for me than him.

Seven

The game Monday night was worse than the previous match. Christina did something she hadn't done in a long time; she turned off the TV before the game was completed, not wanting to see the outcome.

She reached for her purse and searched inside until she found a slip of paper. She might not be getting anywhere with Jason, but Bertie was certainly helpful. She picked up her phone and punched in the number.

"Hello?" inquired a woman's voice.

"Hello, is this Jennifer Noole?"

There was a moment of silence at the other end, and the response held a suspicious tone. "Yes, who's inquiring?"

"My name is Christina Mackey. I'm a friend of Jason Peterson and Bertrand Gauthier. I understand there's been some trouble and I want to help." Christina got the words out in a hurry in case she decided to hang up.

After a few seconds of silence, Jennifer replied, "Yeah, well...I believe you. Your voice is different from that bitch's voice." Christina felt the anger in the woman's tone as it shook with suppressed emotion.

"So, you heard the person who called?"

"Yes, she had the nerve to leave a message on our voice mail, and my husband played it back to me."

"I'm curious, why would your husband believe someone he'd never met, instead of his own wife?"

There was another moment of silence. Christina was sure she was getting too personal and had crossed the line. *Damn, she's going to hang up.*

She ploughed on. "Listen, I know you have no reason to trust me, but you sound like you need someone to talk to. I'm no judge of character, but if my husband accused me of something like this, I'd work really hard to clear my name, by any means. Even if that meant I couldn't forgive him for not believing me in the first place. Isn't there something I can do to help?"

A soft sigh drifted across the line. "You sound like you already know me."

Okay, I'm in. "Just blind luck, I guess. I've never had to deal with jealousy, but I can imagine how bad it must be to lose trust in a relationship."

Jennifer spoke hesitantly, as if trying out the words. "Jason and I were friends before I met Adam. Adam probably thinks I have feelings for Jason, but I don't, he's just a friend."

Christina wasn't ready for that bit of information. "You two dated?"

"No, but at the time I wished we did."

"Oh." For a moment, she was at a loss for words. *Maybe I'm biting off more than I can chew.*

She wished Jason had mentioned the fact Jennifer had been more than an acquaintance. She shook off her own budding seed of jealousy. "Do you still have the recording?"

"No, I erased it. It was probably a stupid thing to do, but I was so furious I wasn't thinking. I've had enough of his crap anyway. When he gets back from Pittsburgh, I'm telling him it's over. I just want to put the whole thing behind me."

"Wouldn't that be the same as an admission of guilt?"

"Not to me. I'm tired of having to justify every move to that man. He treats me like a possession, and I'm sick of it. He's been horrible to Jason, too, from what I hear. I wish I could be more help, but I'm feeling useless right now. Good luck finding the telephone bitch."

Christina felt she'd hit a dead end. "Jennifer, if you change your mind and need help, please call me. I'm still planning to look into this matter, for Jason's sake anyway. Besides, us women should stick together, shouldn't we?"

She heard a small laugh at the other end. "Yes, I guess you're right. If she calls again, I'll let you know, for Jason's sake."

"Thanks, Jennifer. I hope everything works out for you and your husband."

After she hung up, she couldn't resist turning on the television once more to check the final score of the game. She wished she hadn't.

The next afternoon, the sound of his voice on the phone made her fingers tighten around the receiver. "Any chance of having lunch again tomorrow? We can go into Newmarket, it's closer to your place."

"I'll do anything to brighten your day after last night." She kept her tone light, remembering the conversation with Jennifer.

"Yeah, it was another stinker." Jason's laugh sounded forced. "And yes, you will indeed cheer me up. I'll pick you up around noon."

She slowly placed the phone in its cradle and sighed. He seemed dejected. He didn't deserve the crap he was going through.

~ * ~

"Jason, you've got to help me. I'm scared shitless here, and I'm afraid to get out of the car." Sheila's voice held a note of near hysteria.

Jason's customary irritation gave way to concern. She sounded truly frightened this time.

"Where are you?"

"I'm under the Gardiner Expressway…um, I think between Spadina and York. I can see the back of the baseball stadium from here. The car won't start—I think it's out of gas."

"What the hell are you doing under the Gardiner? It's dangerous there."

"Never mind what I was doing. Please hurry, it's scary here."

"Stay put, and keep the doors locked. Keep your head down. I'm coming." He flipped his phone shut.

"Shit," he muttered and turned the car around. He had just finished the morning skate and had almost reached the off ramp to Highway 400 to meet Christina for lunch, but that would have to wait. He wasn't but a few kilometers from where Sheila had described. He quickly punched in Christina's phone number anyway. The line was busy.

I'll call her later. I should be able to make it in time if I hurry.

He pulled a U-turn on Lakeshore drive and headed east, making a quick pit stop at a local station to fill up his spare gas can, normally stored in the trunk. Much of Lakeshore Drive ran under the shadow of the Gardiner Expressway, a dilapidated raised freeway that hugged the shore of Lake Ontario.

The majority of Toronto residents had a love-hate relationship with the crumbling highway. It served as a necessary conduit leading out of the city, but it also blocked an otherwise brilliant view of the lake from the many condos that sprung up along the shoreline. In the words of the current mayor, 'the Gardiner was butt-ugly'.

This stretch was particularly dismal. The winter gloom deepened between huge chipped pylons supporting the Expressway, and the wide expanse of dirt and gravel beneath refused to support much plant life. All that multiplied here were rocks, chunks of fallen concrete, straggly weeds, and squatters.

Jason carefully maneuvered his vehicle off the multi-lane Lakeshore Boulevard and onto a relatively smooth patch of dirt. He parked the car behind a large pillar to hide it from prying eyes. *I don't need a parking ticket on top of everything else…or another broken windshield.*

He climbed out of the car and scanned the area, looking for Sheila's beige Jeep Cherokee. In the dim light, he barely picked it out against a graffiti-strewn retaining wall that ran parallel to the highway, about fifty yards from the road's edge.

It figures, she has it well-hidden. She was probably making one of her little deals. He shook his head with disgust and pulled the gas can out of the trunk of his BMW.

He strode toward the Jeep and saw her wide, frightened eyes as she peered through the glass. He pointed at the gas opening at the back of the Jeep, and she obligingly popped the remote hatch.

After he filled the tank, he leaned against the roof and rolled his fingers at her. She rolled down the window and gave him a breathless smile. Her eyes widened. "What happened to your face?"

He had almost forgotten about the bruise on his cheek. "I'm a hockey player. What do you think happened to my face? Turn it over and see if it starts."

She turned the key, and the Cherokee roared to life. "Thank God! Thank you, Jason—you saved my life." She reached through the window and slid her hand under his jacket.

He pulled away. "Sheila, this is the last time you're ever going to see my face, except on television. Next time you get yourself into a scrape, call somebody else."

Her lips turned into a grim line. Without a word, she put the Jeep into gear and hit the gas. Spinning tires spit gravel into the air as she shot the Cherokee toward Lakeshore. Without stopping, she swerved into traffic. Screeching tires and blaring horns mixed with the hum of traffic from below and above the raised highway.

"You're welcome," he muttered and picked up the gas can.

As he strode toward his car, distant voices drew near. To the east, a group of youths sauntered along the retaining wall, conversing loudly to make their voices heard above the roar of vehicles from above.

Jason immediately tensed when the group detoured and made straight for him. Before he knew it, they surrounded him.

"Hey man, what's a guy like you doin' in a place like this?" The biggest one lifted a brow and reached out to finger Jason's leather jacket.

"Helping a damsel in distress." Jason tried to sound nonchalant, but he felt uneasy. He tightened his grip on the gas can and backed slowly up to a pylon, wondering how many he could take at once. Maybe he could subdue two or three but not five.

"I don't see no damsel here," the apparent leader challenged. "That's a nice jacket you got there. Care to make a donation to wayward youth?" He laughed at his cleverness and the others joined him.

He reached into his back jeans pocket and produced an insanely small penknife. Jason fought the urge to laugh. The thing could still do some damage. With a serious expression, he stalled for time, ready to swing the gas can. "Did you get that thing in the Cub Scouts?"

"Just take off the fuckin' jacket."

The sound of a single siren bounced off the underside of the expressway. Jason's gaze switched from the sea of faces to the welcomed sight of a police car speeding along The Lakeshore. It slowed and drew parallel to Jason and his unwelcome companions, mounted the curb and bounced over rough ground, picking up speed.

Immediately, the teenagers scattered. He found himself alone, still clutching the gas can. He waited patiently for the police car to draw near.

They'll probably want a description. Thank God for passing motorists with cell phones. Somebody must have seen these guys causing trouble.

"Excuse me, sir, would you mind putting down the gas can?" The policeman, unsmiling, strode across the gravel with his hand on his hip.

Perplexed, Jason complied.

The other cop flipped a notebook open. "Your name, sir?"

"Jason Peterson."

"What's your reason for being in this area at this time?" The policeman's eyes darted about the immediate vicinity, as if looking for an accomplice lurking behind a concrete support.

"I was helping an old friend who ran out of gas." Irritation crept into Jason's voice, and he fought to keep it under control.

"And where is this friend now?"

Jason shrugged. "She left."

The first policeman cleared his throat. "Sir, would you mind emptying your pockets?"

"Not at all." Jason dug into his jacket pockets and drew out his keys, wallet, a Sharpie for signing autographs, plus an item he didn't expect.

He stared, nonplussed, at the small zipper-lock plastic bag containing a white powder.

"I think you'd better come with us, sir."

~ * ~

For the twelfth time, Christina glanced out her front window, still nothing. When noon passed, she called Jason's home, no answer, so she left a message. She tried his cell phone only to hear a female voice stating, "The customer you have dialed is not available."

The afternoon wore on. Feeling increasingly anxious, she tried calling Bertie and got the news he'd been to practice that morning with the rest of the team.

"Maybe he forgot. Maybe he's just working outside, or he's at the neighbor's place, checking on his horses," Bertie offered. "I wouldn't worry too much. Maybe he's embarrassed after last night."

Christina didn't want to remember the game the previous night. It was bad but not exactly embarrassing. She asked, "What happened last night besides the loss?"

"Adam walked up to Jason in the dressing room after the game and sucker punched him. I'd never seen anything like it! Two guys had to hold Jason off, he was so mad. The flight back was as quiet as a church."

Christina's heart began to beat rapidly with worry. "What should I do?"

"Sit tight. I'm sure everything's fine. Listen, I gotta go. We have three of these kids in hockey this afternoon, and Corinne and I have to split ranks. Call me tonight if you don't hear anything."

~ * ~

The only other occupant of the holding cell was a tiny man in shredded army fatigues. He looked about ninety pounds of loose flesh hanging on bones, with protruding eyes and a pencil thin moustache drawn crookedly over a fleshy mouth that seemed too big for his face.

The man squinted quizzically at him for about fifteen minutes before he spoke. "Hey, don't I know you? I seen you before somewhere."

Jason kept his gaze trained straight ahead and pretended he didn't hear.

The little fellow slid down the bench, close enough to allow a glorious whiff of stale beer and at least one bodily function. "Yeah," he said with a speculative drawl. "I'm sure I seen you in the papers. Ain't you that hockey player that got shot at last month?"

"You must be mistaken. I, uh, don't know what you're talking about." Jason turned his head away and inspected the graffiti on the wall beside him. To his relief, he heard the metallic clink and rumble of the barred door sliding open.

An officer stood in the doorway with Gord, Jason's agent, close behind him. Gord was a package deal; a sports-loving lawyer who later became an agent.

The policeman said, "Okay, Mr. Peterson, you're free to go."

"I knew it!" exclaimed the leprechaun behind him as Jason hurried out of the cell.

After Jason collected his things, the two men headed for the main exit.

"How much bail did you have to put up?" Jason asked.

"Nothing."

"What? Isn't cocaine possession supposed to be a no-no?" He still didn't know how the bag got into his pocket.

Gord laughed. "That's because it wasn't cocaine."

"What?"

"It was a bag of icing sugar. Someone was playing a pretty sick joke."

Sheila. He remembered her reaching for him and tugging on his jacket after he had filled up the gas tank. *That bitch!*

They burst through the gargantuan double doors of the courthouse, and Jason suddenly had the urge to return to the cell to join skinny fatigue pants. Flashbulbs popped and thirty-odd voices simultaneously shouted questions.

~ * ~

Christina spent an excruciating evening trying to pretend nothing was wrong. During dinner, Mishayla chattered about school, and Christina answered automatically, half-listening.

After dinner, she sent Mishayla to play in her room and sat in the living room with the phone in her hand. She stared at it, willing it to ring. Nothing happened.

She turned on the television to watch the news. Five minutes into the broadcast, she gasped and sat up straight.

"Jason Peterson was arrested this afternoon in a deserted area under the Gardiner Expressway, close to the Air Canada Centre. Initial reports; the star winger was charged with cocaine possession but charges were dropped within hours. Gord Simmons, Jason's agent and lawyer, was on hand to answer questions."

The newscast cut to a frenzied scene in front of the Toronto Courthouse. A man introduced as Gord Simmons stood in front of a silent Jason and said, "The charges were dropped because the whole thing was a practical joke. There was no harm done and everything is back to normal."

The camera zoomed to Jason's face. He looked disheveled and tired. A yellowing bruise discolored his left cheek.

Just before the report cut away to the studio, she heard someone in the background shout, "Is this the same practical joker who spread rumors about Mr. Peterson's love life?"

"No comment," was all Gord Simmons said.

"On to other hockey news…"

"What the hell has he been up to?" Christina's shout rang against the walls.

"What?" Mishayla called from her room.

"Never mind." Christina punched Jason's number into her phone. This time the line was busy.

She dropped the phone in her lap and stared at the television.

"Mom? Mommy."

Mishayla stood beside her chair. She had changed into her pajamas and held the hockey sweater book she had received as a gift from Jason.

"Can you read to me?"

"Yeah. Sure. Okay." Christina placed the phone on the side table and looked at it once more. Reluctantly, she followed Mishayla to her room.

Normally, she enjoyed reading to her daughter and loved encouraging her to sound out the words, but tonight she had a greater urge to return to her worrying. She was halfway through the picture book when the phone buzzed quietly from the living room.

She vaulted off the bed and dove for the door.

"Hey!" Mishayla protested. "We're not done yet."

Christina skidded to a halt and held up one finger. "Just one minute—I'll be right back.

She jogged down the hall and grabbed the phone before the answering machine kicked in.

"Chrissie, it's me. It's okay, I'm all right."

Her chest tightened with relief. "Oh, my God, I was so scared. Well, I was mad at first, then worried, and then scared shitless. Then I saw the news—" A thought suddenly occurred to her. "Why were you in the middle of a vacant lot under the Gardiner?"

The dead air unnerved her. He finally spoke. "I...I was helping Sheila. She, um...ran out of gas. After she left, these guys came up to me and didn't make nice at all. That's when the cops showed up. I thought they were arresting the punks, but they went after me instead."

"They didn't hurt you, did they?"

"Nothing like that—they were very polite."

"Why would Sheila be in such a seedy area?"

"I didn't get around to asking, but I have a pretty good idea."

She just won't leave him alone. "Well. I hope she's grateful for your help. It almost cost you your life." She couldn't keep the sarcastic edge out of her voice.

"Chrissie, she needed my help. The girl has no friends, and if I didn't do anything, I'd have to live with the consequences if something happened to her." He gave a gruff laugh. "And, no, she wasn't grateful. She practically sprayed gravel in my face when she took off to leave me to my fate. So much for the knight in shining armor."

He can't help it. He's just too nice. Even to witches. She softened her stance. "How are you feeling?"

"Like an idiot." His voice lowered and became calm. "Everything's okay. It's over. I told her it was the last time I was going to help her, and I'm sticking to my promise. Now, I think it's time to redeem that rain check on lunch. Shall we try again tomorrow?"

She couldn't shake a lingering feeling of uncertainty. Not to mention her annoyance that Sheila had managed to get her hooks in him again. She wondered if the practical joke was Sheila's doing. "No detours?"

A familiar, delicious low chuckle trickled over the line. "No detours, my dear. Right after practice, I'll aim straight for Schomberg. I'll even leave my cell off, in case I get another call from You Know Who. So...pick you up at noon?"

"Okay," she whispered. She was undone.

Eight

Stood up. Again. She couldn't believe it. This time, she kept busy. It was a great day to clean out the hall closet, anyway. She peeked out the front window again and leaned her hot forehead against the frosty glass. The gloomy weather matched her mood.

She should have known better. Just move on. Maybe she'd call Heather and go out for lunch and a drink. Maybe several drinks.

She wondered why she insisted on putting herself through such torture, time after time. She had no need for a man. She'd be just fine on her own. The thought of abandonment one more time was too much to bear.

Grumbling, she pulled a cardboard box from the shelf and began sifting through the contents. Amongst the old bills and lists, she found a handful of drawings Mishayla had done last year, while she was in Senior Kindergarten.

A crude crayon drawing showed a girl on skates with a crooked X that must have been a hockey stick. Many little circles with smiley faces surrounded the figure, one with long dark hair. She smiled. *That must be me.*

Another picture showed two girls, one big and one small. A third figure of a man wearing a helmet stood off to the side. He was tiny, and his mouth seemed turned downward in a frown. A blue teardrop sprang from one lopsided eye.

It must be Reggie. She'd told her daughter stories about Reggie all the time, making sure Mishayla didn't forget the wonderful man who was more than a father to her. He had introduced her to skates when she was a toddler, and after he died, Mishayla practically lived with blades attached to her feet.

She misses him. She remembered Jason and Mishayla twirling on the ice, and his joy at seeing the little girl, whole and healthy, after her ordeal.

She wasn't being fair. He must have had a good reason for not showing up. After shifting things around in the closet for a while, she finally picked up the phone.

"I'm not up to lunch today." He sounded odd.

"I figured that out when you didn't show up. Is there anything I can do? Do you want me to come over?"

"Do whatever you want. I'm no good to you today. I'm no good to anyone." He abruptly disconnected.

Okay...this was definitely not good. She checked the time. She had about two hours before Mishayla got home. She drove through the dim afternoon to the farmhouse.

She knocked at the front door—no answer. She went around to the side porch and tried the mudroom door—unlocked. Feeling like an intruder, she pushed the door open and called inside, "Jason? It's me, Christina." There was no answer, but the sound of the television in the den drifted into the kitchen.

She slid her feet out of her boots and shrugged off her jacket, leaving it on a stool. Passing through the kitchen toward the den, she hesitantly called, "Hello?"

A flickering light emitted from the den. She paused in the doorway and allowed her eyes to adjust to the darkness. A fire glowed in the fireplace, and the large flat screen television mutely showed a talk show, a soap opera, a commercial. The top of Jason's head protruded above the back of a leather armchair, facing away from her. She walked around to stand between Jason and the TV.

He reclined in the chair with his legs stretched out on the floor and crossed at the ankles. A small cut crystal drinking glass containing a couple of ice cubes dangled from his outstretched hand.

He stared blankly at the television, rapidly flicking through the channels. She stood quietly, waiting. It took a few moments for him to notice her.

He stopped his assault on the remote control and glanced up at her face.

"I came to redeem my lunch date rain check." She fought to keep the tension out of her voice. "Are you all right?"

His gaze slowly focused on her, and he said woodenly, "I've been sent down."

"What?"

"Sent down. Demoted. Gone to the minors. I report to Pensacola tomorrow. After the fiasco yesterday and the fight in the dressing room, Adam told the coach and the general manager that either I go or he wants to be traded. They picked me."

He dropped the remote on the floor and put down the glass, leaning forward in the chair and resting his elbows on his knees. He raked his fingers through his hair. "Jesus...it's bad enough being sent to the farm team, but the one below that? They're all kids there. I'll be the old timer."

"Why didn't he just send you to the farm team here in the city? At least you'd be close to home, and there are plenty of guys your age on the team." She spoke with more hope than she felt. "Why didn't they just trade you?"

"I have a no-trade clause in my contract. I don't get traded unless I ask. However, it can't stop them from sending me down. The point is, they probably want me as far away as possible. If our farm team had remained in Newfoundland, they probably would have sent me there, but now that they're here in Toronto, I'd be too close to the mess. The next step down is the East Coast League and Pensacola's the place, I guess."

He stared blankly at the floor, murmuring, "The East Coast League is full of untried kids or old timers who are either washed out or just don't have what it takes to be in the NHL. I can't believe it's come to this. What the hell is happening to me? I've gone from hero to zero in just a few weeks."

Christina pressed the power switch on the TV and turned on a lamp beside his chair. Kneeling at his feet, she studied his face. His left cheek was still slightly swollen from the fight in the dressing room. She gently touched the bruise with her fingers. He continued to look at the floor.

"We can fix this," she whispered. "They can't keep you there forever. Adam will realize he's wrong, and you'll be back. We'll find out who's behind this." She was sure Bertie would help if she asked. They were like brothers, he'd said. Well, this is his chance to prove it. She smiled hesitantly. "Besides, this'll be a great time to work on your tan."

Jason's blue gaze rose from the floor to lock with hers. Fighting her inner turmoil, she fixed him with a reassuring expression.

He looked perplexed. "Why do you believe in me? Why do you care so much?"

She didn't know why. She'd asked herself the same question over and over again. *He's giving me every reason not to trust him. He misses lunch dates, he lets his ex-girlfriend interfere with his life, and he doesn't want my help.*

She looked at those eyes and knew why. "I just...I just know."

Jason's eyes were sad, but he smiled. He raised his hands and brushed his fingers along her cheeks. Leaning forward, he let his lips touch hers. He kissed her lightly at first, then with more urgency.

Christina immediately melted, arching toward him while still on her knees. He enclosed her in one muscular arm, pulling her between his legs, pressing her body close against his chest. He explored her mouth with increasing intensity, cradling her head with his other hand, his fingers entwined in her hair.

Fused together for only a minute, she whispered against his neck, "For the second day in a row, I imagined you lying in a ditch somewhere."

Jason smiled softly, nuzzling her ear. "Hmmm. That's something only a mother would say."

"Oh, God," Christina exclaimed, pulling away with her eyes wide. "Mishayla. I have to get back."

"Get a sitter," he murmured, skimming his lips along her jaw.

"It's a school night..." She closed her eyes, shuddered, and groaned as his tongue traced down the front of her throat.

"It's my last night," he whispered hoarsely as he found her mouth again.

Christina wavered, and then steeled herself. *This is too soon.* She opened her eyes and promptly played the mother card again. Taking a shaky breath, she pulled back and said, "I...I really have to get back. It's not your last night. Bertie and I will make sure you're home in no time. Trust us. Keep your head up and your stick on the ice and don't let the bastards get you."

~ * ~

Jason groaned. He wanted her now, but in spite of the overwhelming heat in his groin, he had to admit she still made sense. He gazed at her face. God, she was beautiful. He was used to beauty. It certainly played a big role in his relationships of recent years. Now, looking into her steady, serious gaze, he felt a different kind of pull as well, coming from another part of himself. Yes, she was beautiful. She was more than that. He tentatively gave her one more kiss. He felt this was going to be something special, but she was right. He had damned well better take it a little slower, or he'd ruin everything. No more mistakes.

"God, Chrissie..." He pressed his forehead against hers and whispered against her cheek, "Okay, okay. I'll take the flight in the morning." He straightened and raised his eyes toward the ceiling. "Jesus, Pensacola. I can't possibly get into trouble there." At least he'd be out of Sheila's reach. Still, he worried she might make trouble for those he cared for.

~ * ~

She felt a little better. If he had kept campaigning for a consummation of their burgeoning relationship tonight, she would have doubted his priorities. *Little steps.* Although she was sorely tempted to take a giant leap tonight.

She stood on weak legs and pulled him from the chair. "Get packed. Go to Pensacola. Make them regret sending you down."

They walked together to the kitchen and Jason helped Christina with her overcoat. They kissed again and stood for a moment in each other's arms. Christina looked up at his melancholy face and asked quietly, "When's your flight?"

"Ten in the morning."

"Remember what I told you. Don't worry and do your best. You'll be home soon. I'll fix this." She laid her hand on his solid chest. Her fingers felt the hardness of his muscles, even through the thickness of her glove, but she fought the urge to pull his shirt up and kiss his skin. She opened the kitchen door, letting in a blast of cold air from the mudroom. She could feel his eyes on her back as she went through the exterior door and trudged back to her car.

She slammed the car door and sat for a minute, looking through the thickening dusk at Jason's figure silhouetted in the kitchen window. She almost got out of the car again but instead turned the key and steered the vehicle down the driveway. She thought of her promise to fix things. *How the hell am I going to fix this?*

As Christina drove home in the growing darkness, she made a silent wish, one she'd never entertained in her life. She hoped the team that had abandoned Jason would lose and lose often.

Nine

Her wish came true. In the next couple of weeks, the franchise continued its plunge into an impressive losing streak. The newspapers columnists had a field day, speculating on the cause of the losses and the mysterious disappearing act of their star winger. The organization's obvious duress gave her a secret glow of satisfaction, but she still felt sorry for Bertie, left without his line mate and obviously struggling.

For years, she had watched Bertie and Jason display an almost symbiotic relationship when they were on the ice. They read each other's minds as they sent the puck from one stick to the other before anyone on the opposite team knew what was happening. Now, Bertie was forced to deal with wingers who didn't know his next move like Jason did, and they often missed his passes.

Christina returned to work gradually, going into the office a couple of times a week, handling mostly paperwork and reception duties until her hand was strong enough to handle the delicate procedures required of a dental hygienist. During her free time she kept busy with her daughter's school and hockey schedules, plus the increasing desire to dig up as much information as she could about Sheila.

She hadn't yet worked up the courage to speak with the woman directly but would have liked to hear her voice. She decided to try talking to Jennifer again. Maybe she could offer more information.

With Bertie's help, she discovered that although Jennifer had impulsively declared she would leave Adam, she was still living with him. Christina took care to phone their home while the team was away at a game.

Jennifer seemed glad to hear from Christina. Her anxiety had mounted over the last few weeks, and she shared Christina's desire to end the matter.

"I was going to call you. I have more information. She called again, yesterday," Jennifer said with a quaver in her voice. "I didn't erase it, but I plan to do it before Adam comes home tomorrow. I don't suppose you want to listen to it? Maybe you can recognize the voice, because I can't. It seems familiar to me, but I just can't place it." She invited Christina to come over for coffee.

Christina found time the next afternoon to drive over to Adam and Jennifer's home in Aurora, an affluent town just south of Newmarket, before Mishayla was out of school. The woman who answered the door was about Christina's age, with creamy skin, green eyes and honey-colored hair. Her beauty startled even Christina. If Jason had spent time with her, she wondered, why hadn't they dated?

They spent a while in the kitchen with a cup of tea first. Jennifer appraised Christina and asked, "You're the one from the shooting at the arena, aren't you? There weren't any pictures in the papers, but I remember your name."

Christina nodded.

"So, are you two…close?" Jennifer inquired, sipping her tea.

"No, we're just friends." Besides, she wasn't sure what their relationship was, anyway, so it wasn't really a lie.

"Well, you might as well hear what this woman had to say." Jennifer rose from the kitchen chair and led Christina into the living room. A console sat on a desk beside the sofa with telephone, fax, and voice mail combined. She pressed a button and skipped through a few messages until she found the one she was looking for. The voice that emitted from the machine was high and breathless.

"Do you miss your boyfriend?" the voice teased. "Can't kiss him when he's way down there lounging on the beach, can you?" There was a click, and the recording ended. Christina felt a chill when she heard the voice, it was almost as if the woman was talking to her.

"Well, now I have a voice to go with," Christina said. "Can you remember what she said the first time she called?"

Jennifer looked uncomfortable, but replied, "She said something like, 'Where do you think Jason was, Adam, when you were in Raleigh at that charity golf tournament? He was with your wife. You'd better watch your back.'"

"When was the tournament?"

"Last August."

Christina was beginning to feel like an interrogator. She didn't want to hear what the answer might be, but asked anyway, "So…where were you?"

"I was here, at home." Jennifer's eyes strayed to the living room window.

"Where do you think Jason might have been at the time?"

Jennifer looked directly at Christina, her chin slightly raised as if in challenge. "He was here."

Christina felt a jolt in her stomach. It traveled upward through her chest to her head. Her ears buzzed. *None of my business*, she kept repeating in her mind. She was beginning to think those words didn't make sense any more.

Jennifer said, "I asked him to help me to connect a surround sound system in the den downstairs. It was a surprise for Adam, so I never mentioned Jason had been here. I never thought about it until the phone call. I also never thought Adam would react like that! You believe me, don't you?"

Christina closed her eyes and took a deep breath. *Thank God.* "Yes, I believe you." She looked down at the machine. "Do you think there's a way to make a copy of that recording?"

Jennifer opened a drawer in the desk and rooted around inside. She produced a tiny cassette, still in its blister package. "I can put this one in and you can take the original."

"Are you sure you want me to do that?"

Jennifer handed Christina the used cassette. "Yes. I really want you to." She hugged her arms to her body and looked out the window. "I don't know how close you are to Jason, but I want to assure you I care about him very much. I think it's just awful what Adam and the team are doing to him."

She looked at Christina again, her green eyes searching.

I sure hope you know what you're looking for in me, because I sure as hell don't know what it is, Christina thought.

Jennifer must have found something. She smiled and said, "Catch her if you can."

Christina relaxed and smiled. "Just watch me."

The two women embraced and Christina headed back home in time to meet her daughter's bus.

She spent the evening making plans to go shopping the next day for a micro tape recorder and tried to think of a way to meet Sheila in person. She certainly didn't have the experience or authority to look into the damage to the car and the barn, but maybe the tape was one way to discredit Sheila and perhaps get some verbal evidence concerning the other two incidents. She didn't know if it would do any good, acquiring evidence in such a manner, but it was all she could think of. Sure, she watched crime dramas on television but that wasn't real life.

She was still mulling over her plans as she lay in bed. When the phone rang, she reached for the bedside handset, surprised and pleased to hear Jason's deep voice.

"Chrissie."

She felt a rush of relief. "Hi! I was beginning to think you'd never call. How are things going over there?"

"Fine. Well, as good as it can be down here. Weather's nice, though."

Somehow she didn't think he was just calling to discuss the weather. "Is everything okay?" she asked.

"I—I just wanted to hear your voice."

"I'm glad you called. I was just over to Jennifer Noole's house today, and she gave me something that might help your case, a recording of the woman who left the message on their phone."

"I wish you'd just leave it alone," Jason said. He seemed agitated.

"Why? Don't you want to come home?"

"I just have a bad feeling about the whole thing."

"Jason, I've already started the ball rolling here. It's too late to stop now. Besides, Bertie's obviously been suffering without you on his wing, and Adam's wife is beside herself with worry, and she's concerned about you, too."

"Jennifer's worried about me?" he said sharply. "Why?"

"You have more than a couple of friends here, apparently." She hoped he didn't detect the edge that had crept into her voice. She fought to stamp out the tiny sprout of jealousy that kept popping up when she thought of Jennifer, along with Sheila. It was getting pretty crowded in her head.

"Besides, Mishayla misses you," she added.

He said after a moment of silence, "Just Mishayla?"

She smiled and relented, "Me, too."

"Is Mishayla up? Can I talk to her?"

"She's long gone to bed. Don't forget she's only six."

"Oh, I forgot. Well, I won't keep you." He hesitated for a few seconds before stating simply, "I, uh, miss you, too."

Christina had an uneasy feeling as she hung up. While they had been apart, she had a chance to stand back and study their developing relationship with a more objective point of view. He was a sweet man with a sense of humor and an obvious affection for children. He was also practically oozing testosterone, something she could not ignore. She shivered at her memory of the hardness of his arms and his rippling back the afternoon he kissed her. *Christ, what woman could possibly resist him?*

Still, she held a tiny seed of skepticism about his level of commitment, considering his profession and the reputations of many of his peers. Who knows, maybe he did have an affair with Jennifer. Maybe he really was a player, with women as well as hockey.

She shook the thought away. She didn't want to believe it. She decided to give him the benefit of a doubt and draw her own conclusions when the whole thing was resolved. She told herself she was doing this for Bertie and Jennifer, but maybe she was really doing it for herself. She needed to prove to herself that Jason was sincere.

As she settled for the night, she had to admit it was hard to remain impartial, especially when she looked into those round blue eyes. Unfortunately tonight, those eyes were very, very far away.

The next morning as she slowly awoke, her thoughts picked up where they had left off the previous night. She mulled over the phone conversation with Jason. Although she felt a tiny stab of fear at the thought of meeting Sheila face-to-face, she decided it was the only way to reveal the woman's motives. After breakfast, she told her daughter to get dressed; they were going shopping.

Ten

With Mishayla in tow, she cruised the Mall in Newmarket until she found and purchased a small micro tape recorder. Compatible with the little cassette, it also had recording capabilities.

As they sat in the food court, she held the recorder to Mishayla. "Here, say something."

Her daughter leaned over the Formica table and announced loudly, "Hi, Jason, I miss you! Come back soon so we can play hockey."

Later, she gave Bertie a call.

"You wouldn't happen to know Sheila's phone number or address, do you?"

"I don't like the sound of this."

"Come on, Bertie, I'm getting so close. Besides, don't you want Jason back?"

"Sure I do, but I don't want him to get mad at me for getting you in trouble. I don't like that woman. What if she recognizes you? Wouldn't she know you're the one who stopped that Pollard guy from shooting Jason?"

"Yes, my name was in the papers, but I don't think they ever took a picture of me. I can always use an assumed name."

"Jesus, Christina, you be careful," Bertie said. "Okay, she manages a snobby clothing store on Eglinton Street in Toronto. I think it's called Pastimes. I don't have a phone number, but I think she lives in a condo on Front Street, so you can look it up if it's listed. I wouldn't recommend phoning her, though."

"Thanks, Bertie. You won't regret it. How are you getting along without your right hand man? It must be tough for you."

"Holy cow, it's been a nightmare," he exclaimed. "I've only had about two points since Jason was sent down. I hope he's doing okay down there."

"You two haven't talked?"

"Not much. He's playing or I'm playing. We only got to talk a couple of times. I hear he's putting a few in the net, though. After all, he's playing against a bunch of kids and also-rans."

"Don't knock the minor league guys, they're the ones who are really playing for the love of the game, not the money. Go easy on them."

"Whoa, I didn't mean it that way. Who knows, I could be down there one day." She heard an audible sigh. "Maybe I will end up there if I don't start getting a few points soon. It's hard without Jason. It's like he reads my mind when we're on the ice together. I miss the moron."

"Well, Bertie, let's hope we can get him home soon. Good luck tonight."

"Okay, thanks. Be careful."

Christina and Mishayla settled on the sofa that evening to watch the Saturday night game. The team's performance had been abysmal, but Christina felt a sense of obligation to watch Bertie on the ice.

She smiled at Mishayla as the little girl squealed with excitement or dismay whenever the action heated up. The game wasn't going well—not a surprise. Toward the end of the third period, the cameras scanned the ice and picked out Bertie's pointed profile as he glided past the opposing players' bench.

~ * ~

Down at the ice, Bertie's thoughts strayed from the game. He wished vehemently he were somewhere else. He had been enduring verbal jabs by other players regarding his lack of production during Jason's absence. If that wasn't bad enough, on several occasions he had been forced to defend Jason's reputation to his own teammates. Adam Noole had moved to a condo downtown, leaving his wife alone in the large house in Aurora, and they were working on a separation. As a result of his bruised ego, the captain had been directing his own frustration toward the diminutive centre man. *I am not having a good time*, Bertie thought. Every night he couldn't wait to get back to his loving, supportive wife and noisy children.

Tonight, the game was going like a bag of shit. One of the defensemen on the opposing team had been barking at him all evening, and Bertie had just about had enough. As he skated past their bench near the end of the game, the goon leaned forward and shouted, "Hey, Goat, did Peterson sleep with your wife, too?"

Scraping to a halt, Bertie dropped his gloves, reached for the bench and curled his fists around the defenseman's jersey. He hauled the hapless player straight over the boards until he was sprawled on the ice. Bertie straddled him and started punching.

The sounds of the crowd increased in his ears, drowning out the sputtered protests of the player on the ice. He flailed away, his fists scraping and bouncing off forehead, jaw, and nose.

A sudden impact against the side of his nose numbed it for a second, his vision blurred with tears. An arm draped across his shoulders and yanked him up.

He couldn't resist waving at the roaring crowd as the linesman guided him to the bench. *My Corinne will smash the other side of my nose.* He held a white towel against his face on the way to the dressing room. *But I don't care.*

He sat in the dressing room with the trainer, watching the monitor. He grinned with satisfaction when the image of Adam filled the screen, a trickle of blood trailing from his brow to his jaw.

When the dance was over, there were more men in the penalty boxes than on the players' benches. They finished the last couple of minutes of the game in an anticlimactic, desultory fashion until the final buzzer sounded.

~ * ~

Christina stared at the television screen, horrified. She looked down at Mishayla's stricken face. The young girl's wide eyes glistened with tears. She looked at her mother and asked tremulously, "Mommy, why is Bertie so mad? I think he hurt his nose."

"He'll be fine, honey. Hockey players are tough. Um, I think you'd better get to bed." She sent Mishayla off to her room and sat down again. She punched Bertie's home number on the phone.

Corinne answered immediately and launched into her plans to string her husband up for losing his temper on national television. "Just wait till I get my hands on him!" Corinne exclaimed. "A fine example he is setting for his children. I hope Mishayla didn't see that."

"Unfortunately, she did."

She heard a click. "Wait a minute, I have another call. Can you hold for a second?" Corinne asked.

"Sure." Christina waited on the line for about a minute, watching the post-game commentary and wincing as they showed replays of the carnage.

Corinne returned to the line, her voice now soft and calm. "My Bertie is the biggest sweetheart," she stated emphatically. "He fought to defend my honor, isn't that the sweetest thing? I'm going to wait up for my man, broken nose or not."

Christina smiled as she hung up.

~ * ~

On the Monday following the game, Christina returned from work and checked a message on her voice mail. It was Bertie. She immediately called back.

"I feel great!" he responded after she inquired about his injuries. "I never felt better in my life, and I got suspended, too. Three games!"

"I never thought anyone would actually be glad to get suspended."

"Well, it was worth it. You should have heard what the guy said."

Christina's jaw dropped when she heard what had caused the fight. "Well, my friend, I don't normally approve of fighting, but in your case I'll make an exception. How are you going to spend your free time?"

"Well, that's why I'm calling. I'm going to fly down to see Jason. Do you have time to come along?"

Christina hesitated. "Me? Fly down to Florida? Why would he want to see me? You're his best friend." She hadn't heard from Jason since he'd left, except for the single call when he was settling in. She felt as if he was already tuning her out, and his distant behavior didn't surprise her. She was beginning to think the initial attraction between them had been an illusion, just as her sister had intimated.

Bertie obviously thought otherwise. "I know there's something between you two. Before they sent him down, he did nothing except talk about you. I figured you'd want to check on him."

"Do you mean spy on him? Showing up unannounced would probably piss him off."

"We won't be spying on him. I think something's wrong. He hasn't been calling much, and I can't get hold of him. It's not like him to act like this. Have you talked to him lately?"

"The latest call was last week, and he didn't sound like he wanted to talk, so I've been leaving it alone." She wished she had made more of an effort to call him, but every time she did, he was unavailable and hadn't returned her calls. Bertie's concern worried her. "Why hasn't he been back? Who's taking care of his house?"

"Mel's been taking care of things, you know, the cat and the horses, checking the house and all that. I talked to Mel a couple of days ago and in the last week or so he hasn't heard from Jason either."

"It does seem unusual. He seems to love those horses." Now she was really worried.

Perhaps seeing him would quell her fears. She shook off the feeling she might be spying on him—her feelings were just concern. *Yeah, that's it. Concern.*

She was glad that she wasn't at work full time yet and could afford to take a couple of days off. She wondered if one of her sisters would stay with her daughter. "What about Mishayla?"

"The March Break is coming up next week. She can stay with Corinne and the kids. I already talked to my wife about it last night. We can go Saturday afternoon and be back by Monday morning. Corinne thinks it's a good idea for you to go."

"Well, you seem to have it all planned out, don't you? All right, I'll go." As soon as the words were out of her mouth, she started to feel better.

During the rare times when her busy mind was at rest, her thoughts automatically steered toward the last night Jason was home. She still felt a flutter in the pit of her stomach when she remembered his kiss. Were his feelings genuine or was it just an impulse? Did he have feelings for Jennifer the previous summer or was it all just an innocent coincidence? She had no doubt Jason made a big mistake getting involved with Sheila. *It seems as if she's connected to the whole mess. I know I can get the truth out of her.*

What should have been an uncomplicated yearning during their separation had turned into anxiety and uncertainty. She forced herself to think of his affection for Mishayla, and her daughter's trust in him.

Bertie and Corinne were obviously devoted to him, and their children adored him. *Whatever happened before I met him is in the past,* she kept telling herself. *If he had been involved with Jennifer, could a similar transgression happen again? This is driving me crazy. I have to find out more about this damn Sheila.*

Eleven

Since their flight wasn't leaving until Saturday, Christina decided to take the opportunity to see Sheila face-to-face. If she wanted to meet her, she had to make it look accidental and gain her trust. Sheila's clothing store was a good place to start. It was public and Christina could easily make a quick escape if things got dicey.

She called her office to trade shifts with a co-worker, and on Thursday, while her daughter was in school, she made her way downtown to do some shopping.

She entered the busy store and wandered around, brushing her fingers against the expensive fabric of the dresses hanging on the racks. When a sales associate asked if she needed any help, she brushed off any assistance with thanks, saying she was just looking. She hoped she wouldn't have to hang around too long before Sheila came out of her office in the back of the store.

Finally, her patience rewarded. A tall blonde emerged to sign papers at the cashier's desk. Christina smiled at the woman and casually placed herself between the desk and the office door. Fortunately, a scarf display was at hand—if forced to purchase an item, at least she would be able to afford it.

She slid behind the gossamer scarves and waited.

The sales associate, a pretty brunette, stood behind the register. Her pleasant demeanor swiftly disappeared when the boss approached. She seemed nervous and hesitant to speak.

Christina watched her take a deep breath. "Excuse me, Sheila, I have a question about last night's deposit. I counted it again and again, we're $200 short, and I can't figure out what happened."

"Well, I can't imagine what could have gone wrong, Mary," the blonde woman retorted. Her voice had a harsh edge as she continued, "You must have made a mistake. If you can't find the money, it'll have to come out of your pay."

Christina felt a chill when she heard Sheila's voice. There was no mistake. The same voice had uttered the venomous message on Jennifer and

Adam's answering machine.

Sheila crossed her arms and tapped her pointed shoe on the floor a few times. "As a matter of fact, this has been happening too much lately. You must be dipping into the till."

Christina peeked from behind the display case and saw Mary's eyes begin to shimmer with tears. "But Sheila, I—"

"But Sheila, but Sheila." The blonde's voice rose in a falsetto imitation of her employee's voice. "I'll look the other way this one last time, but if it happens again, you're fired."

What a bitch, Christina thought. *Jason actually dated this woman?*

Mary stared at her boss for a brief moment, then rushed to the office, sobbing.

Christina shrank behind the scarves until the store was deserted, except for herself and the fuming manager. She hoped Sheila hadn't noticed her during the altercation, but it was too late to do anything about it now.

As Sheila walked back to her office, Christina let one of the scarves float to the floor, forcing Sheila to stop and pick it up. Christina stooped at the same time, bumping against Sheila and apologizing, "Oops, sorry about that."

The woman picked up the scarf and handed it to Christina. "No problem. Can I help you with anything?"

Christina controlled her revulsion and forced a smile. "I think this scarf is just perfect for a dress I picked up last week. Isn't it a bitch accessorizing?"

Sheila laughed and agreed. Her teeth flashed white behind scarlet lipstick. Impeccably groomed, her hair gathered in a smooth knot at the nape of her neck. Christina kept her involved in light conversation, trying to establish a base to build upon the next time she dropped in. She had to move slowly, not wanting to arouse any suspicion. She probably wouldn't have another chance to come back until she returned from Pensacola.

At a point in the conversation, Sheila narrowed her eyes and inquired, "Haven't we met? I'm sure I've seen you before, you look so familiar."

Christina's stomach sank. She swallowed, quickly flashed a smile and said, "Maybe it was at the benefit gala last month at the Convention Centre. It was a real hoot, all those firefighters!" She made a motion as if fanning her hot neck. Sheila laughed and agreed. At the gala or not, Christina was sure the woman wasn't going to admit she was not involved in a big charity affair.

Christina's heart rate slowly returned to a somewhat normal pace. She didn't think she could keep this up for long.

After closing the conversation with the excuse that she had an urgent appointment, she took the scarf to the front desk. Mary had reappeared and it appeared she had regained her composure. Christina saw the redness in the young girl's eyes and felt sorry for her.

She gave Mary a reassuring smile and paid cash for the scarf.

With obvious forced cheer, Mary asked, "Would you like to fill out a contest form for a free gift certificate?"

Christina accepted the ballot, searching her mind for a fictitious name and address. She settled on the name Kathy Jennings, and wrote down an address, mixing random numbers, street names and towns from addresses she knew, hoping this wasn't a real one.

Waving brightly, she left the store. After the door swung shut behind her, she stood on the slushy sidewalk for a moment and took a shaky breath. She felt like she was going to be sick. As she waited for her composure to return, she felt a little shiver down her spine. Glancing over her shoulder, she was startled to see Sheila's face peering at her from behind a dress rack, her image barely visible behind the reflection in the glass. Her eyes narrowed in what Christina perceived as suspicion. Christina quickly averted her gaze and pretended to adjust her gloves. What the hell was she doing? Turning quickly, she resisted the impulse to run to her car.

When she picked up Mishayla from school, her daughter asked for what seemed like the hundredth time when Jason was coming back. Christina sighed. "Soon, sweetie, soon."

Mishayla picked at a loose thread on the backpack in her lap and stared at the passing landscape. With uncharacteristic maturity, she looked at her mother and very seriously said, "I really like him, Mom. I miss him a lot. He's big and he's funny. Almost like having a daddy."

Christina felt her heart speed up again.

~ * ~

Far to the south, Jason performed his duties automatically. His disappointment with his demotion was apparent in his play. He had tried to follow Christina's advice, but it didn't take long for his confidence to erode. Even the untried rookies were skating circles around him as he half-heartedly went through the motions on the ice. The exasperated coach benched him, grumbling he did not receive a paycheck to be a bloody babysitter.

Saturday afternoon didn't differ much from any other day for Jason. He spent most of his free time between games, practices and workouts in the hotel, eating takeout and watching television without paying much attention to the programming. He considered calling Bertie or Christina, just so he could have somebody to talk to but dissuaded himself, positive his depression would rub off on them. Bertie had tried to call a few times in the past week, but Jason didn't bother to return his calls. *What's the point. He's just going to ask me how I'm doing, and he'll know I'm lying.*

He kept his cell phone off most of the time, but that morning he had left it on after practice. As he sat slouched in one of the uncomfortable straight-backed chairs, aimlessly flipping through television channels, the phone buzzed. He snatched the cell with his free hand and answered it, instantly regretting his action when he realized it was Sheila on the line.

This time she turned the screws, teasing him mercilessly about his exile.

"Jesus, Sheila, give it a rest, will you? If you don't have something useful or concrete to say, just hang up now."

Sheila laughed lightly. "As a matter of fact, I do have something to say. I need a fix, honey, and I need it soon. If you don't come up with something to keep me happy—I don't care if it's your delicious body or my other craving—I'll tell your precious new girlfriend about your selfishness."

"What selfishness?"

"You know what I'm talking about. Brenda. Wouldn't your new girlfriend like to know about her?"

He ignored the remark about Brenda. "What new girlfriend? You don't even know if I'm seeing anyone else." He searched through his mind, trying to recall if any news reports linked him and Christina. He couldn't recall anything specific, and he figured Sheila was bluffing.

Sheila must have sensed she had hit a nerve. She rubbed at the small wound she had created. "I saw her this week. We talked about you. I told you were just a shallow, self-centered jerk who only wants to get a woman in bed. Wouldn't she be interested to hear about your penchant for abandonment?"

Jason knew he should hang up, but he felt the weight of responsibility for Sheila's well-being still resting on his shoulders. He had tried repeatedly to prevent her downward spiral but had failed miserably. He found himself see-sawing between indifference to her plight and the guilt of knowing he could have made a difference. He tried one more time, if only to steer the conversation away from Christina.

"Listen, I didn't abandon you. You pushed me away, hiding behind your drugs and booze. I tried to get you to stop, and you just wouldn't listen. If you insist on ruining your life, don't try to make me feel guilty for giving up on you." It didn't come out the way he'd intended. Now he felt even worse. *Maybe I am a selfish heel. What good am I if I can't get a messed up woman to straighten herself out?*

"I wasn't talking about myself, baby. I was talking about your little nightmares. I found out something really juicy. Ian didn't try to shoot you out of jealousy. It was revenge. He was Brenda's brother. Kind of makes you think, huh? You're not even worth envy. Wouldn't your new sweetheart love to know about that?"

Jason felt a cold chill run down his spine as he listened. *Brenda. Brenda and Ian. Great. Another ghost to deal with.* Now he knew why Ian had looked at him with such hatred only a few days before his death. It couldn't have been mere jealousy. "You're lying," he said weakly.

"Nay, nay, my love. I've got the obituary here to prove it. I can mail you a copy if you like. Or, you can visit me to see it yourself."

Jason felt his stomach turn sour. *Was Ian truly related to Brenda? It was too farfetched. Sheila couldn't have come up with that idea all by herself. It must be true.* He steered the disturbing conversation away from Ian and found himself talking about Christina again. "You don't know if I'm seeing anyone, anyway. If I were serious about a woman, I'd tell her the whole story myself. I told you, didn't I?"

"You only told me because you were talking in your sleep. How long will it be before she starts asking you what those nightmares are about?"

"There's no one to hear me talking in my sleep. That's because I'm not seeing anyone. Why the hell am I justifying my love life with you, anyway?"

She ignored his denial and pressed on. "Don't play stupid with me. I know you're seeing someone, and it's the girl who stopped Ian's bullet. Do you really think she'd believe your story after that fiasco with Jennifer and Adam? Come on, Jason, you know as well as I do that women trust each other more than they trust men. All I have to do is tell her you're a horny, selfish jock who'll do anything to get into her pants, and she'd believe me, too. She'd take her little girl by the hand and run, run, run."

"How the hell do you know she has a little girl?" *Shit. Me and my big mouth.*

She laughed again. "Well, well. You're so predictable. Now I know you're involved with her. Don't be an idiot, everyone knows you're seeing your rescuer. Her name was in the papers the next day, stupid. As a matter of fact, we were talking along similar lines yesterday," she said. "This time I told her you've got a completely different problem. I told her, even though beautiful women in bathing suits surround you, you couldn't get it up because you can't stand the fact you're a loser in a small town league. You should have heard her laugh."

The knot in his stomach twisted to excruciating proportions as he thought of Christina laughing at him. The pain surprised him. He suspected Sheila was bluffing, but a tiny part of him believed her. He felt the heat of anger and disgust rising from his chest to his head. "I felt sorry for you, you could have been somebody, and I tried to help you, but now I have nothing left for you. You're disappearing, Sheila, and nothing's going to save you now. Nothing!" Jason threw the phone across the room. As it rattled across the floor, he realized he could have gone too far.

Christ, this could send her over the edge. She's been teetering enough lately. I'm such an asshole. An unwelcome image of a bottle full of pills filled his head. He could be responsible for yet another life.

He scrambled for the cell and put it to his ear. Nothing. He punched Sheila's number and received a busy signal.

He gave himself too much credit. Why would anything he said have an effect on her? Why should he think anything he did mattered?

He tossed the phone onto the bed and grabbed his keys and wallet.

~ * ~

When Christina and Mishayla arrived at the Gauthier home Saturday afternoon, Mishayla's eyes widened with surprise when she saw Bertie's face. Yellowing bruises surrounded his deep-set eyes, his prominent nose encased in a garish white bandage. He welcomed her with a hug and she shyly touched his bandaged nose. "Whoa, does it hurt much?" she inquired.

Bertie smiled and said, "Only when I laugh." He frowned. "So don't make me laugh."

Mishayla giggled.

"I told you not to make me laugh!" He tickled her and chased her down the hall toward the playroom and his waiting children, and returned to the front hallway to kiss his wife. Christina couldn't help smiling at his appearance.

"Don't you laugh, either," he said sardonically, picking up his overnight bag. "Corinne says it will probably be an improvement."

Their trip required a plane change in Charlotte before arrival at the small Florida airport, and during the flights, they made plans about where to track Jason down. Bertie had the address of Jason's temporary accommodations, a small but luxurious downtown hotel, but not much else. He had studied the game schedule and thought Jason would be in town on Saturday night. He had called Jason's number and left a message that they were coming but hadn't received a response before they'd left.

They planned to check into the hotel and call him, and if they couldn't reach him, they would ask around. "There are a lot of restaurants and hangouts along the beachfront and on the island. We'll just check them all out."

Christina raised her eyebrows in surprise when Bertie mentioned the clubs. Bertie lifted a corner of his mouth, wincing slightly, and commented, "Hey, I know you two might have something going, and personally, I hope to God it happens, but don't forget, he's a single guy, alone in a strange town. I don't see him sitting in his hotel room every night. He might be feeling a little lonely, you know?"

Christina turned her head and gazed out the small window to her right. "Yeah, I know. I'll try to keep an open mind." She didn't really want to think about Jason living a single life in a city far away.

They took a cab to the hotel, checked in, and Bertie inquired at the front desk about Jason's whereabouts. The concierge informed them Mr. Peterson was out but couldn't provide further details.

After they settled in their rooms, Bertie arrived at Christina's room with a list of possible hangouts to check out.

Christina looked at the piece of paper and raised her eyes, regarding Bertie with trepidation. "I'm not looking forward to this."

He patted her shoulder, his eyes serious for once. "Don't worry. He'll be glad to see us."

Christina shook off the uneasy feeling and prepared to go out.

Christina and Bertie took a cab and checked out, one by one, the more popular clubs along the beach. Some of the establishments would not let them in without an invitation, and others recognized Bertie and let them inside to look around. They ran into some of Jason's young team-mates, who provided several suggestions. It took seven tries before they arrived at an old train station converted into an Irish pub. They entered and scanned the room, picking him out at the end of a long, polished oak bar.

Christina felt her heart soar as she saw his profile. She didn't expect such a feeling of euphoria at the sight of him after all these weeks. She eagerly stepped forward, but then hesitated, hanging behind Bertie.

There were two women leaning toward him, obviously campaigning heavily for his attention. He had a polite smile on his face as he sipped on a pint of beer, glancing up at the television screen displaying a hockey game.

Christina and Bertie stood a few feet away from him for half a minute before Jason turned to see Bertie looking at him silently. He straightened in his stool, placing a pleased expression on his face. It was obvious he'd consumed a few too many, but Christina did her best to ignore it.

"Well," he said lazily, "my little buddy came for a visit. Wow! Look at your face! How did the other guy look?" He turned to the two women and quietly spoke to them. They both wore disappointed expressions as they moved on to another part of the room. He turned back to Bertie and must have noticed for the first time Christina standing behind him. His smile faded and he hissed at Bertie, "What's she doing here?"

Twelve

Bertie turned in time to see Christina's stricken expression. *Crap, this was a big mistake.* Christina's eyes filled with tears. She spun on her heel, pushed the crowd of patrons aside, and fiercely shoved the heavy wooden door open, disappearing into the humid night.

Bertie closed his eyes and turned his face to the ceiling for a second. He stepped up to Jason and placed an authoritative hand on his friend's elbow, guiding him off the stool. "Come on, moron, time to go."

Jason stopped every few steps to bid a patron goodbye and waved at the bartender at least three times, forgetting he had done so thirty seconds before. By the time they reached the front door, Christina had already gone. Bertie held onto Jason and hailed a passing cab. Wrenching open the door, he only had to aim Jason toward the opening. The bigger man spilled into the back seat and laid his head back against the tattered upholstery. His eyes were already half-closed and he muttered to himself.

Bertie had never seen his friend like this before. He slid in beside him and gave instructions for the driver to take them to the hotel. It wasn't far, only a few blocks, but Bertie had no faith in his own ability to keep his friend on his feet for long.

Somehow, he got Jason back to his room and pushed him into a small armchair. Jason protested weakly as Bertie pulled off his friend's shoes and switched on a lamp.

"I'll be right back," he said firmly, pointing his finger at Jason. "Don't move."

He left the room and went down the hall to knock softly at Christina's door. It opened a crack to reveal her tear-stained face peering out at him.

"He's safe in his room. I'm going to stay with him a while," he assured her.

Christina's lip trembled as she responded, "Why should I care? He obviously doesn't want to see me." She swiped at her eyes with the back of her hand and sniffed.

"Listen, Christina, you have to trust me. Don't do anything stupid. Just stay here. I'm going to find out what's going on and I'll be back to get you in a while. I'm sure there's a good explanation."

"Yeah, right." She closed the door firmly and Bertie rolled his eyes in exasperation before walking back to Jason's room. *I should be sainted.* He pushed open Jason's door.

Jason was still slumped in the chair. He had turned on the television and was flipping through the channels with feverish speed. He stared blankly at the screen, seemingly paying no attention to the swiftly changing images that flashed before him. Bertie snatched the remote from Jason's hand and turned off the TV. He scraped the other armchair across the floor and placed it between Jason and the television.

"Staring at the TV isn't going to make everything go away. You better tell me right now what the hell is wrong with you, or I give you a crooked nose like mine!"

Jason must have deciphered Bertie's thickly accented rant. He sighed, leaned forward, and looked at the floor, growling. "The bitch called this afternoon, after practice."

Bertie knew exactly who he meant, but he asked anyway, "Who, that Sheila? She called you all the way down here?"

"Yeah. Do you want to know what she said? She said she was talking to my new girlfriend. She said she told my 'new girlfriend' that I would never be able to hang onto a woman, and that I was just an empty-headed jock ruled by his pants. She said my demotion's affecting my performance and that I can't get it up. She said the 'new girlfriend' laughed and agreed." He spat out the words, his malevolence increasing with each clipped sentence.

Bertie stood up and leaned over Jason. He reached down and grasped Jason's shirtfront with both hands and unglued him from the chair. Jason didn't struggle, just stood unsteadily, looking blearily down at Bertie.

"If you believe that," Bertie growled, not in the least intimidated by Jason's superior height and weight, "then you are no longer my friend and not my brother anymore." He finished the sentence in a whisper and opened his fingers with a little push, allowing Jason to fall back into the chair. Jason didn't try to retaliate; he just sat and stared at the wall.

Bertie plunked himself into his own armchair, crossed his arms, and waited for his friend to sober up.

It was past midnight when Jason began talking. Bertie jerked himself awake and listened.

"For the last twelve years," Jason began, "I felt like I could do anything. I was on the top of the mountain, everyone loved me, and I spent a bit too much time loving myself. All those beautiful women following me around—I could take my pick. During all that time, you were the only person who kept me grounded, you, Corinne, and the kids. You were there for me when my parents died and every summer afterward. I left the game behind. I spent time with the horses and went to your cottage up north; swimming, hiking, helping you teach the kids to fish. I didn't need anything else.

"After Sheila showed up, I know I must have acted differently. I saw myself changing. She brought out the worst in me, I guess…then I ended up here. Sure, it's nice and warm but that doesn't disguise the fact I've been sent into exile. The kids on this team are really trying. Some of them will be in the big leagues eventually, but when someone like me gets sent here, it's almost a death sentence.

"Now I feel like the smallest insect on Earth. I'm doing the best I can but it's not easy. Even way down here, the newspapers are painting a picture of me that I don't like. A picture that's not real. They go on about how I'm fickle and unreliable. How I only do my best when it suits me, not for the team."

He stood and stretched, stepping across the room to fetch a bottle of water from the mini fridge. He snatched the sports section of a local paper from the table and handed it to Bertie, sitting again. He took a swig from the bottle and pointed at the paper.

"The rumors are flying around about why I got sent here, and Adam and Jennifer are definitely in the mix. Even some of the little snots on this team are giving me a hard time of it." He stopped himself and rubbed his eyes. "Okay, they're not little snots, they can't help making up reasons why I'm here. It's like freakin' high school."

He raised his eyes and focused on Bertie again.

"Being sent here made me realize the end is way too close, too real. I'm eventually going to have to retire and find something else to do. You have your own life. Soon the kids will be in high school, and you'll have your hands full with driving lessons and college and stuff like that.

"Where am I going to be? Will I coach? Will I be a riding instructor? I don't know. All I know is, I don't want to do it alone. When this thing happened with Sheila, I started to wonder if I had any identity beyond the sport. Would anyone want to spend time with me, by myself, without the crowds, the lights, and the reporters? Is there someone out there willing to grow old with me…scars, bad knees and all?

"I thought maybe Christina would be the one. She seems so brave, thoughtful, and fun. I wish I had spent more time with her and Mishayla before I ended up here. I had such hopes all this would be over, and I could go home and pick up where we left off.

"But the more time I've been spending here alone, my hopes are fading. Why would she want a nobody? She deserves better."

"You're not a nobody," Bertie insisted. "Do you honestly think just because you're not on top of the heap at the moment, that Christina wouldn't be interested in you? She's bigger than that. You're acting like she's written you off. It's not over. Christ, it hasn't even really begun yet."

Jason closed his eyes and leaned his head on the back of the chair. "Yeah, yeah, you're right," he finally conceded. "My self esteem's been taking a real beating lately. All this mess with Sheila—well, she's just screwing things up big time. That woman won't leave me alone. She has her claws in me, and I can't shake her loose. She's running around in my head, bumping into things, and scrambling my brain. Sometimes I think she must be crazy, or maybe I'm the crazy one.

"All the bullshit she said to Christina, or didn't say, made me think. I have to get that woman out of my life before I can begin anything with Chrissie. Sheila knows shit, Bertie."

"What kind of shit? Bad shit?" This was a side Bertie never seen in his friend. He thought he knew Jason inside and out, as if he was another part of himself. Secrets were foreign to him.

Jason's expression switched from contrite to guarded. He shifted in his chair and said nothing. Bertie's unease deepened.

"Jason?" he whispered, "Did you have an affair with Jennifer?"

Jason straightened quickly, and his eyes blazed with their old intensity as he stared at his friend. He firmly stated, "No. I did not." He glanced down again and said quietly, "But that doesn't mean she didn't try to make it happen."

Bertie's eyebrows shot upward in surprise. "She made a pass at you?"

Jason shifted and looked at Bertie again. "It wasn't her fault. I don't want to ruin things for her. She just made a mistake and realized it almost right away. She's a good girl, and I didn't want to get her into any trouble so I didn't say anything. I just don't know how the hell Sheila tapped into that and managed to twist it into something so sordid and tacky."

Bertie said thoughtfully, "Maybe you'd better think back on that day. Maybe you'll remember something. Was there another car outside? Did Adam's dogs bark out the window? Anything would help. She has to be stopped."

Bertie remembered Jason's rant about Sheila's reference to Christina. "Listen moron, if you think Christina believed those things about you—well, I don't know what to think. You can see Sheila is a clever liar, and she's messing with your head big time. I don't even think she knows Christina exists, maybe she just made it all up, to get you going."

"She knows something, but you're right, she probably just took what she read in the papers and filled in the blanks herself. It sure seemed real when she was talking to me, though. Well, maybe you're right. Jesus, Chrissie must think I'm such a bastard."

Jason rubbed his head in frustration. "When I saw her in the bar, Sheila's words were still fresh in my mind. That's why I was out drinking…I just couldn't handle Chrissie thinking of me that way. God, I'm such an idiot. How can I get her to forgive me?" He looked at Bertie; his eyes haunted.

"Well, for starters, you can talk to her. Tell her everything you just told me." Bertie rose to his feet. "Stay put."

"Where the hell am I going to go?" Jason muttered, throwing his head back on the chair.

Bertie shrugged and left the hotel room, returning a few minutes later with Christina. She entered the room with her arms crossed tightly across her chest, wearing a glum expression. She stalked across the room and sat in the chair recently vacated by Bertie, silently waiting and glaring at Jason. As Bertie backed out of the room and closed the door, he saw Jason lean forward to pry Christina's hands loose, holding them gently as he began to talk.

Thirteen

Christina, drained of all energy, listened to Jason. She had spent the last two hours in her room, sobbing uncontrollably at first, but later, simply lying on the bed with a pillow tucked against her chin, tears rolling endlessly into the linen. An occasional hiccup closed her throat. She couldn't imagine why she had been so stupid to expect a joyful reunion, but she was totally unprepared for the look of animosity that had emitted from Jason's eyes when he first saw her.

She had developed a monster headache from the onslaught of tears and wearily rolled from the bed to rinse her face in an attempt to calm down.

She grimaced when she saw her face in the mirror under the harsh fluorescent lamp. Her eyes were red and swollen, and her nose looked almost like Bertie's.

Sniffling, she rinsed her face in cold water. By the time she returned to the bedroom, a soft knock brought her to the door. Bertie stood outside, looking as tired as she did.

"I think he's ready to talk. Are you ready to listen?" Bertie inquired, rubbing his eyes.

Christina looked at him skeptically and frowned. "I think his one look at me in the bar said just about everything."

"Listen, Christina, he has a good explanation, and I think you should hear it."

"Oh, come on, Bertie, I'm so tired—"

"Just a few minutes is all I ask. You'll never be able to sleep feeling like this anyway. You can sleep late tomorrow."

She had finally relented and followed him to Jason's room.

Now she looked searchingly into Jason's eyes as he opened up to her and described his fear of the uncertain future, his frustration with his present situation, and his mistakes in the past. Fresh tears spilled from her eyes when he told her the things Sheila had said on the phone, how he almost believed the woman's vile words.

"I would never think something like that about you," she whispered brokenly, tightening her fingers in his hands. "You have to believe me. She's lying to you. This just proves we have to do something about her." Her voice rose with panic, and Jason cradled her face in his hands, brushing her cheeks gently with his thumbs, trying to calm her down.

He leaned across and gently kissed her mouth, caressing her tear-stained cheeks with his lips. She rose from her chair to curl in his lap, pressing her face into his shoulder and soaking his shirt with slow, tired tears as he stroked her hair.

"I thought for sure you hated me. I thought you'd forgotten me already when I saw you in the bar." She sniffed and rubbed her eyes with the heel of her hand.

"I'm sorry. I was still wrapped up in the awful things Sheila said. I was drinking, and I wasn't thinking clearly. I'm so sorry I made you feel like that." He nuzzled her damp cheek. "I was still stinging from the things Sheila said, and when those women were trying to chat me up, I wasn't really paying much attention. Really, I wasn't."

"I promise I'll get you back home, one way or another," she whispered into his chest. "I promise you."

"Don't make promises you might not be able to keep. This is my problem. I'll work it out somehow."

How are you going to work it out if you're down here, and she's up there?

She eventually became still, drained by emotion. She felt Jason rise from the chair, cradle her in his arms and set her gently on the bed. She was so tired, she didn't protest.

Sometime in the wee hours, she opened her eyes. This wasn't her room.

She heard soft breathing from the other side of the room. Squinting in the darkness, she made out his outline sprawled on the hard sofa near the window.

Later, she felt the bed move as he settled beside her, nesting his body next to hers.

~ * ~

The morning was well advanced when Jason awoke, rubbing his sticky eyes. His head and neck were throbbing, and his mouth felt like he'd been sucking on gravel all night. He unglued his tongue from the roof of his mouth and struggled to rest on his elbow.

Christina was still asleep, obviously feeling the effects of a long day and a late, heart-wrenching night. He felt awful for putting her through such a hard time after she had come all this way to see if he was all right.

She looked more peaceful than the previous evening. Her long, dark lashes rested against her creamy cheekbones while her full lips almost pouted in relaxation.

He lightly brushed her tousled hair from her face with his fingers. She stirred and sighed, her eyes still closed. He bent his head and grazed her earlobe with his lips, letting his warm breath travel across her skin. She frowned a bit and raised her hand to brush the irritation away. Groaning, she murmured, "God, you're worse than a kid, and your breath stinks." A glint of amusement touched her eyes as she squinted at him. "You look like hell."

"Yeah, and I feel like shit." He forced a smile. Last night was a blur. He wondered if he'd said or done too much. *Holy crap.*

"Uh, did I…I didn't do anything inappropriate, did I?

Her lovely forehead furrowed for a moment, but then her brows rose in understanding.

"No! Oh, no. You were the perfect gentleman."

"Good, then we can start from square one." He made another attempt to kiss her.

She laughed and pushed him away. "Go be a good boy and brush your teeth."

Nice. Jason slid out of bed. As enticing as she looked, he was sure she didn't share the same sentiment about him. Besides, he wasn't in any shape to make any advances this morning. Maybe a quick shower and shave would make him feel human again.

~ * ~

Christina listened to the sound of running water and bad singing.

Did he remember what he said last night? He'd seemed so frayed. She thought about his raw, naked outpouring of emotion and couldn't shake the feeling he was holding something back. She had felt like a mime, stuck in an imaginary Plexiglas box, trying to reach him but bumping her head against the plastic.

At least he apologized for that scene in the bar. She struggled to a sitting position and swung her feet to the floor. She considered knocking on the bathroom door to tell him she was heading to her own room but changed her mind. The best thing to do was to freshen up and then face him again with an open mind. She quietly picked up her shoes and slipped from the room.

~ * ~

Jason emerged from the bathroom, a towel wrapped around his midsection. He paused in the doorway when he discovered the room was empty. "Hmm," he muttered. With a sigh, he strode to the closet to find something to wear. When he was dressed, he called the front desk to obtain her room number.

He felt a little more alert than the previous night as he knocked on her door, but he still felt embarrassed. He hoped he hadn't made her too uncomfortable with his ramblings, but somehow he knew he'd needed to open up to her or lose her. Still, he wasn't ready to reveal everything, and the omission made him feel guilty. *There's plenty of time for that*, he assured himself.

The door opened and she looked shyly at him. "Hi."

"Hi." He looked at his feet, his hands, and the doorframe.

"Come on in."

He stepped inside and faced her, nervously running his fingers through his hair. "Listen," he began, "I'd like to apologize for last night. I don't normally drink that much, and I probably said a lot of things I shouldn't have said." He smiled with chagrin. "To tell you the truth, I'm feeling a bit raw from all that heart-to-heart stuff. I'm not used to it."

Christina regarded him for a moment before assuring him, "You didn't say anything to embarrass yourself, and you were just showing your feelings. It happens, you know."

He stepped forward and drew her against him, enclosing her in his arms. He whispered, "I'm glad you're here."

She seemed to tense for a fleeting moment, but then her body relaxed. She rested her cheek on his chest. "Me, too," she said with a sigh.

They settled on the sofa and she leaned against him. He gently encircled her shoulders with his solid arms and rested his chin on her hair. They were quiet for a few moments. Jason felt much better, simply absorbing her presence.

"I saw her on Thursday," Christina murmured as they gazed out the window at the brilliant blue sky.

Jason was instantly alert, looking down at her sharply. "What? Who?" *Was it Jenny or Sheila?*

"Sheila. Who else? I went to check her out, to see what all the fuss was about. I had this image of teeth and claws in my head, but when I saw her, she seemed so ordinary; fancy and polished, but still ordinary."

All Jason could think about was the last phone call from Sheila. The woman was far from ordinary. He shook off the feeling of dread and asked, "What did she say? Did she know who you were?"

"No, I was just a regular customer to her and we just talked about nonsense. But she looked at me in a funny way through the window while I was outside."

"Stay away from her, Chrissie."

"Stop worrying, I'll be careful. Besides, I think I know when someone is playing mind games with me. I'm not stupid, you know."

Jason felt a little jab to his male pride. "Does that mean I'm stupid because she managed to turn me inside out?"

"Of course. I didn't mean it that way, Jason. It's just…I think women are sometimes able to read each other better than men are."

Her comment was eerily close to Sheila's words. *If those two women got together, how much would Sheila say? Probably too much.* "Well, I still think you should just stop poking around," he grumbled and slid out from behind her, rose from the couch, and began pacing.

He felt her eyes on him as he prowled about the room. "You seem to be awfully adamant about leaving this alone," she commented. "Well, I can't let you fester out here when people need you at home."

He stopped. "People?"

"Yes, people. Bertie, Corinne, the kids. Me."

He looked at her. She regarded him steadily with those large eyes that made him feel like he could see inside her. *She's so honest with me. Why can't I be honest with her?* She was wading into territory he didn't want her to venture.

Not yet. He decided to leave the subject alone for the moment. Standing by the window, he gazed at the brightness outside. A few tourists loaded their cars for a day at the beach. His head gradually stopped throbbing, and his stomach finally felt as if it could take some food.

He grabbed her hands and drew her to her feet, enclosing her in his big arms. "Come on, I'm starving, let's find Bertie and get a bite to eat."

~ * ~

She allowed him to lead her to the door, mind still churning. They strolled hand-in-hand to Bertie's room and found the door ajar. Pushing it open, she observed their friend reclining on the bed, surrounded by newspapers, and a pile of empty dishes sitting on the wheeled trolley beside him.

Bertie raised his eyes and looked at them sardonically. "Well, well, look who finally joined the living. Have you eaten?"

Jason strode across the room to inspect the dishes. "There's nothing left!"

"Well, my friend, I have been through breakfast and lunch as well, waiting for you two to wake up. Go ahead, order something, I'll wait." He buried his face in the newspaper once again. Christina leaned against the doorframe and smiled as Bertie peeked over the paper and winked at her.

Fourteen

As Christina and Jason ate, Bertie went through the papers, checking the local outlook on Jason's predicament. It seemed the negative reports had filtered down to the Gulf too.

"You know, I think we have to think back on that day last summer when you visited Jennifer. Maybe someone was snooping around the property or something. If it wasn't her, could it have been that Ian guy?"

Jason shot him a glance that told him to leave it alone, and quipped, "Well, he's dead, so we can't question him."

Bertie insisted, "Well then, you should tell us what was said and if you heard anything outside."

Jason rolled his eyes and said to the ceiling, "I don't want to get into this, nothing happened."

Christina leaned across the table and laid a steady hand on his arm. "Jason," she said quietly, "I have an idea of what happened on that day. I was talking to Jennifer a little over a week ago. She really cares about you and wants us to help. If anything happened between you two, it's not my business, it was before I knew you." She stood and moved to the door. "I've got something in my room I think you should hear."

Jason rose from his chair. "Why are you encouraging her? I don't want her near that woman. She's nothing but trouble."

"I don't know why you're getting so bent out of shape. She's just trying to help." Bertie rose to get more coffee. "She's a smart woman, smart enough to find out the truth."

"That's what I'm afraid of."

Bertie wasn't sure he heard right. "Why would you be afraid?"

Jason returned to the table and rested his head in his hands. "Never mind."

Bertie opened his mouth to protest. At that moment, Christina entered the room with her purse in her hand. She sat down, pulled a small tape recorder out of the bag, and placed it in the center of the table. She motioned to Bertie to come closer and pressed the play button.

The unmistakable voice of Sheila Duffy reached their ears. Jason's eyes widened, and he stared at his friends. Christina pressed the stop button and paced the room. She stopped in front of Jason, still seated, staring at the tiny instrument.

She rested her hands on her hips and spoke sternly. "Listen to me. If something happened, we can't do anything about it, and all we can do is maintain damage control. If nothing happened, or if it was all just a big misunderstanding, we have to do everything we can to put a stop to it and this tape can reinstate you."

Bertie leaned back and let Christina take charge. It felt strange letting someone else steer the moron in the right direction, but she seemed capable enough. She must have felt strange accepting the possibility he could be involved with a married woman, but he knew her suspicions were unfounded. Christina would find out for herself that Jason could be trusted.

Christina continued, "She's a nice girl, Jason. I like her, even though I've only talked to her a couple of times. She deserves our help. So get your head out of your ass and think back, and tell us everything you can remember."

"Oh my God, moron, you've found your match here!" Bertie exclaimed.

~ * ~

Jason shook his head and sighed. If he offered just enough information to satisfy them, maybe it would be enough to silence Sheila and push her out of their lives. He just wished it wasn't Christina doing all the legwork, preferring to do it himself. He proceeded to tell them all he could remember about that day in August when Adam was away at a golf tournament.

"I had just met Sheila back then. We were casually dating by the middle of the summer. She was one of those women who always showed up at the same bar where the guys and I sometimes went after the games. Bertie doesn't remember since he always shot straight home after our games to be with Corinne and the kids.

"Well, we got to know each other a bit, and she came along to a couple of the barbecues at Adam's place in July. I knew Sheila was interested because she laughed at all my jokes. You know, all of them, even the bad ones. Bertie knows I'm not that funny." Bertie raised his eyebrows and nodded in agreement as he lay with his ankles crossed and his hands behind his head.

Jason continued, "Then, in August, Jennifer called me and said she had just bought a new surround sound system for Adam and needed help hooking it up before he got back from Raleigh. So I said I'd help. When I got there, she asked if I wanted a beer, so I said yes and started unpacking the speakers.

"While we were going over the instructions, she kind of got closer and closer, leaning over my arm to get a closer look at the book. I didn't think much about it; she was my friend." He rubbed his eyes, trying to remember more. "Then…then she got this look in her eye, and I know that look. She put her hand on my knee and I stood up right away. She snatched her hand back like it was burning, and her face went really red.

"After that, I hooked everything up as fast as I could, and she sort of hovered around. Even though she thanked me, she looked like she couldn't wait for me to leave." Jason sighed heavily. "She just couldn't meet my eyes after that. I didn't want to embarrass her with questions, so I just left it alone."

"What was her relationship with Adam like?" Christina asked. "Did they ever fight?"

Bertie offered, "Well, we know Adam has a temper on him."

"Jenny would do the usual complaining but don't all women do that?" Jason asked.

"Not all women," Christina said with a wan smile.

"Not my woman, anyway," Bertie bragged.

Christina laughed. "You should have heard her the night you got your nose smashed in, but I don't think she was mad for long."

Bertie closed his eyes and sighed blissfully. "No, she wasn't," he said dreamily.

Jason got back to the subject at hand. "Anyway, not all marriages are perfect and maybe hers wasn't. If she was thinking of doing something, she changed her mind right away, thank God. I don't think I could ever look at her the same way if anything had happened."

"So, do you remember anything else?" Christina prodded. Jason looked at her face. She seemed almost eager. *How can I say no to this girl? How can I keep anything from her?*

Jason screwed his eyes shut and concentrated. *Come on, moron, you can remember that day if you really try. Sheila wasn't there but somebody else had to be.* He straightened and exclaimed, "Yes! There was a car parked on the street. It was a Volvo, a blue one. There was somebody inside but it wasn't Sheila. It was a man." He stared out the window for a moment and turned back to Christina, his eyes round. "Holy shit! It *was* Ian!"

"Are you sure?" Christina asked. A tiny crease appeared between her eyebrows. She peered at him intently, and he squirmed under her scrutiny.

Jason slapped his hand on the table. "Absolutely." He frowned. "I wonder what he was doing there. Was Sheila seeing him back then? We'd just started dating. Hmm, maybe I was the other guy, not him."

He leaned back in his chair and continued pensively, "If he was jealous, I still think it was a bit much trying to put a bullet in me. Overkill, so to speak." He laughed nervously, shrugged, and took another bite of his omelette.

Christina raised her eyebrows, taking a sip of her juice. "Well, there's one way to find out. We get her to talk, of course," she said brightly. "It's obvious she's trying to get you back, and she thinks that threats are the only way. God knows it isn't her charm. Maybe I can use this thing and get some proof." She shook the recorder.

Jason's mind closed like a shutter slamming over a window. "No, no, no. She must know who you are, so she won't say anything."

"She won't know who I am. She didn't the first time."

Jason looked at her with serious eyes. "That's my point. If you go poking around again, she'll get suspicious for sure. I don't want you playing detective while I'm out here sitting on my ass. What if she tries something? The woman's a freaking sociopath."

Bertie spoke from his perch on the bed, "If she's going to go anywhere near that woman, I'll make sure I'm close by. Nothing will happen if she tries something."

Jason wished his friend would stop being so goddamned helpful. He scraped back his chair and started to pace, running his hands through his spiky auburn hair. "The whole thing just creeps me out."

Christina said, "Think of your horses, Mr. Peterson. Think of your lovely cat. What if she tries to do something to them? What if she tries to harm someone dear to all of us? What if she goes after one of the children?"

Jason swiftly turned and shouted, "That's not fair!" His voice bounced off the walls of the hotel room, causing both Christina and Bertie to jump, startled.

Christina stood and said loudly, "Why are you trying to keep me from helping you? Don't you want to put her away?"

Jason wanted it all to go away. Now. He turned so they couldn't see his face. "I want to put a stop to this as much as you do, but I don't want you to be the one doing it. Okay, maybe it's the kids, the cat, the horses, but they aren't going to be on the front lines while this is happening. It's you." He finished his sentence in a hoarse whisper.

He looked at the floor. "You're too involved in this. I'm afraid she'll target you. All the things she has been saying over the phone, everything has been getting more and more crazy and weird and—damn it, I don't think I can go on if that...that bitch hurts you. You mean so much to me—you and Mishayla." He turned around and stared at Christina. His eyes burned into her. He screamed inside...*Just stay away from her. I'll say anything to make you stay away.*

Christina moved close behind him and laid a warm hand on his back.

"Listen, if I promise to be really, really careful, and to have Bertie close by at all times, will you let me help you?"

Jason sat again and rested his elbows on the table. He was tired of fighting them. Rubbing the palms of his hands against his eyes, he hoped for the best and moaned, "Okay, okay."

"Listen," Bertie said, "you don't seem to take this very seriously. I know it's nice down here with the sun and the surf, but do you really want to stay in the minors? Do you think I'm having all the fun in the world being treated like a leper on my own team?" He got up and strode across the room, leaning on the table with his hands. "I need you back, moron."

Jason smiled, reached up and punched Bertie lightly on the shoulder. "I need you, too, asshole."

Christina grinned and held up the small voice recorder, waving it back and forth.

~ * ~

They let the subject lie for a while and spent the afternoon checking out the sights of Pensacola. It was a charming old town with long, blazing white beaches—quiet at this time of year—taking that big, collective breath between Mardi Gras and Spring Break. They strolled along the side streets, gazing in awe at the grand old homes that predated many mansions further north.

The day ended on a high note, a delicious dinner at a nearby restaurant. Bertie smiled as he watched the couple laughing and talking with their heads close together while they sat at an outdoor patio, warm air washing over them. He decided that he was a fifth wheel long enough and declared he was heading back to the hotel to rest his aching nose.

~ * ~

The other two followed suit, but they didn't go back to the hotel to rest. Jason slid Christina's key card into the door and handed it back to her, leaning over her with one elbow on the doorframe. Christina reached out and laid her hand on his chest. She let it slide down, brushing along his side until it rested on his waist. Curling her fingers, she gathered the material of his T-shirt and gave a light tug. She kept her face turned upward, and he looked at her steadily for a moment. Finally, he bent close, cradling her cheek with one big hand as he kissed her lightly, then more urgently. She responded eagerly, clutching his shirt and pulling him into her room. They slid through the door and it softly clicked shut.

Jason felt as if he was invading forbidden territory as he slowly undressed her, brushing his fingers lightly over the curves of her body. He had done this countless times before, but this time it almost seemed he wasn't committing his whole heart and soul to a moment that should be altering his world. He could almost see another part of himself looking down on the pair and shaking an admonishing finger, scowling with disapproval.

He almost stopped, but the sight of her creamy skin and beautiful face swept him over the edge in spite of himself. He shook his conscience loose, telling it to go away, and he took the leap. *I'll worry about the consequences later.* He ran his lips over her smooth, flat stomach.

She was nothing like any other woman he had been with. She approached lovemaking with a refreshing mixture of innocence and sensuality. She wasn't the least self-conscious as she enthusiastically explored his body as much as he did hers.

Afterwards, she slept contentedly, one slender leg draped over him, and her long dark hair adorning his neck.

He lay in the darkness, staring at the ceiling, and wondering how he was going to stop Christina from continuing her crazy crusade. He wanted her to stay away from Sheila. He wanted to deal with that woman himself, before she ruined everything. He glanced down at Christina's sleeping face. *I don't want to lose her.*

He finally closed his eyes, slipping into slumber.

He felt a floating sensation and discovered he was sitting in a small powerboat. Sparkling water surrounded him, and a child's giggle broke through the sound of lapping water. He looked down and saw a little girl, or was it a boy? The reflection from the water obscured the child's face.

He reached out, steadied the fishing rod in the child's hand, and gave gentle instructions. Another voice spoke from behind him.

He turned, and it was Brenda. She smiled at him. He felt his own face tug into a grin and turned back to the child.

The space where the child had been sitting was empty. Suddenly, he wasn't in a powerboat any more, just a little rowboat with a small amount of water sloshing at his feet. He spun around to find Brenda was gone.

He peered over the gun whale at the water. The light burned his eyes. He started to shout, desperately leaning over the edge of the boat and groping in the water with his hand.

He jerked awake with a painful shout.

~ * ~

Christina bolted upright and switched on the bedside lamp. She was surprised to see Jason sitting with his feet on the floor, his head in his hands. She reached to touch his shoulder. It was drenched with cold sweat.

"What's wrong? Jason, are you all right?"

He shook his head, rising to rinse his face in the washroom. "Everything's okay," he called from the other room, "Just a bad dream. Go back to sleep."

"Who's Brenda?"

Jason stiffened. "No—nobody. I don't know."

Christina waited until he was settled once again, before switching off the light, and drew the sheet over him, laying her hand on his chest. It was a while before she fell asleep.

~ * ~

The next morning, Jason accompanied Christina and Bertie to the small airport. Bertie studied a car rental advertisement with apparent interest, and Jason bade Christina goodbye with murmurs and caresses.

She looked into his eyes, searching for something. He fervently wished he could say whatever she wanted to hear, but all he could do was kiss her. *There's time. I'll think of something.*

He offered what he hoped was a confident smile—an expression that would carry them both until they saw each other again.

Bertie ceased his inspection of the poster on the wall and grasped Christina's elbow. "Come on, lovebirds, we're going to miss our flight," he said with a crooked grin.

Christina walked sideways through the security doors, smiling and waving at Jason. He brightly returned the salute, his smile fading as the doors closed.

The cell phone buzzed as he turned away from the gate. Automatically, he flipped it open. "Yeah."

"Well? Have you got a day free for a conjugal visit or a supply run?" Sheila's voice jarred in his ear.

"Bite me." He flipped the phone shut and pushed open the glass exit door with such force, it clattered against the side of the building.

Fifteen

The rest of the week filled with activity; a couple of day trips with Mishayla and two more shifts at the dentist office. When the house was quiet, Christina's thoughts turned to the night she had spent with Jason. She had thrown her reservations aside for the moment, taking a chance to be with him. It may have been too soon, and it should have felt natural for them to be together.

Still, she couldn't help feeling something had been missing. She'd invited his advances with enthusiasm, but while they were together he'd seemed almost detached, as if he was merely filling an assigned role. She found herself making excuses for him. Maybe he was still hung over, feeling the effects of the previous night. Maybe he was annoyed with her for insisting they investigate Sheila's involvement in his exile. Maybe…maybe he wasn't as committed to their relationship as she'd first thought.

She sat up in bed, angry with herself for thinking such a disturbing thought. Throwing aside the covers, she slipped out of bed and moved through the darkness to the living room. Curling up on the sofa with a soft blanket wrapped around her, she leaned her elbows against its back, staring out at the quiet street through the large window.

I should have known better than to get involved with a hockey player. How the hell am I going to shake this doubt?

She felt like Jason was on trial in her head. It was frustrating being judge and jury to a man who was making no effort to defend himself.

It's up to me to finish this. I don't think I could ever make peace with myself if I break this off without a solid reason. It's time to pay a visit to the clothing store again and get an invitation to lunch; a nice, long lunch with lots of wine, but not for myself.

~ * ~

Far to the south, Jason hardly heard the celebratory carousing of his teammates during the bus ride home from a game in Mobile. He sat alone, nodding in thanks when one of the boys congratulated him for scoring a hat trick in the lopsided win. He didn't feel like celebrating; he was too busy thinking about his last night with Christina.

He felt like a fraud. She had willingly welcomed him, but he felt as if another man had kissed her and caressed her body, not him. He wished he could have taken the evening back.

He remembered waking again from the same perpetual dream. He regretted not taking the opportunity to talk to her about it. *I'm such a bloody coward*. The dark horizon sped past. *I have go home to talk to her and set things straight. This has gone on long enough.*

The thought of coming clean frightened him. He worried she wouldn't accept him after he revealed his past, but he had to go through with it before Christina had a chance to see Sheila. He made a mental note to call first thing in the morning to let Christina know he was coming home.

Feeling lighter, he shifted in his seat and accepted a beer from one of his teammates, joining in the festivities.

They didn't arrive in Pensacola until midnight, and it was two o'clock before he finally fell into bed. As usual, he spent a restless night, interrupted by the same disturbing dream. He woke in the darkness, a lingering sound of a crying child in his head. He looked at the clock. *Too early to call. It's only five o'clock.* He punched his pillow in frustration and fell back into a troubled sleep.

It was 10:00 a.m. when he fought his way back to consciousness. He immediately reached for the phone, punched in her home number, and waited. No answer, just voice mail. He hoped she was just sleeping late, and left a brief message.

After an abbreviated late morning practice at the rink, he called the airport to purchase a ticket for a flight leaving that afternoon. He placed another call to Christina's house, still no answer. He tried her cell number, no luck, the phone must be off. Beginning to worry, he called Bertie. Corinne picked up the line and informed him Bertie had taken the kids to a matinee.

"Do you know where Christina is?" he asked.

"I think she said something about taking Mishayla to a birthday party and heading downtown for lunch."

Jason fought a feeling of dread. "Tell Bertie I'm flying in today, and I'll give him a call when I get into town. Kiss the kids for me." He disconnected and tried Christina's number again, slamming the phone down when the voice mail kicked in for the fourth time. Throwing a few shirts and a pair of jeans into a carry-on, he headed for the airport.

Sixteen

That morning, Christina prepared her daughter for an afternoon of fun at her best friend's birthday party. Since the party was four hours long, she would have plenty of freedom after dropping Mishayla off at PlayPlace, a massive game complex, very popular for children's parties. Its location was conveniently close to the city, so she would have enough time to drive downtown and lure Sheila out of the store for a while.

She thought about her promise to have Bertie nearby, and as a courtesy, gave him a call. She was secretly relieved when Corinne told her he was out with the children. *Oh well, if Bertie and Jason give me a hard time, I'll just tell them I tried.*

Mishayla was almost jumping out of her skin with the anticipation of an afternoon of bowling, bouncy castles, video games, and cake. "Gosh, you're making enough noise for five children, just give me a minute to grab my things," she told her daughter as she stuffed her gloves, wallet, cell phone, and the tiny tape recorder into her purse. In her rush to leave the house, she forgot to turn her phone on.

After she dropped her daughter off at the party, she drove downtown and found an empty parking meter close to the clothing store.

"Okay," she said to herself as she stood facing the glass door leading into the store. She took a deep, cleansing breath and yanked the door open.

Sheila was on the sales floor, speaking to a young woman holding an armful of blouses. As Christina moved slowly between the clothing racks, she flashed a smile at the owner. Sheila's eyes flickered toward Christina and she nodded and smiled in return.

Her heart thudding, Christina sidled closer and sighed audibly. Sheila's eyebrows raised in a questioning expression.

"Oh, I just can't decide what to wear to the Red and White Ball next week," Christina said with a forlorn expression.

Sheila laughed. "Why, red or white, of course," she exclaimed.

"Clever you, I've got a gorgeous red dress, but I wore it last year to the Polo for Heart gala. What if someone sees me in it a second time? I'll just die." Christina had no idea how she was going to pay for a dress at this place, but she would somehow make it work. *Maybe I'll take out a loan.*

She glanced at her watch, almost noon. Glancing sideways at Sheila, she sighed again. "Oh God, look at the time. It's lunchtime already? I've been wandering the streets all morning and haven't gotten a single thing accomplished. Boy, I'm starving."

Sheila could smell a big sale approaching and took the bait. "Well, it's almost time for my break. Why don't we get a bite to eat and I can give you a quick rundown of our inventory."

"Sure," Christina responded brightly. "There's a cute little sushi place around the corner."

"Great! By the way, my name is Sheila."

Christina held out her hand. "Kathy Jennings, pleased to meet you."

As Sheila fetched her coat, Christina furtively checked her purse, making sure the recorder was accessible. The two women walked a few doors down the street and entered the restaurant. Christina made sure they had a corner booth so her purse could rest beside her on the cushioned bench.

They giggled over the menu, trying to figure out the difference between nigiri, futo, and maki sushi. Deciding to keep things simple, they ordered a variety platter, a couple of bowls of miso soup, and a healthy dose of saki.

Christina eyed the miniscule saki cups and wondered how she was going to get Sheila to relax and talk with such tiny servings of rice wine. She didn't take any chances, only allowing herself little sips and constantly refilling Sheila's cup with the warm liquid.

It wasn't long before Sheila was comfortably tipsy. Maybe it was the warm serving temperature of the Japanese wine, but the woman was definitely relaxed halfway through the meal. Christina decided this was the right time to steer the subject around to hockey.

"You know, next spring there's a benefit dinner at the Royal York. They're planning to have a lot of hockey players there. God, they're hot, aren't they?" She leaned sideways, pretending to swoon and surreptitiously reached into her purse to switch on the tiny recorder, pushing it deeper inside. "I wish I could have some of that."

"Sure, they're hot. I dated one," Sheila responded with wicked pride. "Man, he was *so* delicious, a real tiger in bed."

Christina felt a twinge of jealousy but forged on. She swallowed and forced her eyebrows up, responding with mock curiosity, "Was?"

Sheila smirked and waved her chopsticks around. "Oh, he moved on. The big asshole couldn't keep his mind on one woman for more than five minutes."

Christina could feel her face getting hot. "Men. Talk about fickle, huh?"

"Well, this one was a real piece of work. You know, he had the nerve to dump me just when I needed him most. Remember the shooting incident a couple of months ago?"

"Yeah, it was all over the papers. I can't believe that guy actually got a gun in the arena, with all the extra security they have these days."

"Well, 'that guy' was a good friend of mine. Well, he was more than a friend, I guess. We were pretty tight, Ian and I. The guy he tried to shoot was Jason Peterson, my boyfriend at the time. I think Ian was jealous of Jason, and when I told Jason that Ian was my...friend, he dumped me. Right on the spot! I was furious."

Sheila's voice was getting loud, and Christina nervously looked around. The restaurant, which had been hopping with activity when they first arrived, was almost empty after the lunchtime rush. Sheila giggled and spoke more quietly, leaning close to Christina. She confided in a slightly slurred voice, "I got back at him, though. I let his precious BMW have it with a baseball bat." Sheila's eyes were slightly unfocused as she sighed, resting her chin on her hand. "I waited for him to come running to me for sympathy but it didn't work. So I called him and he just yelled at me. The stupid jock."

Christina fought to keep her hands from shaking as she poured more saki. "You must have been really mad."

"You bet I was mad. How dare he treat me like trash? A couple of weeks later, I tried to see him at his farm, but he wasn't at the house. I thought maybe he was in the barn with his stupid horses." Her expression changed from self-righteous to pensive. "I thought I'd wait for him in the barn. You know, I've always wanted to make love in a barn..." Her eyes closed dreamily and she looked as if she were going to drift away.

Christina knew the night in question—she remembered lying in the guest room of Bertie's home, thinking about the man downstairs. She prodded Sheila, "Did he come home and find you?"

Sheila frowned. "No, I waited forever, smoked almost a pack of cigarettes, and then left." She covered her mouth and giggled sheepishly. "The stupid barn burned down. Oops."

"Oh, my God, were the horses okay?"

Sheila waved a hand in dismissal. "Yeah, yeah, they were fine. Thinking back, I realize he probably wouldn't have welcomed me with open arms, anyway. He had enough on his mind already." She picked up the saki cup and took a healthy swig, no longer bothering to sip. Setting the cup down with a clunk, she leaned forward and whispered confidentially, her slur more pronounced, "A week or so before that, I let a little story leak out. I called the team captain's house and left a message that Jason had been sleeping with his wife. Boy did the sparks fly!"

Christina allowed her eyes to widen with surprise. "Wow! Was it true?"

"Of course not, I just wanted to punish him for leaving me high and dry." Sheila drooped a little, almost in tears. "I don't know what I'm doing half the time. I want him back, but I want him to suffer too."

"How the heck did you get a story like that?"

Sheila shook off her melancholy and continued. "Well, Ian, you know the guy that killed himself? Well, he was more than a friend. He'd moved to Toronto from somewhere out west, and I met him just a little while before I managed to hook up with Jason. Ian and me were pretty tight, and he must have been pissed when I started going to team events with Jason. But Jason is *so* much hotter." Christina noticed that Sheila was getting repetitive and was thankful that the recorder was picking up every word, repeated or not.

Sheila belched delicately and continued, "Anyway, Ian started following Jason around and mentioned he'd been to the captain's house, but I knew darn well that the captain was at a golf charity event in Raleigh." She pronounced the city's name with a long drawl and giggled. Christina feared that she was going to lose Sheila soon; she was starting to sway in her seat.

"He was following Jason around? Why?"

"I guess he was cooking up an excuse to break us up. He was pretty jealous. He told me they were just in the house together, but he didn't really say they slept together. I blew it off when Ian told me because I know Jason's not into married women, but I thought it would be a great idea to use that information to get back at him for not coming back to me. So, I called the captain's house, left a message, and I kind of embleshed...em–embellished things a bit." She giggled and straightened, rubbing her eyes.

"The icing on the cake was when I set 'im up with the cops a few days later. My knight in shining armor..." Sheila glazed over for a moment.

Christina prodded, "What? Did he have to rescue you from something? What cops?"

"Oh. I got him to help me with my car and planted some white powder on him, the goof got himself arrested!" A spurt of laughter almost sprayed Christina with saki. "I called the cops and told them there was a deal going down."

"Sheila!" Christina did her best to keep an admonishing tone out of her voice, although she was appalled. She had totally forgotten about the arrest and subsequent release. Jason's demotion the next day had chased the event right out of her head.

She rearranged her features and attempted to appear astonished and impressed. "Was the stuff real?"

"Are you kidding? The real stuff is expensive enough. I love him but not that much."

Love him? This is one mixed up broad. Christina didn't know whether to hate her or feel sorry for her. She began to understand Jason's fickle feelings about Sheila. The woman alternately presented vastly different sides in a haphazard fashion. Little Lost Girl vs. Bitch of the Century. Christina felt herself sliding into the sympathy void and gave her head a mental shake. "How did he react to that?" she asked.

"He was so pissed!"

She wanted desperately to escape, but something about Ian's role in the shooting made her backtrack. *Was it just jealousy or something deeper?* "Why would Ian be mad enough at Jason to shoot at him?" she asked.

Sheila rested her cheek in her hand, pensively tapping the cup of saki with a chopstick. "Yeah, that's strange to me too. Ian was a hothead, but he'd always kept his temper around Jason and didn't even talk to him much. Sometimes I'd talk about Jason just to get his blood boiling, but he was usually just annoyed. Then, a week or so before the shooting, I joked about Jason's nightmares, something about a kid. Ian started to act really strange after that."

"What kid?"

"Oh, that's not important. Ian went ballistic and tried to take Jason out, but got himself shot. What a psycho. But Jason was the real deal. I really liked him. I wish it could have been different, but I think he's moved on. He's seeing someone else."

"Who?"

"Some widow with a kid. I could tell you about his fixation with brats but that's another story."

Christina's feeling of apprehension quickly developed into panic. She regretted leaving Bertie behind and wished he were in the next booth. She mentally kicked herself for being such an idiot. *I don't know how long I can keep this up.* To give herself a chance to calm down, she rose from the cushioned bench. "Whew! What a story. Can you excuse me a minute, I just have to make a quick call."

She reached into her purse for her cell phone and furtively switched the recorder off, shoving it deeper into her purse. In her haste to leave the table, she left her purse on the seat and moved to a small hallway leading to the washroom area.

Looking at the cell phone, she realized she'd forgotten to turn it on. Cursing herself, she hit the power button and called Bertie and Corinne's home to inform them she was on her way to pick up Mishayla. Corinne picked up and immediately launched into a lecture about leaving cell phones off when one was out and about by herself.

"Sorry I left the phone off. We were in such a hurry this morning, I totally forgot about it. I wanted to let Bertie know I was going to see Sheila today, and I'm sorry I didn't tell him sooner. I know he'll be furious, but if he had been hovering around, she would have been suspicious for sure."

Corinne's voice was high with agitation. "You bet he's furious. He's been worried sick since he got home with the kids. To top it all off, Jason called, and he's on his way home. He wants to see you."

"Oh, Jeez. Where can I get hold of him?" Christina peeked around the corner to see if Sheila was still seated at the table. She was there, her forehead resting on her hands.

"He's probably just landed. Mel is picking him up and taking him to the farmhouse to pick up his car. Leave your phone on, he'll probably try to call you as soon as he's home. You're not with that woman now, are you?"

Christina pretended she didn't hear the question. "Okay, thanks, Corinne. I'll call back later." Christina flipped the phone shut, drew a deep breath, and made her way back to the table.

~ * ~

Sheila took a deep breath and tried to brush the cobwebs from her brain. *Fucking saki does it every time.* What was she thinking? She had allowed herself to open up a little too much to this woman. She didn't even know her. *God, I must be a real mess.* She reached for her bag to find a tissue, and her eyes rested on Kathy's purse. Glancing at the back of the restaurant, she noted the woman was nowhere in sight.

Was her new best friend willing to extend a little loan? Greed overcame caution, and she let her fingers slide inside the purse, plucking out the wallet sitting on top. Keeping a cautious eye on the doorway, she flipped the wallet open. She couldn't help glancing at the driver's license that peeked from behind a clear pocket in the wallet. The name jumped out at her and everything suddenly made sense.

That's why she's asking so many questions. Her eyes narrowed. *That bitch! She's the one he's been seeing.*

She glanced up and saw Christina's shoulder emerge from around the corner. Letting the wallet drop inside the purse, she swiftly covered her eyes with her hands, resting her elbows on the table, her mind churning with suppressed rage.

By the time Christina returned to the table, Sheila had become outwardly calm. She dabbed at her eyes with her tissue and apologized for being so maudlin.

"I'm so sorry for ruining your afternoon with my sob story…*Kathy,*" she emphasized the name, "but I really think I should get back to the store."

Christina glanced at her watch. "Oh, dear, we talked for so long I completely forgot about my appointment. Could I take a rain check on the shopping? I promise to come back tomorrow."

"No problem," Sheila responded with a toothy smile that didn't quite reach her eyes. "Drop by tomorrow, I'll have a couple of nice gowns for you to try on."

Together, they walked back toward the store. Christina unlocked her car and gave a friendly wave before sliding inside. Sheila wiggled her fingers in return, stepped inside the store and shouted to her sales girl, keeping an eye on the car pulling into traffic. "Mary, I have something to take care of. Would you mind watching the store for a while longer, there's a dear." She swiftly darted outside and clattered unsteadily in her high-heeled boots to her nearby Jeep, noting the direction Christina's car had taken. Firing up the engine, she caught up to the Escort and followed at a discreet distance. As discreetly as she could while seeing double. Somehow, she managed to evade disaster as she followed the Escort northward.

PlayPlace was just outside the city in a large mall complex. The two vehicles hummed along the highway, exiting on a ramp leading directly to the mall. Sheila allowed Christina's car to pull ahead to a parking space close to the main entrance, and she guided her Jeep to a spot near the ramp to the highway. She waited fifteen minutes before she observed Christina's car emerging from the sea of vehicles, heading for the exit. Sheila fired up the engine, wondering what kind of urgent appointment brought her rival to this location.

Sheila followed the car, keeping her Jeep a few car lengths behind as they continued north. It started to drizzle, a wan, depressing mist—not quite snow and not rain, either. She switched on the wipers and headlights as the late afternoon light faded to a grayish-blue twilight. She edged a little closer as Christina made for the ramp to Highway Nine, humming eastward on the four lane regional road.

~ * ~

Christina had been shaking with dread throughout the interview but it was over now. She breathed a sigh of relief and allowed herself to relax, feeling a warm rush of anticipation at the thought of Jason's return. *I wonder why he's flying into town? No matter, he's back, and I can't wait until he hears this damning tape.* She smiled and began making plans for the evening. *I'll run into Newmarket, get something for supper, and invite him over.* Bypassing the turnoff to her house in Schomberg, she continued eastward, toward Newmarket.

As darkness gathered, her cell phone chimed. Keeping an eye on the road, she groped around in her purse to find the phone and flipped it open. Jason's voice cut through the hum of the engine.

"Where the hell have you been?"

His angry tone took her by surprise. Feeling a stab of irritation, she retorted, "Well, I missed you, too."

"Sorry, I was just worried. Where are you?"

"I'm on the road. Where are you?" She stalled, wondering how to tell him she had been with Sheila, but he already knew.

"I've been home for about an hour, phoning all over the place. Corinne told me where you were. Why the hell didn't you get Bertie to come with you, and why was your phone turned off? We've been going crazy."

"Bertie was busy, and I couldn't pass up the chance. Sorry. I forgot to turn on my phone, but it's just as well, I couldn't have you guys phoning me while I was getting that woman drunk."

She laughed, pleased with herself. "Anyway, it paid off! I have her, Jason. She totally admitted everything on tape!" Mishayla sleepily protested from the back seat. Christina continued in a more subdued voice, "She mentioned both the car window and the barn fire. She also knew there was no affair last August, but she used Ian's information to fabricate it."

"That's all she told you? There wasn't anything else?"

Christina made an impatient noise. "What else could there possibly be? Isn't this enough? Oh, and she mentioned being behind the arrest. Funny, you didn't get around to telling me about that one."

"Listen, Chrissie…" There was silence on the line for a second. "Can you come straight over here before you take Mishayla home?"

"I've already passed your house, but you know I can't wait to see you either. Listen, I'm heading into Newmarket to pick up some groceries before going home. Why don't you come over and I'll cook you some dinner? Then you can listen to the tape."

A bright light in her rear view mirror made her squint as she approached the Glenville curve. She interrupted him, "Jason, I have to put the phone down for a bit, someone is tailgating me something awful. I have to be careful. I'm coming up to Glenville Pond. You know how much I hate this curve."

She placed the cell phone on the passenger seat beside her and concentrated on the sweeping bend in the highway. She blinked. The vehicle behind her didn't slacken its pace, creeping closer to her rear bumper and almost obliterating her vision with the glare from its high, bright headlights.

The reflection abruptly swung to her left, disappeared from her center mirror and filled the side mirror.

The impact drove her head against the headrest. She cried out and gripped the steering wheel, trying desperately to keep the vehicle on the road, but her car flew with alarming speed toward the low concrete barrier. She hoped the Escort would simply bank off the accumulation of ploughed snow against the barrier, but instead, it kept going.

The car launched into the air. For a few seconds, all she saw beyond the windshield was blackness interspersed with specks of moisture hitting the glass. It seemed like minutes before the underside of the vehicle made contact with the steep incline on the other side with a lopsided, stomach-turning thud.

The air bag deployed, slamming into her face with unbelievable force. Dazed, Christina thought it was over, but the Escort slid drunkenly sideways and slowly rolled, picking up speed as it approached Glenville pond at the bottom of the slope.

~ * ~

At first, Jason didn't recognize the sounds coming from the cell phone. Then he heard a high, metallic screech and Mishayla's voice, crying "Mommy!" A sickening, crunching noise accompanied by the sound of shattering glass followed, lasting about twenty seconds. He shouted into the phone, "Chrissie! Mishayla! Shit!"

Feeling helpless, he listened intently. After the massive noise, he heard nothing. He screamed into the phone again, disconnected, and punched 911, muttering over and over, "Oh, God, oh, God."

After giving the particulars to Emergency Services, he grabbed his jacket and called Bertie while striding to his SUV.

Corinne answered the phone. "Bertie! Get Bertie now!"

He heard her shout to her husband, "Bertrand! Jason's in trouble! Pick up the phone!"

Bertie picked up an extension. Before he spoke, Jason blurted "I think Chrissie's been in an accident."

"What the hell?" Bertie exclaimed.

"I think she went off the road. I called 911 and they'll check along Highway Nine near Dufferin Road. I'm going there now, I'm closer." He disconnected and shoved the vehicle into gear. He knew without asking that Bertie would join him at Glenville pond.

~ * ~

Bertie dashed up the stairs, calling to his wife to find his keys.

Corinne was stunned when he told her what had happened. "Are you sure?" She asked, her brown eyes wide and frightened.

"If Jason says there was an accident, there was definitely an accident. I'm going to see if I can help." He grabbed his jacket from a hook on the wall and burst through the back door, sloshing through the early spring drizzle to his vehicle. He gunned the engine and sped through the darkness along Highway 7, north to Nine, and rushed westward.

Seventeen

Christina struggled toward consciousness and blinked against an onslaught of moisture beating against her eyes. She squinted and barely discerned dark, gray-black clouds illuminated by the lights of Newmarket a few miles away.

This unlit stretch of Highway Nine curved north as it rose, dissecting a twin set of high, tree-clad hills before bending eastward again. All she remembered were the bright lights reflecting from her rear view mirror and obliterating her vision, and Mishayla's terrified scream as the vehicle behind her accelerated, making violent contact with her left rear bumper, pushing her car over the barrier and down the embankment toward Glenville Pond. Everything turned upside down and around with a loud crunching noise mixed with Mishayla's screeches. The windshield had smashed and this was the result of her unobstructed view of the silent sky.

Her joints protested, and her face throbbed. She felt as if she'd been punched. Instinctively, she ran her tongue across her teeth to make sure they were all there. She dabbed at her mouth and felt something wet and sticky.

It was too quiet. *Mishayla.* She struggled sideways to peer into the back seat. In the darkness, she could barely see Mishayla's silent silhouette in the booster seat. "Mishayla? Mishayla! Oh, God…"

She unhooked her seatbelt to reach behind her and check for a pulse. She found it, faint but steady.

Sobbing with relief, Christina used her fingers to feel around the front passenger seat in the darkness, searching for the cell phone. She couldn't find it. It must have flown through the broken windshield. She squeezed between the front seats to the rear passenger compartment and felt all around the girl's limp form to see if there were obvious injuries. She didn't detect sticky warmth indicating blood, but her daughter's condition still made her frantic with worry. The shattered window beside her daughter's head gaped open, cold drizzle pelting their faces. The buckled roof hovered only a few inches from Mishayla's head. She must have had quite a bump.

It seemed like ages but her daughter stirred and moaned. "Mom, I feel sick."

Christina caressed her daughter's damp cheek. "Try not to move, sweetie. I'm going to see if I can get us some help. Can you move your fingers and toes?" She tried to keep her voice steady, but wanted to sob out loud.

Her daughter wiggled and gasped with pain. "Everything hurts, Mom." A tiny wail rose from her throat, and Christina's heart wrenched.

I shouldn't have been talking on the cell.

She peered through the cracked side window and squinted toward the road above her. She saw the glow of passing headlights. Someone must have seen the accident. She tried the door but it was jammed.

She gave her daughter one last glance, returned to the front passenger seat, and crawled through the windshield. She made a quick circuit around the car to make sure it wasn't too close to the edge of the pond. Thankfully, the car had come to rest only two feet from sure disaster.

She turned and studied the embankment. It was steep but she figured it wouldn't be too difficult to climb if she used her hands as well as her feet.

She wished she'd brought gloves. Cursing her forgetfulness, she stumbled up the embankment toward the highway, wiping her bloody nose with her sleeve.

The early spring drizzle gave the dirty snow a granular texture. The incline leading to the road was steep, and the half-thawed snow scraped her hands as she attempted to claw her way up the slope. She made it up halfway and lost her grip. She slid back to the bottom, shouting with aggravation and pain. Now she was soaked and her hands and knees were raw.

She tried yelling for help, but her voice merely echoed off the steep hill hugging the pond. Besides, the closed windows of passing vehicles wouldn't ever allow her cries to be heard.

She tried climbing again, and once more slithered to the base of the embankment. She rested her aching forehead against the cold ground and screamed hoarsely in frustration. Pushing herself to her feet, she gave up and stumbled back to the twisted wreckage of the car.

She studied the condition of the pond. The surface glowed white in the darkness, but patches of darker gray meandered across the surface. She would have considered crossing the pond to get to the dirt road on the west side, but she was sure the surface was little more than a thin sheet of ice covered with slushy snow. It wouldn't support her weight.

Thank goodness the car hadn't rolled on the ice. Glenville Pond wasn't large but it was deep. On the east side of the pond, a tree covered slope rose sharply out of the water. At its base lay a tangle of deadwood, crisscrossing in jagged heaps sticking out of the ice. *No sense trying that way, either.*

She mounted the hood of the car and crawled back through the windshield to check on her daughter. Her baby was still fuzzy and incoherent. She pulled off her jacket and laid it carefully over Mishayla. Turning her eyes to the road far above, Christina prayed someone would see the skid marks leading to the barrier and investigate. The throbbing in her head and neck increased, but she refused to give in to her pain until they were both safe.

It seemed like hours passed, but only ten minutes later the glow from a set of headlights slowed and stopped on the shoulder above. Christina gasped with relief and scrambled out of the vehicle again, stumbling through the slush to meet the figure sliding down the embankment.

"Oh, my God!" she sobbed. It was Jason. He threw his arms around her, peering at her face in the faint light. His face twisted in sympathy when he saw the trickle of blood on her upper lip. "Oh, sweetie, are you okay?"

She nodded and choked out, "Mishayla's not doing so good." She tugged on his sleeve and guided him back to the wreck. He followed her and ran his hands over the side of the car, finding a spot where his gloved fingers could grab hold. He gave a mighty heave and wrenched the back door open, reaching inside to check Mishayla's condition.

His voice drifted from the interior of the Escort, "Did you see what kind of car was following you?"

Christina shivered in the darkness and tried to remember, rubbing her aching forehead. "It had really high, round headlights, like a Jeep."

~ * ~

Jason immediately made the connection. Sheila. He removed his gloves and quickly checked Mishayla's pulse, placing his warm hand on her cold cheek. She stirred lightly, whimpering. He whispered to her, "Keep still, pumpkin, somebody's coming to help." He adjusted Christina's jacket on the little girl and scrambled out of the vehicle, swearing to himself.

Turning to Christina, he grabbed her shoulders. He wanted to shake her and kiss her at the same time. "What did I tell you about going to see that woman on your own? Jesus, Christina." His voice trailed off, and he enclosed her in his arms again, pressing his cheek against her damp hair. He slipped his gloves onto her shaking hands and wrapped her chilled body inside his coat.

Christina's muffled voice drifted from the folds of his jacket. "I'm sorry, Jason, I just had to do it, I couldn't wait any longer. I missed you so much..."

Jason fought to control his panic. His heart was racing, and he was almost dizzy with the realization that both Christina and Mishayla could have been gone forever. And it would have been his fault, not Christina's. Not even Sheila's.

He took a deep, shaky breath and murmured in a cracked voice, "I'm not mad at you. I'm just glad you're okay, and I'm sure Mishayla will be fine too. Come on, she's asking for you."

He assisted her into the back seat and glanced back to the roadside. The car must have cleared the fence, so there was no visible damage to the barrier. A scar ran down the incline. Squashed tufts of dry grass and piles of granulated snow indicated where the car had rolled. *My God, what a mess.*

Jason slid inside and wrapped both of them in his jacket, holding them close. He gently dabbed at Christina's lip, trying to clean off some of the blood.

Christina waved his hand away and nestled against him, reaching out to hold her daughter's hand. "How did you know we were here?" she asked.

"Don't you remember telling me you were coming up to this curve? The one you don't like. I remembered what you told me about this pond. I saw the tire tracks. The ambulance is on its way, they'll see my truck parked up there."

Christina leaned close to her daughter and murmured words of encouragement. Five minutes later, blue and red lights flashed from the roadside above, and paramedics and firefighters scrambled down the slope with ropes and gurneys.

Only requiring one, the paramedics used a body board and strapped Mishayla securely. They hauled the gurney up the slope with speed and efficiency. Jason didn't let go of Christina's hand as the firefighters assisted them up the embankment.

As they approached the summit, they saw a familiar silhouette leaning on the roadside barrier. It was Bertie.

Jason stopped in front of him, ready to tear into him for letting Christina go off alone, but the look on Bertie's face stopped him. His expression was murderous as he swept past Jason and faced Christina.

"I don't know what to do with you! How do you expect me to help you if you go off by yourself like that? You're worse than one of the children. Don't you ever do that again young lady, I don't think I can take it. If anything ever happened to you, Corinne would kill me, and the moron would finish me off—"

His voice broke, and his shoulders shook. He gathered Christina into his arms with a muffled sniffle.

Christina's eyes met Jason's over Bertie's shoulder. She lifted one eyebrow. "I think I've been adopted," she said with a wan smile. She gave Bertie a peck on the cheek and accepted a blanket from one of the paramedics, moving toward the waiting ambulance to be with her daughter.

"We'll be right behind you," Jason assured her and turned to face Bertie. Bertie kept his face down, violently scrubbing his face with his gloved hand. "I'm sorry, moron, I should have been watching her more closely." He laughed nervously through his tears. "She's a slippery one, though. I hope the kid's okay."

Jason clapped him on the shoulder and assured him, "Everything'll be just fine. Let's go, I have to talk to Chrissie about something and it can't wait."

They strode to their vehicles, but were interrupted by a police officer. She apologized for the delay, asking if they had any information regarding the crash.

Jason blurted, "Sheila Duffy."

"Excuse me?" the officer asked.

"I have a strong feeling the vehicle that hit her was a beige Jeep Cherokee driven by a woman named Sheila Duffy. If you want, I can give you her address and the license plate number of her Jeep," Jason offered.

Frowning skeptically, the officer took down the information and told them she'd be in touch.

The regional hospital was in Newmarket, a short drive along Highway Nine. Jason followed Berties' SUV into town. Arriving soon after the ambulance, the men parked and entered together through the Emergency entrance.

Bertie glanced sideways at Jason. "What do you have to talk to Christina for?"

"Something I should have told her a long time ago. It's been bugging me for a while."

Jason looked around, expecting her to be in the waiting room. An elderly man slumped on a chair with a young woman beside him. They stared at the small television mounted near the ceiling. On another chair, a teenage boy sat with his mother, holding a bloodied towel to his hand. Christina was nowhere to be seen.

He inquired at the Triage desk, and the nurse told him, "The doctor is giving her a quick examination to make sure she didn't sustain any injuries during the accident. You know how mothers can be; they tend to ignore their own symptoms if their children are injured. She should be out soon." She called out to the mother and son.

A few minutes later, Christina stepped out from one of the examining rooms, looking tired and sore. Jason rose to his feet and walked toward her. She lifted her arms as if they each carried a heavy weight and clutched his jacket, burying her face in his chest. He enclosed her in his arms, resting his cheek on the top of her head. They stood still, eyes closed, oblivious to the frenetic activity around them.

"They're giving her an MRI and moving her upstairs," Christina told him. "They told me to wait."

Jason led her back to the waiting room and settled at her side, letting her lean on his shoulder. He wished they were alone so he could finally get to the reason for his impromptu return to Canada but there were too many people rushing back and forth, and Christina looked so exhausted and forlorn, he didn't want to upset her.

They had almost dozed off when a representative from the provincial police force paid them a visit. Christina turned, wearily listening to the female officer as she reported that they visited the home of Sheila Duffy, but nobody was at the residence.

Christina closed her eyes and turned her face into Jason's shoulder, sighing. Jason laid a gentle hand on Christina's hair and said, "I think you should find this woman. She's dangerous."

The officer protested mildly, "Mr. Peterson, we have no evidence proving Ms. Duffy caused the accident, other than your tip. If you would like to visit the station as soon as you are able, maybe we can put our heads together and find enough evidence to issue a warrant."

"It'll happen," Jason assured her. "Let's just get through this first."

The officer nodded gravely and continued her report. Handing Christina a plastic bag, she said, "We recovered your purse and cell phone, and the car has been towed to a forensics lab for inspection. We'll go over it carefully, and if there's been any contact with another vehicle as you stated, we'll find traces of it on your car. We're doing the best we can." She gave both of them her wishes for Mishayla's speedy recovery and left the hospital.

Two hours passed, and the attending physician informed them of Mishayla's transfer to upstairs. The three of them wearily relocated to a small, hard sofa in the hallway outside Mishayla's room, sleeping in fits and starts.

It was midmorning when Jason's cell phone chimed. He jerked awake and answered it, trying not to wake Christina and Bertie.

His coach's voice was tight with anger. "Peterson, you're supposed to be at practice. Where are you?"

"I'm in Canada."

"What? Do you think you can just pick up and take off whenever you feel like it? You're not untouchable, Peterson."

Jason knew he'd been pushing the limits with the team, but at this point he didn't care. "Sir, it was a family emergency. Yes, I realize I have no immediate family, but trust me sir, someone I really care about is in the hospital. She had an accident."

The coach's voice rose in agitation. "I don't care if your mother is in the hospital. You get your ass back here or you're suspended."

"She's six-years-old, for crissakes. I'll be back tonight."

Jason flipped the phone shut and nudged Christina. She fought to open her eyes and looked at him.

"I've gone AWOL," he said quietly, his eyes focused on hers, and his hand gently cradling her cheek. "I'll have to get back, but I want to make sure she'll be okay before I get on the next plane."

"Are you in trouble?" she asked drowsily.

"Not really. This coach sputters a lot, but he's more lenient than the old one."

The doctor finally approached with an update on Mishayla's condition. "She has a pretty bad bump on the head and a bit of whiplash, but she's awake now. We did an MRI to check for damage, and it looks like she had a significant concussion."

Christina said, "She plays hockey. Will she be able to continue?"

The doctor shook his head. "I wouldn't recommend it. If she had another head injury, it could do irreversible damage. You can see her now."

Christina visibly drooped. Jason laid his hand on her shoulder and gave a reassuring rub. She stood and stretched, ready to enter the room. She turned and looked at him. "Are you coming in?"

He waved her on. "Go ahead, I'll be in soon."

She nodded and went inside. Jason sat, looking at the floor, thinking about how close they had come to tragedy, all because of that woman. He hoped the police found her first, because if he did, his fingers would gladly close around her throat.

Ten minutes later, he entered Mishayla's room.

The little girl was pale but alert, her neck encased in a soft, white brace. Her face brightened when she saw Jason, but a shadow fell over her eyes. She regarded him sadly and said, "Mommy says I can't play hockey anymore. I wanted to be just like you, Jason. Just like you and Bertie." A slow tear trickled down her cheek, and Jason had to fight to keep from crying himself.

"We'll find something fun for you to do, baby. I'll bet you'd be great at anything you try," he responded with false brightness.

Christina sat on the other side of the bed, holding her daughter's hand and gently stroking her forehead. "You're having a heck of a year, aren't you, honey?"

Mishayla grinned weakly. "Coach says, 'What doesn't kill ya makes ya tougher.'" She furled her eyebrows in imitation of her coach and winced. "Ow."

Christina reached to smooth her daughter's brow. "I think I'm going to have a little talk with Coach," she said with mock severity. They waited as Mishayla's eyes drooped and she fell into a relaxed slumber.

When the nurse entered, Christina asked, "Is it okay for her to sleep?"

"As long as we check her regularly, she can sleep."

After the nurse left, Jason opened his mouth, about to say something, but Christina held up one hand as she rooted around in her purse for her phone. "I'm just going to check my messages. Maybe the police called the house." She tapped a few buttons. "Oh, here's one from just after the accident." She listened intently.

He watched her face as she frowned, eyes widening in shock, and then narrowing in fury. She glared at him and flipped the phone shut. "Why didn't you tell me?"

Jason's stomach felt like it had fallen through the floor. "Who left that message?"

~ * ~

She stared at him with disbelief. She thought she knew him, thought he could be trusted.

"It was her." Christina looked down for a moment, taking a deep breath. She looked up again, her anger still churning through her like bubbles of heat. "I don't know how she got my home phone number but she did." She fought for control, and whispered, "She said you got a girl pregnant, abandoned her, and she died in childbirth. Is it true?"

"It wasn't like that, it was—"

"So it *is* true. What the hell possessed you to leave a big detail like that out of our relationship?" Christina kept her voice quiet but emphasized her words with a wide wave of her hands, and then stood and paced around the room, swinging around to face him once again with both hands clenched in her hair. "If you had said something earlier, I would never have wasted all this time with her, asking questions, sneaking around. I was doing this for you!"

Jason flushed. "I didn't want you to do anything for me. I didn't ask you to go and talk to her. It was driving me crazy, knowing she was a nut job and could be telling you anything to make me look bad!" He stood and raised his hands, entreating. "I was going to tell you, but the time was never right."

"How long were you going to wait? Were you going to tell me at my baby's funeral? She almost died because you dragged your ass, waiting for the right time. Christ! How could you be so stupid?"

Jason's face darkened. "Don't call me stupid. I didn't want you snooping around. This was my business, not yours. How do you think I felt sitting down there in Florida, on my ass, while you ran around on your crazy crusade? I was the one who should have been finding out the truth, not you."

"Which truth? I don't know what's true anymore. I had second thoughts about dating a hockey player, but I took a chance on you. I guess I was wrong. Maybe you *are* just a jock who thinks with his pants instead of his heart! Get out. Go play your hockey and date your women. Those are the two things you're good at."

She gasped and turned away, appalled at the awful words she'd just uttered. She squeezed her eyes shut but couldn't stop the tears.

She didn't turn around as Jason stepped around the bed and stopped beside her. His fingers brushed her shoulder, and she stiffened and shrank away, keeping her eyes averted.

She heard him retreat and stole a look over her shoulder as he stopped beside Mishayla's bed. Her heart lurched as she watched him lay his hand gently on the girl's cheek. He left without another word.

~ * ~

Bertie's eyes flickered, and he raised his chin from his chest in time to see his friend striding past with a stony look on his face. "What the heck happened?"

Jason ignored him and pushed open the door to the stairs with a crash, not bothering to wait for the elevator.

Eighteen

Bertie hesitated, torn between following his friend and going inside to ask what had transpired. He made up his mind and pushed open the door to Mishayla's room. He glanced at the bed to find she was still asleep. Christina stood across the room with her forehead pressed against the fogged window. He quickly moved around the bed and brushed her arm lightly with his fingers. "What happened?"

She turned her face to him, her eyes bright with tears. She buried her face in his shoulder and sobbed out the cruel words Sheila had revealed over the phone.

Bertie didn't believe it, not for a second. "No, no, you can't be right. It couldn't have happened like that. There has to be an explanation. He would have told me."

Her response came out in fits and starts, intertwined with hiccups and sniffles. "I don't know what to think. I thought for a second it was just another one of her lies, but the look on his face when I asked him about it— well, it just confirmed it."

Bertie patted her back ineffectually and steered her out of the room, glancing at Christina's sleeping daughter. "Come on, she's resting. Let's go get a coffee and calm you down."

He sat with her in the cafeteria, trying to think of something to say to reinstate her faith in Jason. He had no doubt the whole thing was just a big misunderstanding and was determined to get to the bottom of it. In the meantime, he decided to remind her she was not alone.

Cradling his coffee cup, he looked at her earnestly. "Listen, Christina, I care about Jason. I've known the guy since we were teenagers, and I trust him with my life. If he made a stupid mistake, I'm inclined to give him the benefit of a doubt, but I'll understand if you can't." He studied her face, not detecting a response. He sighed and murmured, "I'll try to find out what's going on, and in the meantime, you should concentrate on Mishayla."

He paused and took a sip, gazing at a family gathering at the other end of the restaurant. They huddled together at a corner table, obviously in duress. "Corinne and I will be with you while this shit with Sheila is going on. She's bad news, not only to you and Mishayla, but also to Jason. She deserves to be put away, even if it's just for causing the accident. But, personally, I'd like to nail her for other stuff as well. She took away my best friend."

Christina sighed and rubbed her eyes. "Remember when we were talking to him in Florida? He was trying to talk me out of seeing Sheila, telling me it was because he was worried about us. Now I realize he was only thinking of himself." She looked glumly at her cup. "I don't know if I can trust him again. I had my doubts when I met him."

She looked at him directly. "I realize not all professional athletes are self-centered people who think they're God's gift to the opposite sex. Most of them are loving, generous people. You're a prime example of that. I was willing to believe Jason was just like you, but you've been married for eleven years. He hasn't. You two are different, even though you think he's a brother. Maybe he isn't as strong as you are. Maybe he's as shallow as Sheila."

Bertie scowled. "I'm going to ignore that last comment. Give it time. I'll find out what's going on, but let's concentrate on the woman from Hell for now."

~ * ~

Sheila had been sitting in an all-night coffee shop for hours. After pushing Christina's car off the road, she had experienced a brief flash of horror at what she had done but it was short-lived. The Japanese rice wine had not quite worn off, and her befuddled mind had no trouble justifying her actions. The bitch had been lying to her all along. Her Jason didn't deserve a woman like that. She was the one for him.

She glowed with satisfaction, hoping the car had disappeared in the depths of that pond. It would be months before anyone checked it out.

Sipping coffee after coffee, she sat at the booth by the window and slowly became aware of one of the patrons talking to the man behind the counter.

"Yeah, there were cop cars and ambulances all over the road at Glenville Pond," he explained to the attentive employee. "They managed to rescue them, a woman and her little girl. Boy, that was a close call, I tell ya."

Sheila straightened in her seat, keeping her eyes focused on the table. She listened intently.

"I heard she's been seeing Jason Peterson. He's in town, can you believe it? Mack saw him going into the hospital just after the ambulance got there. You know, she's the girl who stopped that guy from shooting him a couple of months ago."

The patron leaned across the counter. "She's the girl? She's from Schomberg, right? Christina Mackey. My son is on her daughter's hockey team." The man smiled. "Well, good for her. She deserves a little happiness after what happened to her husband. Nice kid, too."

Sheila slid from the booth, her mind racing. *He's in town?* The fact Christina was still alive and her daughter was involved in the crash flew out of Sheila's head as she thought only of Jason. She felt a rush at the realization he was only a few miles away. As she strode to the exit, the news Christina was still alive sunk in. *He's with her. She'll tell him everything. He'll never come back to me now. I have to stop this. I have to stop this.*

She pushed through the glass door to the vestibule, a public telephone fastened to the wall. Quickly skimming through the phone book, she found Christina's home number and took a chance. Punching the number, she waited for the beep after the welcome message and launched into her story.

"Hello, Christina. I just wanted to tell you that I knew it was you at lunch today. You know, there was something I left out of our conversation. Do you think you know everything about your precious Jason? Well, I know something that might change your mind. He's not the noble knight you think he is. He told me himself that he got a girl pregnant, and then the bastard just abandoned her. She was so devastated she didn't take care of herself and died in childbirth. The kid's dead, too. So if you think you're going to clear his name, just remember what kind of a man he really is. Do you think he cares about that kid of yours? He just wants to fuck you and move on. Watch your back, sister."

She slammed the receiver into its cradle and swept out of the building to the parking lot. She was about to climb into her Jeep, but stopped and looked at the front right bumper. It was slightly crumpled, with a scrape of blue paint embedded in the dent.

Stealing a cautious look at the two men inside the coffee shop, she rubbed at the bumper in an unsuccessful attempt to wipe off the paint. Frowning, she stared at the damage for a few more seconds and then quickly moved away from the vehicle, walking along the front of the shopping center and entered an all-night grocery store. She decided to leave the Jeep where it was, hoping the coffee shop patron hadn't noticed her proximity to the vehicle.

Flipping open her cell phone, she called a man she'd met a few weeks ago, planning to hang with him until she felt it was safe enough to go home.

Nineteen

Two days passed, and Sheila still had not been located. Christina opened the Wednesday newspaper, scanning the sports section out of habit. The headline jumped out at her: Jason Peterson Requests Trade. She sighed as she read the Chicago team was negotiating a deal for Jason, and a trade was imminent. The spring trade deadline was upon them and teams shuffled their rosters in search of the best combination of winners as the playoffs loomed.

On Thursday, the phone rang. She hesitated before picking up the receiver.

"Ms. Mackey, this is Officer Cam Willis. We found a beige Jeep Cherokee at the Tim Horton's on Davis Drive in Newmarket. It had damage on the right front quarter panel and paint transfer. It matches your Escort. I'm informing you that we've issued a warrant for Ms. Duffy's arrest."

She thanked the officer and glanced nervously out the front window. She hopes she was arrested soon and not outside right now.

~ * ~

Rob was making coffee while Sheila was in the shower. It had been a crazy couple of days, but he didn't mind—her sudden appearance took the blah out of a long, cold winter.

He took his coffee into the living room and glanced at the television. The image of Cam Willis filled the screen, his florid face as cheery as ever. Rob liked to listen to the veteran cop as he extolled the virtues of safe driving and the judicious use of safety belts. *Thank God, he isn't on the vice squad; otherwise he'd be knocking on my door*, Rob thought with a chuckle. The bag of pot he kept in his sock drawer remained a secret. He didn't tell Sheila about it, knowing she'd have polished it all off without any concern for his finances.

Today, Cam was informing the public about a nasty accident on Highway Nine, near Dufferin Street. It turned out to be a case of attempted murder.

His coffee cup halfway to his lips, Rob looked at the screen with shock when Sheila's face appeared, large as life.

To hell with this, he didn't know her that well. He picked up the phone. The cops were at the door within an hour, reading Sheila her rights as she stood in the kitchen, her hair still damp from her shower and a look of furious disbelief on her face.

~ * ~

The next day, she appeared before the court for her bail hearing. The judge looked through her file and studied the woman in front of her. She raised her chin defiantly as the judge revealed two of the accused had been charged previously with assault drug possession six months prior but had never appeared in court for her hearing. She rolled her eyes with disgust as the judge declared her be held without bail until the trial.

~ * ~

Bertie and Corinne sat in the kitchen, discussing the upcoming trial.

"He's going ahead with charges against Sheila for vandalizing the car and starting the barn fire, but I don't think he's going to get anywhere with that," Bertie told his wife. "He waited too long, and the evidence is probably long gone."

Corinne leaned her elbows on the table and regarded Bertie intently. "Would Christina's tape help?"

Bertie scowled and answered, "No, I don't think so. The lawyer said something about the tape being procured under false pretences or something like that."

"Okay, so the crazy woman is behind bars for now, but we still have those two to think about." She reached with her fingers and brushed Bertie's chin with affection, scratching the half-grown crop of black hairs that constantly adorned his face. "They both deserve what we have."

Bertie grinned and leaned forward to brush her lips with his own. "Okay, ma Cherie, I'll try again."

The next day, he phoned Jason to give him an update on Sheila's status. After that was out of the way, he tried again to discover what had happened in the hospital.

Jason didn't want to get into it. "Never mind about that, I don't want to talk about it."

Bertie gave up and got back to business. "Okay, then, what about pressing charges for the damage to the BMW or the barn fire? How did it go?"

"Don't even bother. Just as we thought, my lawyer said the tape probably won't be admissible in court, and the evidence is long gone by now. It's just good enough for me that the truth about the so-called affair got out in the papers. The coach already called to apologize."

"It wasn't the papers that made the coach call you. It was Christina,"

Bertie admitted.

"What?" How?"

"Remember the tape she recorded? We couldn't use it in court, but she came with me to see the coach and made me play it back to him. Boy, was his face red."

"Why would she do something like that for me?"

"I was wondering about it myself, seeing as you two seem to be so mad at each other. I asked her why, and she said something about a promise." Bertie waited, hoping for some kind of declaration Jason would aim for reconciliation with Christina, but his friend didn't speak. He sighed and asked, "What about the trade? Can't you back out of it? Aren't you coming back home?"

"Bertie, you know I love you like a brother, and I'll miss seeing Corinne and the kids, but we all have to grow up sometime. We'll see each other in the summer, I'm sure." Jason's deep voice held a note of resignation and sadness.

Bertie tried again. "What about Christina and Mishayla?"

There were a few seconds of silence. Bertie thought he had lost the phone connection, but Jason's voice finally drifted to his ear, "They'll be better off without me. Tell her thanks for me. I gotta go now, Bert. Take care." He abruptly hung up.

~ * ~

After the trade, he made the move from Pensacola to Chicago.

His first game in Chicago was bittersweet. After the warm up skate, the players re-entered the arena for their introductions. The lights and thunder from the crowd came up simultaneously as Jason's name was announced.

He felt no satisfaction. He had the devotion of the fans again but missed the best wishes of the person who meant the most to him. Strike that, the *two* most important people.

He pictured Chrissie and Mishayla rooting from the stands. He kept the image in his head for each game afterward. It helped.

Shortly after, during a weekend charity gala in Detroit, he found himself face-to-face with his former captain, Adam. He wondered whether the man would haul off and punch him right there in the lobby, but instead, Adam grunted and nodded. They warily circled, then finished up with an awkward guy hug accompanied with slaps on the back.

Jason looked around the foyer, searching for Jennifer, but she wasn't there. He considered asking Adam about her but decided against it, merely wishing his former captain good luck.

As the season picked up its pace in preparation for the playoffs, he almost returned to his old form, banging the puck into the net with regularity.

At least one shadow was lifted from his professional life, but he still felt an emptiness that couldn't be filled. His new team-mates had no trouble lining up dates for him. He was too polite to put them off, so he went out a few times with some very nice women but each time the evening ended in affectionate embraces, but nothing more.

His frustration mounted with each game, and the only outlet he allowed himself was the physical punishment he dealt to his opponents. After twelve years of finesse play, members of the opposite teams were unprepared for his increased physical play as he bore down on them, eyes blazing.

At times he was too reckless, missing his checks and painfully slamming into the boards. He picked his share of fights as well, his inexperience in that department evident on his face when he reluctantly returned to Newmarket to deliver testimony at Sheila's trial.

He sat in the witness stand, sporting a set of stitches over a black eye and a swollen cheek as he told the court what had transpired during his cell phone conversation with Christina. The defense attorney tried blaming the use of a cell phone for the accident, but Jason firmly insisted Christina had set the phone down beside her to concentrate on the difficult curve in the road.

Later, the prosecution asked Jason to relate further details of the conversation on the cell phone. In order to build sympathy for the victims, he asked Jason, "Mr. Peterson, please tell the court what you heard after Ms. Mackey set the phone down on the seat."

Jason knew he would be asked such a question, but he still hadn't prepared himself for the answer. The memory of those sounds on the phone still haunted him. He took a deep breath and told the court, "Ms. Mackey set down the phone because she knew she was coming up to a difficult curve in the road, and she mentioned someone was tailgating her. While I waited, I heard a thump, and then a long scraping sound followed by a screech. I heard...I heard a scream. It was Mishayla calling for..." He fought for control and tried again. "She was calling for her mother. There was an awful big thump and a lot of noise like breaking glass and the car rolling." He closed his eyes and rubbed his forehead. "Then I didn't hear anything after that."

~ * ~

Christina had managed to avoid eye contact with Jason throughout most of the proceedings. Whenever he had tried to move toward her, she withdrew and started to speak to her attorney. While he was on the witness stand, however, she couldn't help looking at his face while he described the accident. The pain in his expression sent a jolt through her stomach so excruciating she almost cried out.

His gaze locked with hers just as he finished his testimony. For an instant, his eyes glowed, as if embers had suddenly burst into flame, but the illusion faded immediately, a wisp of smoke in its wake, replaced by a distance that left her feeling bereft. She swallowed and looked down at the table in front of her so he wouldn't see her tears.

Sheila was her usual, inconsistent self during the trial, alternating between tearful remorse and self-righteous indignation. She took every available opportunity to stare imploringly at Jason and to appear lost and vulnerable to the press. On occasion, she looked at Christina, poisonous hatred seeping out of her eyes.

Reconstruction experts revealed the contact with the rear left bumper of Christina's vehicle was severe enough to prove it was deliberate. They had matched the paint transfer from Sheila's vehicle to Christina's wrecked car.

The jury convicted Sheila of dangerous driving causing bodily harm, and leaving the scene of an accident. The charges of impaired driving didn't stick since she was already sober by the time the police had picked her up. A sentence of only twelve months was swiftly passed, with a chance of parole in seven months.

As the bailiffs led her away, she screamed obscenities at both Christina and Jason. Jason stood at the back of the room with his arms tightly folded across his chest and swiftly left the room as soon as court adjourned.

Twenty

While he was in the region, he engaged a real estate agent to put his century farmhouse on the market. He also arranged to have his horses transported to a farm in Illinois where he was negotiating the purchase of a nearby country home. He took the time to have dinner with Bertie and Corinne before heading back to Chicago. Before accepting their invitation, he warned them not to get any fancy ideas about inviting Christina, although a small part of him wished they would go against his orders and invite her anyway.

He felt a twinge of disappointment when he arrived at their stone farmhouse and discovered he was indeed the only guest.

The season ended early for both Jason and Bertie; their respective teams were knocked out of the third round of the playoffs in early May.

During the early summer months, Jason kept himself busy with living arrangements. He had chosen a Cape Cod style home in the rolling countryside east of Chicago, with a roomy kitchen and a welcoming family room on the first floor. *She would have loved this kitchen.* He ran his fingers along the mosaic tile on the countertop. A long island structure adorned the middle of the room, its butcher-block pine surface buffed to a velvet patina from years of use. He pictured friends and family sitting on stools around the island, laughing and talking, drinking wine or coffee. It seemed like the perfect place for a gathering, not unlike Bertie's kitchen with the long harvest table that had hosted many an impromptu party.

He leaned against the enamel sink and gazed out the window. A cedar rail fence enclosed a perennial garden already bursting with color, and beyond the back gate was a small paddock beside the barn. Near the kitchen window, a dilapidated tree house still clung to an ancient, twisted apple tree. He visualized Mishayla peeking out of the crooked window.

His thoughts often wandered toward Mishayla and how she was doing. He tried to analyze his fondness for the little girl and wondered if his affection was misplaced. Was it because of his attraction to Christina or just his general affinity with children? Why was he able to connect with children so easily, when he had been raised without siblings? Was it because he was always there for Bertie's kids, sharing in their every milestone? Was it because he was just a big kid himself, always playing games? Or was it because of the child he had lost? The child he never knew he had.

He clearly remembered the magic year when he was just starting out in the professional league. He was only twenty-two when he'd met nineteen-year-old Brenda. They dated for an unprecedented six months when she announced her mother was remarrying and they were moving to Saskatchewan. The parting disappointed Jason, but he'd bounced back with the resiliency of youth, hitting the dating scene within a few weeks. It wasn't until a year later that he discovered, through a mutual friend, the young lady had died in childbirth and the baby had not survived.

Shocked and saddened, he mentally did the math and was certain he'd been the father. The discovery put him into an emotional tailspin.

Bertie was his close friend at the time, but Jason couldn't bring himself to tell his line mate about the pregnancy. Bertie and Corinne were expecting their first child, and he didn't want to upset them.

Years later, while dating Sheila, he had begun to have disturbing dreams about a lost child, and when Sheila had listened to his nocturnal mumbles, she'd asked him about it. He let his guard down and told her everything. He was still glowing from the bloom of their new relationship and had mistakenly thought opening up to her would help him grow as a person. By that time, he was tired of the carousel of women and started to think about settling down.

He didn't think about the incident again until their relationship soured and she began using the information to torture him. During her heated phone calls the previous winter, she released the shocking truth about why Ian had attempted to shoot him. She'd seen Ian's obituary, and it revealed a sister, Brenda, predeceased Ian. Sheila put two and two together and discovered Brenda was the same girl Jason had dated so many years before. Ian wasn't jealous. He was looking for revenge.

It was too bad he was dead, Sheila surmised, but she had no problem picking up where Ian had left off, delighting in making Jason's life miserable. She intensified her actions by twisting his sad past to suit her own needs, planting seeds of malice wherever she could, alternating between cruelty and then attempting to make amends as if nothing had happened between them.

He knew it was the drugs causing her wild mood swings and tried to take her abuse with a grain of salt, but it was hard. She may have been messed up, but he wasn't far behind.

Jason was glad she was in jail and hoped she would stay behind bars for a long while. *She's a real piece of work*, He moved to the mudroom to slide on a tall pair of rubber boots. The air was warm and fragrant, quickly changing to pungent as he entered the barn to saddle one of the horses. Three heads popped over the partitions, each of his friends heavily campaigning for an outing.

"Sorry, Paladin," he murmured as the nearest gelding stretched its neck to poke Jason on the side of his head. "It's Jerry's turn today." He led the bay out of its stall and started to brush the smooth coat.

As he worked, he wondered why Christina had taken the trouble to see the coach and play the tape, even after she had basically written him out of her life. He had no idea such an omission about his past could have such a devastating effect on a relationship. Thinking back, he could see her point. The way Sheila had delivered the news, it was no wonder it made him appear as an insensitive womanizer who used women and discarded them. It didn't help that his reputation was already compromised by the episode with Jennifer. *God damn Sheila. What a psychopath.*

The horse snorted and stamped, suddenly uncomfortable with the extra pressure on its flanks. Jason realized he was getting too rough with the brush, and he apologized gently, patting the horse's neck.

Grabbing the saddle, he outfitted Jerry and led him into the sunshine. Mounting, he and Jerry ambled through the paddock gate. Nudging the horse to a trot, he made his way through an orchard to the fields beyond and slowed to a walk.

He thought he knew everything about women, but boy, he had a lot to learn about love. Maybe it wasn't too late. If she heard his side of the story, maybe she'd forgive him. He had to explain everything to her. Even if they couldn't be together, maybe she would at least remember him in a different light. He had to try, or the look of disgust on her face would be the only thing he would see for the rest of his life.

Now that he had made his decision, he felt a new rush of hope. Squeezing the horse's ribs, he pushed Jerry into a spirited gallop, feeling a rush of wind in his ears and a smile returning to his lips.

Twenty One

One hot day in late July, he worked up the nerve to give her a call. He rehearsed what he was going to say and picked up the phone. There was no answer. When a third attempt brought no results, he called Bertie and asked him if he knew where she was.

"They've taken a month off and they're visiting relatives in England," Bertie revealed. Jason felt his stomach sink with disappointment.

"How is she? Does she say anything about me? Is she dating anyone? How's Mishayla?"

"Cripes, Jason, slow down. She's fine, she still doesn't want to talk about you. She's not dating anyone as far as I know, and Mishayla was as chipper as ever the last time I saw her."

He invited Jason for a week-long stay at his cottage in Muskoka. "Just like the old days."

"Well, not quite, but I'll be glad to come," Jason responded with a shadow of his old grin tugging at his lips.

August was hazy and humid in northern Ontario, but at least the mosquitoes were less vicious than during the earlier months, when they relentlessly feasted on hapless vacationers on the many lakes and rivers in the area.

Bertie's sky blue wooden cottage perched on windswept rocks on Lake Muskoka. Larger than his farmhouse in Uxbridge, it sported a raised, wraparound deck, a huge boathouse and a roomy dock.

Shards of mist had barely cleared from the lake's glassy surface as Bertie and Jason settled with their coffee on a couple of weathered cedar Adirondack chairs on the dock. Jason gazed lazily at a pair of loons as they dove beneath the smooth water, bobbing alternately to the surface. It was unusually quiet—the children were not awake yet, having stayed up extra late the previous night to toast marshmallows over an open campfire. They had been ecstatic to see Jason again, and he was surprised at how much they'd grown in just a few months.

Bertie set his mug down with a stretch and a sigh. "I know you come here every summer, moron, but this year seems a bit different."

Jason lifted a corner of his mouth in a wry smile and shrugged. "It sure feels different to me. Sure, we're not on the same team anymore, but it still feels like something else is missing."

"Yeah, buddy, and it takes a smart fellow like me to tell you what it is; a certain dark-haired beauty and her little sprite. Are you going to tell me what really happened, or do I have to keep Sheila's version in my head?"

Jason felt his coffee rise in his throat. "You sure don't waste time getting to the point." He didn't look forward to this conversation, but it was inevitable Bertie would want to know everything.

He swallowed and told Bertie what happened during their rookie year. He added the details of how Sheila had been using the information to torture him, and the reasons for his reluctance to tell Christina about it.

"It turns out, Ian was Brenda's stepbrother, I guess from a second marriage."

"What second marriage?"

"Her mom got married again and that's why she moved away. I didn't make the connection because his last name was different, but Sheila did, and telling me about it sure gave her a lot of satisfaction. God, now I actually feel sorry for the idiot—he must have really built up a lot of hate over the years."

"How did he find out about your relationship with the girl? Didn't he know about it before?"

Jason knit his brow in speculation. "That's what's so weird about the whole thing. He never acted any different around me.He'd been with the team for a few years after transferring here from out west. But now that I think about it, a few days before the shooting, I ran into him in the elevator, and he just glared at me."

"Maybe it was just a random thing, and Ian made the association."

Jason sighed. "Sheila probably let something slip. After all, she knew about my relationship with Brenda. Maybe she made the connection and sent him over the edge. Well, it's too late now; the damage is done."

Bertie shook his head. "Moron, moron, moron. Why the hell didn't you tell me about this thing with Brenda way back at the beginning?"

"Bertie, you and Corinne were about to have your first baby. I didn't want to saddle you with this, or upset Corinne, either. She was nervous enough already. Then, you know, three more babies later and it was never the right time. To tell you the truth, I'd almost forgotten about it, except in the last couple of years I started having nightmares. They brought it all back."

"What kind of nightmares?"

"I had dreams about me fishing with a little kid, and he or she would suddenly disappear. I remember dreaming I'm calling out over and over again and I remember feeling panic, and then I'd wake up in a cold sweat. That's how Sheila found out. One night I had the nightmare while Sheila was with me, and like an idiot, I told her all about Brenda. It was just like her to make it sound like I was some shallow asshole who didn't care about that sweet girl."

He wandered from the dock to pick up a flat stone and hurled it. It skipped across the water and broke up the few remaining tendrils of mist curled around an outcrop of rocks jutting into the water. The loons, disturbed by the stone, disappeared under the surface with a flip and a ripple.

He continued. " And then I met Chrissie and got to know Mishayla. I started wondering what my kid would have looked like at that age, and if he or she would have played hockey. If I hadn't been such a stubborn jerk, if I'd either helped Christina or had the guts to tell her about Brenda, Sheila would never have gone as far as she did, and Mishayla would never have been hurt." Jason stood still, gazing at the distant trees emerging from the retreating mist.

He murmured, "I think about her all the time. It's my fault she can't play hockey anymore, and she's just six years old."

Bertie took a sip from his brew. "There's hope for her yet. They've been giving her regular checkups and the damage might not be as bad as we thought. She could be in the Olympics yet."

Jason smiled. "What a relief." He was silent for a while, and then returned to his chair. He leaned forward and turned to his friend. "What am I going to do about Chrissie? She deserves to know the truth. I don't want her to spend the rest of her life thinking guys like me are only out for one thing. Even if she can't forgive me, I wouldn't want Mishayla to grow up thinking all men are like that, either."

"Would you get back together with her if she knew the truth?"

"I dunno. That's up to her, I guess. To tell you the truth, the things she said to me at the hospital still hurt."

"What did she say?" Bertie urged him.

"When you two showed up in Pensacola, she told me she would never think of me as an empty-headed, horny jock. In fact, she promised me. Well, in the hospital room, she pretty much told me what she really thought of me. She called me stupid, and she said I was only good at dating women and playing hockey. I was stunned. I felt like my whole world was collapsing." He stood up and paced around the floating dock, causing it to sway gently in the water. He turned back to his friend. Bertie could plainly see the pain in Jason's eyes when he murmured, "She promised me, Bert."

"Come on, Jason, you can't base a whole relationship on a few angry words in a hospital room. She was under a lot of strain that day, banged up, dead tired, and pissed off. She probably regretted saying those things right away. You should have seen her after you left. She was a wreck. If you'd stuck around instead of asking for a trade, you two would have worked it out eventually. Anyway, I'm sure enough time has passed for her to listen to your side of the story. She's a reasonable girl." He remembered their phone conversation just before the trial last spring. "Remember when you told me the coach called you to apologize? Remember what I said?"

Jason bowed his head. "You said Chrissie was the one who made you take the tape to the coach so he would clear my name."

Bertie raised his eyebrows. "Do you remember why she did it?"

"It was a promise she made to me just after I got sent to the East Coast League."

"Well, there you go, a promise. She's not in the habit of breaking promises. Give the poor girl a break."

Jason sat silently for a moment. Bertie sipped his coffee and waited. The only sounds were the gentle lapping of the water, the splash of the loons diving for fish, and the constant hum of the cicadas.

"I guess I jumped the gun on the trade thing. Then I guess I sat on this a little too long before finally deciding to call her too. Now she's out of the country. I'm such a goddamn loser." He leaned back in the warm wooden chair and gazed at the sky, huffing with frustration.

Bertie's hands flew up in the air. "Cripes, do I have to think of everything? You know how to write, don't you? Get out a pen and paper and write it all down. She'll be sure to understand if you explain things to her."

"Write a letter? Jesus, Bertie, I'm not good at stuff like that"

"If I can do it, you can. You're not such a moron, you know. Maybe it's time for you to learn a new skill for your retirement." He raised his eyebrows and gave his friend a crooked grin.

Jason sighed and stood. "Well, big brother, you know best. I'll give it a shot." He suddenly felt the tightness around his chest dissipate, and he could breathe again. "Well? Are we going fishing today?"

"As soon as the kids are up," Bertie announced, heaving out of the comfortable chair to head back to the house for breakfast.

At the end of the long, hazy day, after the campfire and marshmallows, after the children had finally gone to bed, Jason retreated to his room. He sat at a little pine table beside a window that looked out onto the dark lake. The warm breeze drifted in from the darkness, rippling the bits of paper on the wooden surface. He wasn't the letter writing type and had no idea what to say. Leaving it up to the gods, he grabbed a piece of stationery and wrote in a strong, flowing script.

Christina,

I think about you all the time and hope you and Mishayla are well. I want you to read this letter to the end; don't throw it out, so you will see I'm not the heartless monster you think I am. You heard Sheila's version, and I hope you trust me enough to read mine, which is the truth.

During my rookie year, I met a nice girl named Brenda and dated her for a few months. I was twenty-two and she was nineteen. Anyway, one thing led to another and I thought we were getting along great. But she told me she was moving away with her new family, and I accepted it and moved on. A year went by, Bertie and I were making headway with our careers, and Corinne was about to have their first baby. Then a friend told me Brenda had passed away a few months before. She had died in childbirth—full term, and the baby didn't survive either.

Honest to God, I didn't even know she was pregnant, but I'm pretty sure the baby was mine. I was devastated. I didn't know who to turn to and didn't want to bother Bertie with such bad news. I don't know why Brenda never told me, and I guess I'll never know. It turns out, Ian was her stepbrother, and he was mad enough to try to shoot me, I guess. I suppose I'll never know the truth behind that, either. I hadn't made the connection because his surname was different from Brenda's last name.

In the past year or so, I started to have bad dreams about a lost child. The dreams are pretty vague, and I still have them. One night, Sheila managed to get the story out of me, and she didn't mention it again until one of her rants last spring. I figured she must have told Ian about my nightmares, and he finally had a person to blame for his stepsister's death.

Then when you started making plans to talk to her, I was paralyzed with the fear that Sheila would tell you. I wasn't ready for you to know about it. That's why I kept trying to talk you out of seeing her. You were so insistent, I finally just gave up and decided to help in the hope we would get Sheila out of the way before she did any more harm. I tried to put the past out of my mind, hoping it would go away on its own. But it didn't. It kept haunting me, and then I decided to risk your anger and tell you myself.

I really tried to tell you about Brenda several times, but we were always interrupted. I flew home, just for that purpose, but by then it was too late. I don't blame you for being angry with me, just believe me when I say you and Mishayla are very important to me, and I would never knowingly cause pain to you or to that sweet little girl. It was selfish of me to withhold such important information—I was only thinking of myself. I was so afraid of losing you to that woman's lies, I didn't think of the consequences.

Well, Sheila is in jail now, and hopefully she won't bother us any more. She sure did enough damage while she was loose. Getting mixed up with her really seems to confirm I'm a dumb jock—I should have known she was bad news, and I was stupid enough to let her control me.

I regret requesting a trade, but at the time, I couldn't bear the thought of being so close to you when you hated me so much. When I saw you in the courtroom, I wanted the whole roomful of people to disappear so I could scream out my explanation, but the look in your eyes stopped me.

I miss you both terribly and I sometimes grab the crazy hope we can somehow start again. But I'll understand if you can't trust me again. Sometimes I wonder if I can trust myself.

Take care of yourself and Mishayla, and try to think of me in a better light.

Jason

He sealed the letter and held it in his hands for a moment. The warmth of the evening and the sound of the crickets was a world away from that winter day when he'd looked in her eyes as she squinted merrily up at him through drifting snowflakes.

He carefully set the letter on the little pine desk and slipped quietly downstairs through the silent house. He let himself out of the cottage through a side door and felt his way down the needle-strewn path to the lake's edge. He needed no light; he already knew the way by heart.

The dim rectangle of the floating dock beckoned. He stepped onto the still warm surface and settled into one of the cedar chairs.

The moon had set, and the lake reflected an explosion of stars. He leaned his head on the back of the chair and stared upward. He felt as if he was floating in a sea of stars above and below him.

The pair of loons called to each other in a plaintive howl that echoed off the trees. No matter how many times he heard the haunting sound, it sent chills of pleasure down his back. He wished Christina were there to share the feeling.

He mailed the letter on the day he left for Illinois, feeling marginally hopeful.

Twenty Two

August drifted into September. Mishayla met the challenges of school with her usual enthusiasm and was cleared to play hockey once again. Christina performed her duties automatically. Neither happy nor sad, she simply drifted through her days in a neutral gray mist. She settled into a regular routine at the dental office, making light conversation with the patients and responding with false brightness to her co-workers' conversation.

The trip to England was a gift from her parents, a brief diversion from her apathy. Her boss, Dr. Woodside, had been glad to give her the time off, attributing her recent melancholy to the strains of the trial.

"Dr. Woodside's a great boss," Christina commented to her colleague, Trish, as she dropped metal dental instruments into the sterilizer.

"You're lucky to have people like us around you, considering the crappy year you've had," Trish responded, checking a bill of lading against a new box of supplies. She stowed packages of gloves, masks, and new toothbrushes into drawers. "How was the trip to England?"

Christina smiled briefly. "It was fabulous. We spent a week in London, and then we went to Manchester, and took a drive around the countryside, staying at these cute little cottages."

"Did you meet any cute British guys?" Trish teased.

Christina raised her eyebrows and responded in a slightly mocking tone, "Yes, I met some cute British guys." She shrugged. "My sister was constantly trying to fix me up with some of my cousins' friends during almost every stop we made. Cripes, I didn't realize we had so many cousins out there with single friends. It's almost as if they were lying in wait for me at every village."

Trish giggled. "So? Did you date any of them?"

Christina's grin faded. "No." She frowned. "Well, maybe. Yeah, a couple but it just didn't feel right."

"Why the hell not? Country men with British accents, what's not to like?"

"I think I'll just take a break from dating for a while. No point starting anything while Mishayla needs me."

"What about Jason, that hockey player you went out with last winter?"

At the mention of Jason's name, Christina's heart fluttered briefly, struggling back to life like a wounded bird, then resumed its sluggish, plodding rhythm once again.

"He was a mistake." Christina washed her hands and left the room to take the next appointment.

~ * ~

Jason quickly consulted a slip of paper before steering the rental car left onto a long, straight dirt road that stretched toward the horizon. It took a half hour of driving before he finally saw the sprawling ranch house, perched on a small rise that barely made a bump on the vast, flat land that was Saskatchewan.

He stopped the car in a cloud of dust and climbed out, hesitating before taking the few steps to the front porch. The door opened as he raised his hand to knock, and a small woman in her early sixties observed him with unreadable eyes.

"Mr. Peterson."

Dipping his head with respect, he greeted her. "Hello, Mrs. Pollard. Thanks for letting me come out to see you."

She held the door open for him. "Well, it's about time you came." She led him into the front living room and offered coffee. He declined; sure his churning stomach wouldn't accept it without a fight.

After a few stilted pleasantries, he got down to the reason for his visit. Taking a deep breath, he said, "Mrs. Pollard, I wanted to personally offer my condolences for your loss…both of them."

The older woman sighed and fiddled with the cushion in her lap. "Ian was always on the edge. He let his emotions dictate almost every decision he made. He cared very deeply for Brenda, even though they were only brother and sister for a short time." She looked at him directly, a mix of sadness and an old bitterness in her eyes. "Why are you here now, after all this time?"

"I guess I was afraid. I was hiding from my responsibility, even though it was too late, anyway. I thought you'd be too angry to forgive me. Why didn't you tell me about her death?"

"We had no reason to. We didn't know who the father was. She refused to tell us."

Jason's eyes widened with surprise. "She didn't tell you?"

"Why didn't you come to her if you were the father?"

"I didn't know about it either. She never told me. When I found out, it was too late."

Mrs. Pollard closed her eyes. "Oh, God, I thought you knew all along."

"If neither of us knew, how did your stepson find out?"

"That's what's been bothering me. Ian took her death really hard. After a couple of years, he finally put it behind him and moved to Toronto. Maybe it was a coincidence he joined the same team you were on. He never mentioned your connection to Brenda until last year. We got a phone call last winter. He was ranting about you, saying you were the father. He started talking about revenge. We tried to talk sense into him, but he wouldn't listen."

Jason looked at the floor. "Well, that confirms why he tried to shoot me. I thought at first he was just jealous." He looked back at Mrs. Pollard and explained, "I think he found out through my ex-girlfriend. She'd been dating both of us at the same time, and she probably told him about my nightmares."

"Nightmares?"

"I didn't find out Brenda had died until a year after. A friend of mine who lives out here was visiting, and told me about it. I never knew she was pregnant. I was young and stupid and should have talked to you about it as soon as I got the news, but I was petrified. I felt so guilty and bottled it up inside myself. A couple of years ago, I started getting nightmares about losing a child. I didn't know if it was a boy or a girl, but I just remember it disappearing, and I'd be chasing after it, calling it, and then waking up in a sweat.

"I finally told my girlfriend about Brenda, and I didn't think about it until recently. She must have told him about it, and he made the connection." He gazed at her with haunted eyes. "I wish Brenda had told me. If she had, I would have been out here on the next plane."

"Maybe she was thinking of your career and didn't want to interfere."

He sighed. "It's just like her. Unselfish to the end." He rubbed his face. "Now it all makes sense."

"None of it really makes any sense. Two people I loved are dead." The older woman finally broke down and sobbed. Jason immediately moved to sit beside her and did his best to comfort her as she unleashed her grief.

Twenty Three

The biting winds of early November rattled bare branches and windowpanes before Bertie had a chance to talk to Christina. He met her in Newmarket for coffee on a blustery day between road trips to discuss Sheila's upcoming parole. Nervous about the outcome of the woman's impending release, they both hoped she had finished with them and moved on.

Bertie watched Christina's face as she sipped her coffee. She looked refreshed from her trip, but there was still a melancholy dullness around her eyes. He had tried to talk to her over the summer about Jason, but she was always quick to change the subject. He tried again. "Jason's been trying to reach you."

"Yeah." Her response was noncommittal. She kept her eyes focused on the traffic outside the coffee shop.

"He told me what happened. Everything. Christina, he wants to make it right."

"Make what right?" Christina frowned. "He wasn't taking the situation seriously enough, and his omission put my kid in danger. True, I probably should have left Sheila alone, but I really thought I was helping him. If he didn't tell me about his old girlfriend, how many other things did he not tell me? I thought we had something special, and then the doubts crept in. Rather, they galloped in, full steam. Who knows, maybe he had other girlfriends while he was with me."

"No, he didn't. You know, he never brought a girl to our house before. You were the first one."

"What about Sheila?"

"I only saw her at team functions. She probably invited herself most of the time. Now, listen to me, young lady, Jason is serious about you, whether you believe him or not. That's why I told him to write everything down."

"Write everything down? What does he have to say to me that he didn't say already?"

"He wrote you a letter, last August while he was visiting our cottage. Didn't you get it?"

"No. What did it say?"

"Man, I thought you'd already got it, so I never asked. I didn't see it, but I'm pretty sure it says something about what happened with his old girlfriend and the baby. He said he wanted to explain things to you. I'm sure he mailed it before he went back to the States."

"Christ, after all this time…"

"Try the post office, maybe there's a lost mail file or something."

Christina looked at her watch and rose from the booth. "The main sorting station is on Mulock Drive. Maybe they're still open."

"Want me to come along?"

"Sure, if you want to." She shrugged on her coat and the two left the restaurant, driving in tandem across town to the regional sorting station. The clerk asked a few questions and consulted a computer, quickly scanning the files of undelivered mail in the last three months.

"Here's one," he replied, indicating a letter with a smudged address. "We got a partial postal code, so we forwarded it over to the Schomberg postal outlet. You might try there."

Christina thanked the clerk, leaving the building with Bertie. "I guess I'll head home and stop at the post office in Schomberg. I'll call you later, okay?"

Bertie bade her goodbye and drove westward to Unionville.

The next day, she called the Gautier home, asking if she could drop by. Bertie and Corinne welcomed her, and Mishayla rushed off to Jeanette's room while the adults settled in the kitchen. Sitting at the large harvest table, Christina pulled the letter out of her purse.

"I haven't opened it yet. I was afraid to."

Bertie urged her, "Go ahead, open it. We'll wait."

She tore open the envelope and smoothed the paper on the table. As she scanned the page, her eyes softened and then began to brim with unshed tears. She covered her trembling lips with her hand and continued to read.

Bertie dug a napkin out of the chrome holder beside him and handed it to her as Corinne rubbed Christina's shoulder.

Christina kept her face down as she wiped her eyes. Resting her forehead on her hand, she shook her head and said quietly, "I'm such a moron."

"Only room for one moron in North America and he's in Chicago," Bertie said. He leaned forward and peered at her face. "You gonna be okay?"

She sniffed and muttered, "Yeah." Raising her face and scrubbing at her eyes, she asked, "So what do I do now? He's there, I'm here."

Corinne said simply, "Buy a plane ticket, for starters. We'll figure out a way for you to see him. Don't worry about Mishayla, she can stay with us for the weekend, see how it goes."

Christina smiled at them through her tears. "You two should be sainted," she said.

"That's what I keep telling everyone!" he exclaimed, getting to his feet to make some coffee.

Over the next few days, she made arrangements to have Mishayla stay with the Gauthier family while Bertie made some calls to obtain a ticket to the weekend game. His sense of drama didn't waver as he refused to tell Jason that Christina was coming for a visit.

The thought of arriving unannounced made her understandably nervous. "Remember what happened last time I showed up unexpectedly?" she reminded Bertie as he drove her to the airport.

He grinned. "Trust me," he assured her. "Now, remember, you're to call this number and ask for Maxine Templeton. She's an old friend and she handles the security at the rink. She'll have someone take you to the dressing rooms after the game." He produced a slip of paper along with her plane ticket.

Christina was amazed. "Wow. You really do think of everything."

They arrived at the airport and Bertie enveloped her in an affectionate hug. "Good luck, my girl. Everything will be fine."

Christina still looked troubled. She thought of Sheila's impending release. "You've got my cell phone number, right? Sheila could already be on the streets."

"Don't worry, she's never had any contact with my family. There's no connection, so there's no reason for her to bother us. Plus, you and Jason will be in the States, she can't follow you there. She's on parole."

~ * ~

It was a long bus ride from Milton to the Bay Street bus station. For the first time in years, Sheila took a streetcar to her condo. When she unlocked the door and stepped inside, she noticed the apartment smelled stale and felt cold. Cranking up the heat, she picked up the pile of mail on the floor and started to go through the bills and brochures. She tossed the pile on the glass-topped dining room table in disgust and checked the refrigerator. Nothing. She should have reminded Mary to pick up some groceries in preparation for her return.

She considered herself damn lucky she got through the last few months relatively unscathed. She was still the owner of the clothing store, although forced to borrow heavily against the business to pay her lawyer fees. Her lawyer had somehow managed to negotiate the return of her Cherokee instead of losing it to the next police auction. The vehicle was waiting for her in the underground parking garage, its bumper still askew from the contact with Christina's Ford. So what if her license was suspended. The Jeep was available when she needed it.

Sheila rummaged through the cupboards and found an unopened can of tonic. Opening the freezer, she was pleased to discover a half bottle of vodka still nestled inside.

Mixing a drink, she moved to the living room and slid open a drawer in a side table, plucking Ian's old appointment book from the mess of restaurant takeout menus. Leafing through it, she found what she was looking for, a list of names and addresses from the team roster.

She ran her finger down the list until she reached Jason's name. She brushed the handwritten words lightly as if it was his face. Sighing, her eyes scanned upward until she found Bertie's name. Smiling, she drained her drink, quickly assembled another and downed that one, too. She slipped the address book into her purse, flipped on the television and found the satellite station carrying the game in Chicago. Settling on the sofa, she watched Jason as he wove gracefully around his opponents. She started to talk to him as if he was in the room.

"I missed you, sweetie. Sorry I can't visit you, but maybe we can get together when you play in Toronto."

After her third drink, she stopped measuring. She splashed vodka into the glass, topping it up with a hint of tonic. Soon she was out of mixer and continued to take shots of chilled vodka until the bottle was empty. Before the game was finished, she fell asleep on the sofa.

~ * ~

Christina flew to Chicago with a mixture of soaring hope and paralyzing dread in her heart. The two-hour flight was over before she knew it, and she took a cab to a hotel near the United Centre, where Jason's team played. She quickly checked into her room, dropped her bag on the floor, and promptly set out to take another cab to the arena.

Bertie had obtained a good seat for her, and she tried to enjoy the game. Every time Jason hit the ice, her heart raced almost as rapidly as his own must have been beating, playing hard and fast. Since the rumors about him proved to be false, he had regained his old enthusiasm on the ice, weaving past the opposition with ease and finding the back of the net with astonishing regularity. His tendency to pick fights had passed, and his public behavior off the ice had become more gracious, if not somewhat subdued.

As arranged, an usher guided Christina down the hallways surrounding the dressing rooms just as the game ended. Tonight, Jason was the subject of a brief interview just outside his dressing room, so he paused under the bright lights to have a chat with a television sports personality.

He was politely responding to the commentator's question when Christina turned a corner in the hallway. She stopped short, suddenly afraid to venture further.

As she hesitated among the waiting fans, her small figure hidden by the crush of bodies, Jason finished his interview and swiftly entered the dressing room. She shifted with impatience as the team members slowly exited the room, rejoining their families and friends in the hallway before making their way to the exit.

The crowd of fans didn't diminish; it grew more congested in the hallway as Jason finally stepped through the door. His eyes scanned the crowd. He focused on someone, but it wasn't Christina. He smiled and stepped toward the knot of people to greet someone, bending down to kiss her cheek. As he gave her a gentle embrace, she laughed, exclaiming, "It's about time you finished primping. How about a late dinner?"

Christina recognized the voice. She backed away and retreated into the crowd, ready to turn and run, when she saw Jason's gaze rest on her. His eyes widened with surprise, then something that looked like dismay. Christina gulped and dashed for the elevator.

Twenty Four

As Jason emerged from the dressing room, Jenny broke from the waiting crowd of fans and smiled.

"Are you up for a late dinner?" She stood on tiptoe and gave him a brief peck on the cheek.

Jason opened his mouth to speak and glanced at the crowd. Christina stood among the fans with a look of horror on her face. He made a move toward her, but she was already gone.

"Wait in the dressing room, Jenny." Jason pushed through the surprised group of fans and sprinted down the hall.

He reached Christina just as she stopped in front of an elevator leading to the main level. She reached out to hit the elevator button and he grabbed her wrist. "Chrissie, wait!"

She turned on him, attempting to shake her wrist free while slapping at his arm with her other hand. "Let go of me!"

"Chrissie, stop it! What the hell are you doing here?"

"I came here to tell you—oh, it's too late anyway." The elevator door opened and Jason pushed her inside so they could be alone for a moment.

"You're not kidding, it's too late. Why are you here now, after all these months? I thought it was over."

The doors slid shut but the elevator didn't move. Christina retreated to the corner and glared at him. "I got your letter."

Jason's mouth opened in surprise. "You just got it now? I sent it last August."

"Well, I just got it a few days ago."

"Chrissie, I thought you received it ages ago. When you didn't call, I figured you just didn't want to see me anymore."

"So you moved on."

"What do you mean?"

Christina tossed her hair with impatience. "Jennifer, you idiot! It didn't take you long to hook up with her."

"She's going through a tough time, Chrissie. She needs a friend."

"She sure came a long way to be with a 'friend'," she retorted and pushed past him to stab at the elevator button. The elevator started to move. "It's just what I suspected all along. I was just a passing interest. She must have been your true love all along. I hope you two will be happy together." Her voice broke.

She reached into her pocket and shoved a crumpled piece of paper against his chest. He allowed it to flutter to the floor. As the doors slid open, she pushed him aside with difficulty and squirmed past him to exit the elevator into the main foyer.

Jason watched her as she ran through the thinning crowd toward the exit, torn between dashing out into the street to catch up with her and returning to Jennifer, who was waiting downstairs. With a frustrated roar, he punched the elevator button, almost sending it through the panel. Several passing patrons turned, startled by the noise, but the doors had already slid shut.

He leaned his forehead against the panel, sighed and picked up the paper, recognizing the letter he had written. He strode back to the dressing room and pushed the door open. Jennifer stood near the coach's office door, inspecting a series of old photographs of the team. She turned and regarded him with curiosity.

"Well?" she asked. She settled on one of the benches and patted the spot beside her. Jason sat, his elbows on his knees, turning the piece of paper in his hands. Without a word, he handed it to her.

Jennifer shrugged and started to read. Jason didn't look at her, but he heard a little sniffle as she finished the letter. Sliding a hesitant look at her face, he found her gazing at him with tears in her eyes.

"When did you send this?"

"August."

"When did she get it?"

"A few days ago."

She waved the wrinkled letter. "You never told me about this."

"I never told anyone until this summer." Jason sighed and leaned against the wall. "I was hoping it would make her see me in a different light, but even after that effort, it didn't work. She still thinks I'm running around, sleeping with every woman I see."

"Oh, come off it! I know you're not like that, and you know it, too. You just have to let her know it."

"What about you? Didn't you fly down here for more than just moral support?"

"What about me? I can take care of myself. Listen Jason, I'm crazy about you, but I'm sure as hell not going to stand between a good friend and the woman he really loves. I could never live with myself." She turned her face away and swiped the tears from her cheeks with trembling fingers.

Jason stood and took her damp hands, pulling her to her feet. He gave her a gentle kiss and drew her against him, stroking her hair as she softly sobbed. After a few minutes, she pushed him away, smiling through her tears.

"You're a fantastic guy," she declared in a wavering voice and dug in her pocket for a tissue. Wiping her eyes, she sniffed and told him, "Will you get the hell out of here and find that woman? I'll be fine. I'll take a cab to the hotel." Reaching up, she kissed him on the cheek.

"Are you sure?"

"I'm sure, I'm sure, now get going," she laughed shakily and gave him a playful push.

Jason smiled at her gratefully and dashed from the room.

~ * ~

He burst out of the sports complex onto the busy street before he realized he had no idea where he was going. He swiveled and headed for the underground parking area to retrieve his car. After driving to two hotels and inquiring at the front desks, he decided he was wasting too much time.

Back in his car, he pulled over beside a telephone booth at a gas station and grabbed his cell phone. Inside the booth, he flipped through the yellow pages and used his cell phone to call downtown area hotels.

After five calls, he smacked his hand against the booth glass and swore at himself. *Idiot.* He quickly punched Bertie's number on his cell phone as he strode back to his car.

Before Bertie spoke, Jason cut in, "What hotel is she staying in?"

His friend's voice blurred with interrupted sleep as he answered, "Lost her already, moron?"

"Shut up! Which hotel?"

"The Sheraton. Water Street. Good luck," Bertie mumbled.

"Oh, and by the way, thanks a bunch for the heads up, idiot." Jason abruptly disconnected.

He wheeled around and headed back to the booth to obtain the phone number. The night desk clerk informed him she was checking out and should be leaving soon. "Can you please get her to wait? Tell her a friend is coming to see her. Tell her it's Jason."

There was silence on the line as the concierge hesitated. *He must think I'm a stalker or something.*

Finally, the concierge relented. "I'll do my best, but I can't guarantee anything."

Jason flipped the phone shut and slid back into his car. The hotel was just a few blocks away so he took liberties with the gas pedal and prayed he wouldn't be stopped for speeding.

As he pulled in front of the hotel, he saw her standing on the sidewalk. An airport limousine had just pulled up to the curb and she was about to place her overnight bag in the back seat.

Jason exploded out of his car, shouting, "Chrissie! Chrissie, wait!" He reached her, snatched the bag from her hand and grabbed her wrist with his other hand.

"God damn it, let go of me! What is it with you and grabbing?" She struggled, and the limo driver looked on with concern.

"Ma'am? Should I call a security guard?"

Jason and Christina froze, realizing they must look like maniacs wrestling on the street. Jason let go of her wrist but hung onto the overnight bag. Christina made a feeble attempt to grab it, but he held it out of her reach. She looked at him balefully. He raised his eyebrows and stalked to his car. He heard her stomping footsteps behind him and a little growl rising from her throat.

He tossed the bag in the back seat and opened the passenger door for her. She plunked into the seat, folding her arms in defiance.

He slid into the driver's seat and reached across her to fasten her seatbelt. She shrank from his touch but didn't resist, keeping her eyes focused on the front windshield.

He pulled into the street and guided the BMW toward the freeway, heading east. The speedometer needle inched to the right as he pushed the car a little harder than usual. After twenty minutes of driving, he finally eased off the gas pedal and took the exit in a more sedate fashion. As he drove, he worked his brain, trying to think of a way to break the thick silence.

Finally, he ventured, "I waited after I sent the letter. I really hoped you'd see things differently. When you didn't answer or call, I asked Bertie about it. He said he hadn't discussed it with you. He said he was tired of babysitting me and told me to work it out for myself. So I waited some more."

She glared at him in the darkness, the glittering tears in her eyes reflecting the ghostly glow from the dashboard lights. "You waited a lousy couple of months!"

"What the hell do you want from me?" He slapped the steering wheel with frustration. He heard her startled gasp and continued more quietly, "I'm not making excuses. I thought you'd already read the letter. I thought you'd moved on, so I made a half-baked attempt to do the same thing."

"That's exactly what I'm talking about. What's Jennifer doing while you're dumping her and kidnapping me?"

"You haven't got a clue, have you?" He peered at her and shook his head. "I didn't dump her. I never had her in the first place. She told me to come and find you." He steered the car off the two-lane highway and turned onto a snow-covered side road, rising and falling through dark hills lined with ghostly white fences.

~ * ~

Christina tried to digest what she'd just heard. She wiped her eyes on her sleeve and glumly stared out the front window as he drove a short distance along the country road and made another turn. A long driveway wound through tall pine trees, finally revealing a Cape Cod house with a small barn set off to the side.

Jason cut the engine, got out and stepped around the car to open her door. Still angry, she didn't want to move. Grumbling, he reached across her waist and unhooked the seatbelt before pulling her out of the car. Christina kept her eyes on the ground and leaned against the side of the car with her arms crossed. She didn't look up when he stepped close to her and stood still. She could feel his gaze on her. She raised her eyes and focused on his chest, inches from her face.

He took her chin in his hand and forced her to look up at him. He spoke firmly, his deep voice cutting through the cold silence, "She told me to find you because she knows you're the one for me. She knows how I feel about you, and she doesn't want to come between us. That's what friends do."

She gazed up at him, her anger slowly dissolving into uncertainty. He stared back; his eyes seemed to enlarge in the darkness, becoming more visible than the surrounding vapor that rose from his open mouth. "For Christ's sake, say something," he whispered hoarsely. She continued to study his eyes until he stood back and raked his fingers through his hair until it stood up in spikes. He began to pace back and forth.

Christina didn't know what to think. Was he really sincere? She didn't have time to reflect as he grabbed her hand and pulled her toward the house. He strode swiftly, heading for the side door. She ran to keep from stumbling. He fumbled with his keys in the lock, guided her into the kitchen and slammed the door so hard the glass panes rattled.

He leaned against the wooden frame and whispered, "I know I've been a selfish jerk. I made plenty of lousy judgment calls and hooked up with the wrong people. I feel responsible for what happened to Brenda. I should have been there when she needed me, and I wasn't. I should have saved her, and my baby, but I couldn't. No one blames me, nobody except myself...and Ian, and but now he's dead, too." He raised his hands, as if warding off the guilt that consumed him. "I'm going to have to live with that for the rest of my life. But the one thing...the one thing I don't regret is you. And because of my stupidity, I'm losing you."

He crossed his arms and spoke to the floor. "Chrissie, I promise you this, and I'm going to keep this promise, no more secrets, no lies, and no omissions. This is me, all of me. I'll never hide anything from you again. You mean too much to me. I love you, Chrissie, and I owe you everything. You saved my life. Not just from a bullet but from everything. Nothing really had any meaning until I met you."

He blinked hard and appeared to study his own feet with concentration. He raised his eyes and continued in a shaky voice, "And if you want to keep saving me, I won't stand in your way. God knows I need the help."

She leaned against the butcher-block island, looking steadily at his face. His eyes held her with blue heat, shimmering with unshed tears. She kicked off her boots, stepped forward and grabbed the front of his jacket, pulling him close so she could reach his mouth. With a sound somewhere between a laugh and a groan, he pulled her against him. He kissed her deeply, winding his fingers in her hair and letting his tongue explore the softness of her mouth and lips. She responded hungrily, clutching at his jacket and standing on tiptoe to bring her face closer to his.

He placed his hands around her slim waist and deposited her on the butcher-block island in the center of the room so he could hold her closer. He shrugged off his jacket, letting it fall to the floor and pressed his body against hers. She straddled him and held his face, running her lips over his brow, his chin, his neck and then returning to his mouth once again.

He pulled his T-shirt over his head and flung it behind him, turning his attention to her jacket and the buttons of her shirt. "Oh, Christ," he breathed, as she nipped at his earlobe, the soft sound of her exhaling breath sending a shiver down his neck.

She ran her hands over his upper body, brushing her fingers along the muscles and sinews on his arms, gliding lightly up his abdomen and chest. He in turn, marveled at her smooth, creamy skin and delectable curves. The night in Pensacola now seemed unreal. They had been two different people. Her image obscured by his self-doubts, he now saw her clearly, and he felt unworthy. But she accepted him anyway.

He whispered, "Do you want to go upstairs?"

She shook her head and reclined on the smooth wooden surface, allowing him to slip off her jeans and panties. She covered her eyes with her forearm and stretched out on her back. She kept her eyes closed, straining with her ears and listening to the rustle of his clothing as he finished undressing. She relied on her other senses as he moved silently around the table, lightly brushing her body with his fingers, his lips, his tongue.

She shivered with anticipation, never knowing where his next touch would alight; her neck, the crook of her elbow, the soft hollow on her hip. A mist surrounded her, floating without sound, each brief contact against her skin spinning her gently in every direction. He slipped his hand in the space under the small of her back, brushing with his fingers and causing her to arch, her soft gasps turning into little animal sounds. He finally slid her hips to the edge of the butcher block. Her eyes flew open and an involuntary cry burst from her lips as they joined. He raised her shoulders and held her close, moving with slow deliberation. She curved her arms around him and buried her face in his neck, shuddering as wave after wave of sweetness washed over her.

He lifted her easily, making for the narrow kitchen stairs. She hung on as he stumbled up the steep steps, muffled laughter ensuing when he almost tripped and stopped his abrupt descent with one hand. They slowly progressed to the bedroom to continue their exploration.

They made love as if they had been starving, hungrily devouring each other. This time there was no ghost watching with disapproval. There were no shadows, no doubts. Eventually, they lay exhausted, her body draped on his, her cheek resting on his solid chest. He brushed her long hair from his face and traced a lazy finger along her slender back, slick with perspiration. "Time to hit the showers," he whispered.

She rested her chin on his chest and grinned at him. "Sure, Coach."

He laughed and rolled her to the edge of the bed before scooping her up and moving to the shower. They made love again, this time more slowly, the warm water pelting their bodies as they leaned against the smooth tiles.

Refreshed and sleepy, they curled together and slept until the pale blue light of morning crept through the windows.

~ * ~

Christina stirred, but then lay still with her eyes closed.

He knew she was awake but didn't speak. He smiled and let one finger trace down her neck, brushing her hair aside as he kissed her smooth shoulder. His fingers continued, traveling lightly to the swell of her breast.

Her eyes were still closed, but her lips parted as she inhaled sharply, letting her breath out in a slow moan. She awakened fully and turned her head toward him, looking steadily at his face.

"Your eyes," she murmured. "Your eyes called to me when I first met you. They almost made me jump out of my chair in the courtroom. I wanted to run to you up on that stand, but then your eyes stopped me."

"Is that why you were looking at me so intently last night? What were you trying to see?"

Her own eyes began to glisten with tears. She reached up and lightly passed her fingers over his eyes, brushing his lashes. He blinked, and continued to stare at her face. Her voice wavered. "I was looking for the ghost. Even though I knew you wanted to be with me, there was always something between us when you looked at me. If I saw it, I tried to convince myself it didn't exist. But it still haunted me, filled me with doubt. Now it's gone. Now your eyes are clear." She sniffed and smiled through her tears.

He dipped his head and kissed her, caressing her mouth tenderly. He tasted her tears. She raised her hands and buried her fingers in his auburn hair, pulling him closer.

They made love languidly, his large muscular frame moving with restrained and gentle rhythm. At length they lay rumpled and content. Christina slipped into slumber once again, and Jason let her sleep as he rose from the bed. There was work to be done.

~ * ~

After a leisurely breakfast at a nearby upscale crepe house and an appointment with a manicurist, Sheila returned to her apartment with a paper bag tucked under her arm. In the kitchen, she laid out the prescription bottles along the counter. Lighting a cigarette, she pensively scanned the parade of pills, her long, red fingernails tapping her teeth. She mixed a quick screwdriver and picked out two pill bottles, taking a healthy sample from each and chasing them down with the drink.

Grabbing her coat and keys, she scooped up her purse containing Ian's appointment book and headed for the underground garage. Coaxing the reluctant Jeep to life, she exited the parking area and headed for Lakeshore Road, finding a route north, toward Unionville.

~ * ~

It was midmorning in the hills east of Chicago when Christina awoke. Stretching luxuriously, she drowsily rolled over to discover Jason was not in the room. She yawned and shuffled across the bedroom to the window. The scene outside was quiet and still, until Jason emerged from the open barn door. He pushed a laden wheelbarrow toward a steaming pile of straw and manure beside the small barn. His faint, tuneless whistle crept through the closed window as he worked.

Smiling, she rooted through her overnight bag he'd brought to the room. She climbed into a pair of jeans and a warm sweater and skipped down the back stairs.

~ * ~

By the time Jason entered the kitchen, the smell of brewing coffee welcomed him. Christina crossed the kitchen, prepared to embrace him.

He backed away and protested, "I'm all stinky. Don't touch me."

She chased him around the island. "I don't care. I like the smell of horse poop."

He allowed her to catch him and playfully rubbed a grimy hand on her cheek. She squealed and relented, letting him wash his hands.

They took their coffee to the living room. Jason fiddled with the fireplace and soon had a warm blaze going, then settled on the long, leather sofa with a contented sigh.

Christina leaned on Jason's chest. She twisted around and reached for his face, letting her fingers brush along his strong jaw. "When we first met, were you attracted to me, or was it because you missed your own child that you accepted Mishayla without any reservations?"

Jason smiled. "Hopefully last night showed I was definitely attracted to you. When I saw you in that hospital room, it was as if I'd known you all my life. That wonderful kid is a bonus. I have to admit, I had a lot of time to think about it, wondering if I was using Mishayla as a substitute for the child I never had, but after all this time, I've come to the conclusion that she's special in her own right." He smiled wistfully. "It helps that she plays hockey."

"Do you think Jennifer will be all right?"

"She'll be fine. She was being perfectly honest when she came to see me. She said she had no expectations. I was still feeling pretty raw when you didn't answer my letter, and it seemed natural to try going out with Jennifer. After all, she was single and so was I. But looking back, it felt a little weird. We were both trying too hard to make something happen, but I somehow felt like I was with my sister." He looked at the ceiling. "We never even kissed, except when I kissed her goodbye before coming to find you."

"Hmm." Christina took a sip of coffee, set down her cup, raised herself, and straddled him, leaning against his chest. She held his face in her hands and nuzzled him playfully. "Now I'm the number one fan of two hockey players."

He chuckled and gathered her closer, tasting her lips. Interrupted by a tinkling cell phone ring, Christina rolled off his lap and strolled into the kitchen to retrieve the phone from the countertop. Jason followed, pausing in the doorway. He watched her face as she gasped in shock.

"What? Oh, my God! No, sit tight, I'm on my way. Stop it, it isn't your fault. Just wait, I'll be there as soon as I can. Yes, I'll call with the flight time. Okay, okay…"

She flipped the phone shut and stared across the kitchen at Jason. He immediately tensed. Her eyes shone with tears and she covered her trembling mouth with her hand.

He was across the room in three strides and laid a palm on her cheek, brushing a tear with his thumb. "What happened?"

Her voice rose to a panicked squeak. "Mishayla's missing."

Twenty Five

Sheila parked the Cherokee at the end of the driveway and ensured the beige vehicle was obscured by a tangle of leafless shrubbery. She cut the engine and cracked the window, taking a long draw on her cigarette. Through the haze of smoke, she observed a knot of people at the front of the house. Two adults and five children were busy constructing a snowman out of the soft, pliable white stuff. She vaguely remembered her own childhood, when she was told wet snow was the best for making snowmen, its flexibility more suitable when the weather wasn't too cold.

She counted the children again. Five. She thought she had it wrong; the Gauthiers were only supposed to have four kids. *The little frog's wife couldn't possibly have spit out another one so soon.*

At length, the dark-haired woman carried a toddler and herded another small one into the house, and Bertie climbed into his SUV. A wave of alarm washed over Sheila until he pointed the vehicle toward a track behind the house. He disappeared over the hill and she relaxed again.

The sound of the three remaining children's voices drifted through the frigid air. The older boy shouted to a girl with light-colored hair, "Mishayla!"

Sheila's face broke into a wide smile. *Oh, this is just too perfect.* She stabbed out her cigarette and opened the window further.

"Mishayla, get some branches for the arms," the boy called out.

The girl yelled, "Okay," and ventured close to the bushes near the end of the driveway.

"Hello, Mishayla," Sheila called out in a friendly voice. "Can you come over here for a minute? I have a message from Jason. He misses you, and he wants to see you. Would you like to surprise him with a visit?"

Mishayla stopped her twig hunting expedition and straightened, looking at the blonde woman with suspicion. At the mention of Jason's name, her face brightened. "You know Jason?" she asked.

"Yes, he's a good friend of mine."

"Hey, my mom's visiting him. I thought he was far away."

"He came for a visit, and your mom doesn't know about the surprise. She's probably on her way back right now to join you."

Sheila glanced at the other two children. The boy froze in place and stared in her direction, then turned and ran toward the house. She had to hurry or the opportunity would be lost.

"Yes, sweetie, he misses you a lot and wants you to help him buy a present for your mom. Do you want to go shopping?"

Mishayla seemed to digest this for a moment and apparently came to a decision. "Okay, but let me go and tell Mrs. Gauthier first."

"Oh, there's no time for that, the stores will be closing early today." Sheila's eyes darted from the girl's face to the house.

"Well, okay, but I have to be back in time for lunch. We're having grilled cheese sandwiches!" The little girl obligingly climbed into the back seat of the Jeep.

Just as the front door of the house burst open, Sheila plunged her foot on the gas pedal and steered the Cherokee down the country lane.

~ * ~

They found an early flight, and barely made it in time for the plane's takeoff. Christina sat beside Jason during the two-hour flight and gripped his hand with incredible force, her feet tapping the floor in agitation. She was hardly aware of Jason's low voice as he uttered soothing words, and his solid shoulder offered little comfort. She knew, in the back of her mind, he was doing his best to help her, but all she felt was a thick, suffocating cloud of panic.

Bertie met them at the airport. He was so frantic Jason quickly said, "Get in the back. I'll drive."

Christina maintained her grip on Jason's arm as he drove. She listened to Bertie as he explained the events of the morning. "She was outside with the two older kids and Corinne was in the house with the little ones. I just went down to the pond to check the ice. I was only gone for ten minutes, and when I got back, Corinne was crying and the kids were all yelling at once. They said some blonde lady in a Jeep took Mishayla. It happened at 11:00 this morning. She's been gone three hours, and the police are combing the area. My God, Christina, I'm so sorry, it's my fault. I should have been watching them."

Christina fought her own terror and looked over her shoulder at his stricken face. She let go of Jason's arm long enough to reach between the front seats to grasp Bertie's clenched fists. "It's not your fault. Don't beat yourself up. Let's just see what the police have to say."

Bertie slowly calmed and was back in control as they rejoined his distraught wife at the farmhouse. The local police were busy scanning the area and had already received the description of Sheila and her vehicle, broadcasting it to all divisions. An Amber Alert was on throughout the region.

Christina huddled in Jason's arms on the living room sofa when her cell phone rang. The room became quiet as she answered. She sprang from the sofa and yelled into the phone, "Mishayla? Honey, where are you?"

She heard her daughter's voice crackling faintly over the line, "Mommy?"

"What happened, honey, are you all right? Where are you?"

"The lady came to get me. She said she was your friend and was going to take me to see Jason and so we could get a present for you. I'm in the lady's car, Mommy, but I'm stuck. She bumped into a fence and she's not awake."

"Whose phone are you using, honey?"

"I used the lady's phone. I remembered your number!" The girl seemed proud of her accomplishment; there was no fear in her voice. "Are you still visiting Jason?"

"No, sweetie, I'm home now." She struggled to keep the shaking out of her own voice. "Can you tell me where you are?"

"She drove around forever, Mommy, and she just talked and talked. She was talking about Jason, so I listened for a while. But I didn't understand most of it. I got sleepy and stopped listening, but then she got sleepy too and bumped into this fence. We're on the ice."

"What ice, honey?" Christina's heart raced as she strained to hear her daughter's fading voice.

"The ice you don't like. I'm sorry, Mommy, you told me not to go with strangers, but she said…" The little girl's voice faded one last time and the phone disconnected.

Christina flashed a look at Jason. "I know where she is." She rushed to the front door and grabbed her jacket from the stair railing. "Come on, hurry up."

~ * ~

Jason had a good idea where she was heading.

"Give me your keys." He held his hand out and Bertie immediately snatched the SUV keys from the hall table and slapped them into Jason's palm. "Get the police out to Glenville Pond."

Jason drove to Highway Nine and sped westward. Christina's legs were shaking as her feet tapped impatiently on the floorboards. As they approached the curve from the east end, she strained to see over the concrete barrier on the south side of the road. Jason jerked the steering wheel to the left and they skidded onto the small dirt road that skirted Glenville pond. Sheila's Jeep sat in the middle of a wide expanse of ice surrounded by dark, densely packed trees. A long, jagged scar traced along the thin scraping of snow covering the ice. Wet spots scattered about the surface, indicating thinner ice.

Christina scrambled out of the vehicle and hesitated on the bank, straining to see the interior of the Jeep. The rear door opened and Mishayla peered out at them.

"Mommy! The car keeps shaking, I'm afraid to get out!" the little girl shouted across the ice.

Jason's voice wavered with fear as he said, "The ice won't support that Jeep for long. I'm surprised it hasn't gone through already. Damn it, where are the police?"

"Oh, my God!" Christina cried as she heard a crack in the middle of the pond along with Mishayla's startled squeak. The girl stretched a foot downward, touching the toe of her boot to the slushy surface.

Jason called out, "Mishayla, get down on your belly and crawl like a snake!"

Mishayla followed his instructions, sliding gently from the doorway and getting on all fours on the ice. She slowly started to shimmy toward them, pushing the wet snow before her with her elbows.

Another loud crack caused the little girl to glance over her shoulder. The Jeep shifted, and she made a move as if to jump to her feet.

"Stay down!" Jason shouted, and as the Jeep's weight pushed down on the ice surface behind Mishayla, he vaulted out onto the ice, throwing himself on his stomach as he approached her. He slid a few feet and just managed to reach her hand as the surface crumbled behind her, submerging her feet. He pulled her toward him and scooped her up, running frantically for the bank in an attempt to outrun the cave-in. The collapsing ice caught up to him, causing him to stumble and sink to his knees. He struggled the last few feet, plowing through the slush, and crawled up the snowy bank, still gripping Mishayla.

Christina tore her eyes from the Jeep as it swiftly sank below the surface, bubbling and steaming. She ran to Jason and Mishayla and fell to her knees. Her daughter stood in front of Jason, who kneeled on the snow-covered bank. He held the girl by the waist as if he was afraid to let her go. Mishayla gazed serenely at his face, carefully brushing tears from his cheeks with her damp mittens. He leaned forward and buried his face into the front of Mishayla's jacket, shaking with muffled sobs.

Mishayla rested her cheek on top of his spiky auburn hair and patted the back of his head. "It's okay, Jason, don't cry, everything's all right." She turned her gaze to her mother.

Christina leaned forward and held out her arms. Jason smiled through his tears and relinquished Mishayla to her mother.

Moments later, she heard the distant sound of sirens, and a convoy of emergency vehicles plowed to a halt behind Bertie's borrowed SUV. Bertie himself flew out of the passenger side of the foremost police car and ran to the pond's edge, accompanied by the police officer who had been at the house. The rest of the emergency personnel were already at work, with divers ready to recover Sheila's body from the black water.

Christina welcomed Bertie and they all stood on the bank, gazing out at the jagged wound in the ice. Mishayla quickly tired of watching the flashing lights and rubber clad divers. She had already switched the well-oiled mental gears of childhood and asked if they could go back to the house so she could have grilled cheese sandwiches.

Christina asked Bertie, "Do the police need to talk to us now or can we give our statements later? Mishayla's cold and hungry."

Bertie had a quiet word with the police and returned with the news that they could visit the police station in the morning. Leaving the authorities to their investigation, they climbed into the vehicle, heading back to the Unionville farmhouse.

Mishayla rode in front with Bertie, chattering about Sheila's ramblings as they had driven about the countryside. Christina leaned on Jason's shoulder in the back seat, both of them listening carefully to Mishayla's comments as Bertie prompted her with seemingly innocent questions. They would need every bit of information available to them in case there was an inquest.

Jason glanced at his watch. "I was supposed to be at practice two hours ago." He leaned his head back on the headrest. "I guess I have to make another call to another coach about going AWOL."

Christina smiled wistfully and held him tighter. "Hopefully this one will be as understanding as the last. I wish you didn't have to go back."

"I know, honey," he replied, taking her hand and squeezing it gently. "I wish I didn't have to leave you guys with this big mess." He watched the passing landscape with sadness.

Christina peered at his profile with concern. "What are you thinking?"

He turned back to her and patted her hand. "A lot of stuff. I was thinking I was an impulsive idiot for asking for a trade, but I can't really do anything about that now. I have a job to do, and I have to live with my decisions."

He turned back to the window. "I was thinking about Sheila, too. She may have been misguided and a little bit nuts, but I don't really think she was that evil. She didn't deserve to die like that."

"Hmmm." Christina muttered neutrally. She understood but found it difficult to be so forgiving. The woman had tried to kill her, after all. She kept her opinion to herself, accepting and appreciating Jason's generous nature.

They gathered at Bertie and Corinne's boisterous home. All of the adults participated in the preparation of a warm meal, dispatched with efficiency around the big pine kitchen table. Afterward, as the light outside turned soft and blue, they gathered in the large family room. Mishayla climbed without hesitation onto Jason's lap and took his face between her small hands. She looked directly into his eyes and declared, "Jason, I'm glad you're back."

Jason settled the girl more comfortably in his arms and earnestly gazed at her in return. "I'm glad I'm back, too."

"Are you going to stay?"

"For a few days."

"A few days? Why? You just got here."

"Sorry, sweet pea, I have to go back to my team. I have an important job."

Mishayla's face fell. She rested her head on his chest with her lower lip trembling. He heard a little sniffle and he peered down at her face. "Mishayla?"

"Yeah..." She responded in a tiny voice as she tried not to cry.

"If you like, you can visit me in Chicago. Would you like to learn to ride a horse?"

"Yeah!" she piped with renewed enthusiasm and snuggled closer with a contented sigh.

Jason closed his eyes for a moment and rested his hand lightly on her cheek. He gazed across the coffee table, giving Christina a wide smile, his eyes glowing with promise.

Later, Mishayla didn't react with surprise when both Christina and Jason's bags were dropped into the guest room. She simply bade them both goodnight with a kiss and a hug and happily skipped to Jeannette's room where she normally slept during her overnight stays.

For the first time in many years, Jason spent a peaceful night of uninterrupted slumber, comfortably entwined with the woman he loved.

~ * ~

The lead sky sullenly released a few drifting snowflakes, barely stirred by the almost nonexistent breeze. Sheila's parents gazed at the casket as it slowly sank into the freshly dug rectangle in the almost frozen ground. Despite their attempts to maintain contact with their daughter, she hadn't spoken to them for a few years. On a day when they should have been shaking with tears and grief, the only expression they shared was one of resignation.

The only other attendees of the funeral were Jason, Christina, Bertie, and Corinne; as well as Mary; the unfortunate sales clerk who had been employed at Sheila's clothing shop.

Jason had insisted they pay their respects. He didn't want Sheila's parents to be alone while they said goodbye to their daughter. He was fully aware of Sheila's tenuous relationships with others and suspected the turnout would be sparse. He felt her parents would appreciate the support. He had never met them personally, but had spoken to them a few times on the phone during the most turbulent times in his relationship with Sheila. The calls were usually a result of his attempts to help her, but her parents were generally at a loss, offering little advice. They had given up on their daughter long ago.

As the ceremony ended, they bade Mary goodbye, and she walked alone to her car. Christina, Corinne, and Bertie started to move toward the parking area, but Jason hung behind, hesitant to end the afternoon so soon. He regarded the quiet older couple, wondering if he could possibly say anything to help them with their loss. He had tried his best to haul Sheila out of the chasm she had fallen into, but the idea of attempting to convey his regret with a few spoken words felt impossible. In the end, all he did was reach for them in turn, embracing them without a word.

During the drive to Christina's house, Jason remained quiet. Christina accepted his silence, allowing him to be alone with his thoughts. She hadn't wanted to attend the funeral; the memory of Sheila's last attempt to ruin their lives was still fresh and raw. She wondered why Jason had felt so strongly about his need for closure in this manner, but she still respected his decision. Sheila may not have deserved their support, but her parents certainly did. So if he wanted to go to the funeral, she'd be there for him.

Her thoughts were interrupted by Jason's deep, pensive voice. "For the past few months, I kept asking myself why I let her manipulate me when I should have ignored her. Why did her words affect me so much? I almost let you slip away. I think I have it figured out. I'd failed to protect Brenda and the baby. When I should have been there for them, I wasn't. Then when Sheila started to slide, I thought I could make up for my past failure by saving her.

"It turned out, I just wasn't good enough. When she told you about Brenda, it may have looked like she was twisting the whole thing out of proportion, but it was probably closer to the truth. I started to believe Sheila when she said I had a penchant for abandonment. I thought that if I failed with Brenda and Sheila, I would probably fail with you and Mishayla, too."

"You didn't abandon anyone. You didn't know about Brenda, it wasn't your fault. You didn't abandon Sheila...you kept trying to help her even though she was driving you crazy. She really abandoned you. Most importantly, you didn't fail with us. We didn't need saving."

"I'm sorry, I thought you needed saving from me. In my mind, I was the biggest, most selfish jerk. I made all the wrong choices, and after the accident last spring, I saw anything we'd built crumbling away. I figured I was just going to make things worse if I stuck around, so I bailed." He released the steering wheel with his right hand and reached for her.

She took his hand in hers, studying it, stroking his palm with her fingers. He enclosed her hand in his, squeezing gently. He glanced at her briefly, and his eyes were bright with unshed tears. "You're right. You didn't need saving. I'm the one who needed saving. And you did it. I fought you all the way, but you were so goddamn stubborn. I'm glad you were."

She smiled. "I'm glad, too. Keep your eyes on the road."

Twenty Six

Christina and Mishayla made a rare trip together to watch Jason play in Chicago after the Christmas break. The game was fast-paced and exciting, and Mishayla jumped out of her seat every time Jason hit the ice, screaming his name along with the rest of the fans. Christina grinned at her daughter and followed the action. The game ended on a positive note, with a narrow win for Jason's team.

Just as the final horn sounded, an usher stopped beside Christina and handed her a package.

Puzzled, Christina held the small box in her hand and looked up at the usher. "What is it?"

The usher smiled. "It's a special award assigned to your seat number from the organization."

Mishayla interrupted, "Hey, Mom, look! We're on the big screen!"

Christina glanced up as her fingers pried the box open. She blinked. Her face filled the gargantuan four-sided screen hanging from the rafters. Embarrassed, she dropped her gaze.

She squealed and almost dropped the box.

Mishayla tugged at her arm. "What is it, a mouse?"

"No…no, sweetie, it's not a mouse."

An emerald cut diamond ring peeked from a dark blue velvet nest. Her heart jolted and thudded so hard she hardly heard the crowd around her.

She swallowed hard and stood to scan the ice surface. Jason and his teammates had not left for the dressing room. He was alone at center ice, slowly gliding to the near corner, looking up at her with round, blue eyes that almost blazed with their own light.

The team stood in a line at the bench, their sticks hanging over the boards. Simultaneously, they banged the sticks in a steady rhythm against the battered wood surface, as if they were some ancient tribe encouraging a fellow warrior.

She grasped Mishayla's hand and they both descended the concrete steps. The usher, who had hovered nearby, followed and obligingly opened the large gate that opened onto the corner of the ice surface.

~ * ~

Jason was there to meet her. He let his gloves slide from his hands and he tore off his helmet. She lightly skipped down the stairs with her daughter hopping to keep up. As she got closer, he saw the smile, then her eyes. They glistened in the bright light. He felt a strange tightening in his chest. It felt great.

Finally, she stood on the raised wooden threshold and held out the little box. He took a deep breath and flipped it open. He extracted the ring and took her hand.

The ring slid onto her finger with ease. He paused for a moment and looked at the old scar on the back of her hand. It was almost the same shape as the glittering diamond. He turned her hand over and touched his lips to the smaller scar on her delicate palm. Gathering her close, he lifted her from the gateway. Christina wrapped her arms around his neck and gave a little hop. He held her against him and slowly pirouetted, allowing her feet to hover above the ice surface. He searched for her mouth and kissed her deeply, listening to the swell of the crowd around them. She laid her cheek against his perspiring neck.

His ear picked up her soft voice over the crowd. "Ow."

He suddenly remembered his shoulder pads and gently lowered her. Mishayla stretched her arms up to him. He reached down and scooped her into his arms. The girl giggled and planted an affectionate kiss on his cheek.

The crowd roared.

About Sandra

Born in Montreal, Sandra Cormier accompanied her family to many communities across Eastern Canada including Northern Ontario, Quebec and the Maritimes, as well as other destinations like Trinidad and Spain. She finally settled in Newmarket, Ontario with her husband and two teenage children. Her many passions include writing, art, horses and of course hockey. Bad Ice is her second novel.

Visit our website for our growing catalogue of quality books.
www.champagnebooks.com